'Enger delivers this rich and episodic narrative in short, punchy chapters of beautifully written and quietly mesmeric prose ... superbly eulogises stymied heroism and quiet, decent crookery ... a worthy dirge for the brave, young, and handsome cowboys of old'

Sunday Business Post

'The novel captures effectively the romance, roughness and roguery of the early 20th century. A delightful read'

RTÉ Guide

'[Leif Enger is] a formidably gifted writer ... possessed of a seemingly effortless facility for the stiletto-sharp drawing of wholly believable characters ... *So Brave, Young, and Handsome* is affable and human as all get out, homespun and sophisticated at once, wise and knowing about the ubiquity of the human condition and the vagaries of the human heart'

Chicago Tribune

'*So Brave, Young, and Handsome* is a sharp and brainy redemption tale, with all the twists and turns and thrills of a dime-store western. . . . [Enger has] laid claim to a musical, sometimes magical and deeply satisfying kind of story-telling'

Los Angeles Times

Also by Leif Enger

Peace Like a River

SO BRAVE, YOUNG, AND HANDSOME

Leif Enger

Quercus

First published in Great Britain in 2008 by Quercus

This paperback edition published in 2009 by

Quercus
21 Bloomsbury Square
London
WC1A 2NS

A CIP catalogue record for this book is available
from the British Library

ISBN 978 1 84724 790 2

10 9 8 7 6 5 4 3 2 1

Typeset in Bembo by Ellipsis Books Limited, Glasgow
Printed and bound in Great Britain by Clays Ltd, St Ives plc

For Robin, Ty, and John
the brightest colors I ever saw

SO BRAVE, YOUNG, AND HANDSOME

A THOUSAND A DAY

Not to disappoint you, but my troubles are nothing – not for an author, at least. Common blots aside, I have none of the usual Big Artillery: I am not penniless, brilliant, or an orphan; have never been to war, suffered starvation or lashed myself to a mast. My health is adequate, my wife steadfast, my son decent and promising. I am not surrounded by people who don't understand me! In fact most understand me straightaway, for I am and always was an amiable fellow and reliably polite. You, a curious stranger, could walk in this moment; I would offer you coffee and set you at ease. Would we talk pleasantly? Indeed we would, though you'd soon be bored – here on Page One I don't even live in interesting surroundings, such as in a hospital for the insane, or on a tramp steamer, or in Madrid. Later in the proceedings I do promise a tense chase or two and the tang of gunpowder, but here at the outset it's flat old Minnesota and I am sitting on the porch of my comfortable farmhouse, composing the flaccid middle of my seventh novel in five years.

Seven novels, you exclaim – quite right, but then I didn't finish any of them. I'm grateful for that, and you should be too. Number Seven featured a handsome but increasingly bilious ranch hand named Dan Roscoe. A right enough pard to begin with, he became more arrogant page by page.

No laconic wit for Dan! It was himself I was writing about, with many low sighs, the morning I first saw Glendon Hale rowing upstream through the ropy mists of the Cannon River. What a cool spring morning that was – birdsong, dew on the blossoms – I yearned to be on the river myself, but Dan Roscoe had rustlers to catch and a girl to win. Neither seemed likely. How often I sighed in those days! I needed a revelation but you know how it is. I would have settled for a nice surprise.

Hearing the groan of oarlocks I peered downriver. A white-headed fellow was rowing up out of the haze.

He rowed standing, facing forward, a tottery business; twice as I watched, one of his narrow sweeps missed the water completely and he lurched like old Quixote, hooting to himself. The truth is he appeared a bit elevated, early though it was. As I say, he was white-haired with a white mustache and he wore white shirtsleeves and his boat too was white above the waterline, so that he had a spectral or angelic quality only somewhat reduced by his tipsy aspect.

Forth he came through the parting mists. To this day I don't know what took hold of me as he approached. I stood from my work and called hello.

'Hello back,' said he, not pausing in his strokes.

'Pretty vessel,' I called.

'Pretty river,' he said, a simple reply that made me ache to be afloat. But he wasn't slowing, as you might expect a polite person to do, and I stepped off the porch and jogged down to the stubby dock my son had built for fishing.

'Can you stop a minute? There's coffee,' I said – sounding pushy, I suspect, though I am no extrovert; ask Susannah.

'Maybe,' he said, yet he was already well past me and in

4

fact the haze was closing round him again. I had a last glimpse of his boat – its graceful sheer and backswept transom. Then it disappeared, though I could hear in the fog the dip of the old man's oars, his screeling oarlocks, and what might have been a laugh of delight, as though he'd vanished by some mystic capacity that tickled him every time.

I went heavily back to the porch. My boy Redstart was there grinning – he was eleven, Redstart, catching up with his papa in all kinds of ways.

'Who was that man?' he inquired.

'I don't know.'

'Was he drunk, do you think?'

'Anything's possible.'

'He rows standing up,' said Redstart. 'I never saw that before. Did you talk to him?'

'No, I didn't.' I couldn't look at the boy for a moment or two. I was embarrassed at how much I'd wanted to visit with the man in the boat, and how unaccountably sorry I was that he'd just rowed away. I sat in my chair and lifted pages into my lap. Dan Roscoe was waiting for me in those pages – boy, he was morose. Who could face it?

'I can still hear him,' Redstart said, 'out in the mist. Can you hear him rowing, Papa?'

I looked at my son, the lover of mysteries. You could never guess what Redstart might say, for his mind was made of stories; he'd gathered all manner of splendid facts about gunpowder and deserts of the world and the anchoring of lighthouses against the furious sea; he knew which members of the James gang had once ridden into our town to knock over a bank and been shot to moist rags for their trouble;

5

and about me he knew some things not even his mother knew, such as the exact number of novels I had abandoned on that porch. He whispered, 'How many words today, Papa?'

I made a quick and not altogether honest guess. 'Two hundred or so.'

'It's early still, that's pretty good,' he replied, then sat and shut his eyes and leaned awhile. I knew he should go take the horses to pasture or mulch the tomatoes but I didn't want to lose his company. I picked up my pen and wrote: *As Dan Roscoe branded each bawling calf with the Moon Ranch insignia, he recalled how Belle had clung to the arm of his hated rival* – a moribund sentence that announced the death of my seventh novel. It didn't surprise me. I had the grim yet satisfactory thought that it wouldn't surprise Dan Roscoe, either. Well, let him moan! I was sick of Dan and his myriad problems.

'Red,' said I, 'here's an idea. Why don't you go in the house and lay hands on a few of your mother's orange rolls. Let's climb in the boat and head upstream.'

'Hmm,' said Redstart. He dawdled to his feet; he said 'Well' a couple of times.

'Well, nothing,' I said. 'We don't even need the rolls. Let's catch up with that old man. I want to talk to him.'

Redstart went to the door. Poor reluctant boy; long my joyous accomplice in distraction, he had lately been run to ground by his efficient and lovely and desperate mother. He didn't want to shame me, but what choice did I give him?

'I guess we better not, Papa. You got to get your work done. Remember what Mama said?'

2

What Susannah said was, approximately, *If you don't soon finish that book of yours, we'll have to start selling the furniture.* Lest you read in her words a tone of panic, let me assure you there was none. She was only letting me know where things stood. The end of money didn't mean the end of much – the end of our marriage, say, or even of Susannah's obstinate confidence in me. At worst it meant the end of pretense. The end of my little run at distinction. To say it truly: the end of pride.

I was the one who panicked.

Here's how I came to this sorry pass. In the fall of 1910 I published a short novel called *Martin Bligh,* which became so popular I quit being a postman and started calling myself an author. Who knows how these things happen? The book was just an adventure tale. Nothing ambitious. I only wrote it for entertainment and to gratify a sort of wistful ache – Martin Bligh was a postman too, though as a Pony Express rider he had a better shot at glory and peril than I in my tinctured cell at the Northfield P.O. It was a story to make a boy lean forward; it had Indians and great ships and the buried gold of Coronado and two separate duels, including one with sabers. I also added a black-haired senõrita because my own Susannah loves a romance, yet *Bligh* was reviewed in a Chicago newspaper as 'disturbingly real,' no doubt because some of the Indians adorned their pintos with bloody blond scalps. That the haggard and venerated Buffalo Bill Cody read my story and praised it in newspaper interviews did not hurt the book at all, though it hardly explains why the first printing of three thousand copies disappeared in two weeks. My publisher, Hackle & Banks, New York, was startled enough to wire me congratulations and print another four thousand, which sped from the warehouse in exactly twelve days. At this I received a second telegram: BLIGH OUR FASTEST SELLER. THANK YOU. GRACE. I was ignorant at the time that Grace was Grace Hackle, the generous and canny widow of Dixon Hackle, who had founded the publishing firm twenty years before.

Then letters began to arrive. I was still employed at the P.O. and was startled in the sorting room when envelopes bearing my name began crossing the desk. I rarely received mail – when I did it was apt to be from my mother, whose letters were straightforward offerings of gained wisdom. These on the other hand were praise from strangers who had read my little tale. To call these readers charitable doesn't touch it. They were lavish and interpretive; they were 'stirred.' The daunting and completely unforeseen fact was this: They had mistaken me for a person of substance! I blushed but kept the letters. When I did hear from my mother, sometime later, she suggested I cling to my place at the post office and not let publication make me biggity. Fine advice, you will agree, yet vanity is a devious monkey. While some labeled my story naïve or my diction purple, I clove to a review calling it 'an enchanting and violent yarn spun in the brave hues of history.' A famous ladies' journal claimed I'd crafted 'the ideal popular tale.' By the time Mama wrote I was miles past her advice. By then Grace Hackle had sent me several elegant personal notes. She had paid for Susannah and me to ride the Great Northern from St. Paul to New York City, where she registered us in a hotel with frescoes and high ceilings. She had accompanied us to a stage play, then to a restaurant lighted the amber of sunsets, where we ate fresh sea bass and talked of books and authors.

'It is destined timing,' Grace declared. 'You have dared paint a romance on the sterile canvas of our age.' She was a perfectly beautiful tidy small woman with the metropolitan habit of placing events in the big picture. She believed romance was no mere ingredient but the very stone floor on which all life makes its fretful dance. Having traveled once as far west as the Black Hills she still awoke from dreams of rock and prairie. She confessed to a fascination with the architecture of tepees. William Howard Taft might be president, Grace noted, but who did not miss Teddy Roosevelt? 'The strenuous life,' she sighed.

Looking back, I have to laugh. You know why Martin Bligh was strenuous? Whenever I didn't know what to write next, I put a swift river in front of his horse and sent the two of them across!

'And now,' Grace added, 'tell me you plan to write another book.'

I looked at Susannah, who was squeezing my hand under the table. I had never thought about another book.

Grace sipped tea. 'You have some ideas, I suppose.'

'Why, yes,' I said, though my lone idea at the moment was the fragile sweetheart Grace herself had just planted: that I was an Author now, that I had new Business upon the Earth, that the tedium of sorting mail might be exchanged for something more expansive or — dare I say it? — Swashbuckling.

'*Can* you write another book?' she asked, rather baldly.

I thought about it. *Martin Bligh* had not been difficult to write; whatever I wanted to do, that's what Martin did. He rode in all weathers, flouting night and blizzard; he defied the wicked; he kissed the pretty girl. How hard could it be to do something similar again? I said, 'Indeed I can.'

Grace's eyes were unconvinced. Perhaps she saw what I could not.

Wanting to please her I made a hasty claim. 'I shall write one thousand words a day until another book is finished.'

'You dear man,' said Grace Hackle. In memory she blanches at my naïve pledge, but maybe not.

'Jack London sets down a thousand a day before breakfast,' said I. Why do the foolish insist? But I was thinking of the modest dimensions a thousand words actually describe — a tiny essay, a fragment of conversation. 'How hard can it be?' concluded your idiot narrator, lifting his glass to the future.

3

We didn't see our tipsy oarsman for weeks – I'd have forgotten him entirely if Redstart hadn't kept bringing him up. 'I bet he's a vagabond. Clive says they get a vagabond at the door every week.'

Clive Hawkins was Redstart's most stalwart friend. The two of them would spit on their hands and shake. They were presently in agreement that vagabonds were the most alluring terror locally available.

'Vagabonds don't have rowboats,' I pointed out.

'He might be a new strain,' Redstart said. 'He might've stole that boat just before we saw him. He was laughing about something, remember?'

'Maybe he recalled a good joke,' I said – I am one of those people who can never remember a joke, on the rare occasion I feel like telling one.

'That wasn't a joke laugh. It was a pleased laugh. He was pleased by something clever he'd done. He probably stole that boat. Any vagabond would be happy to have a boat, after walking for weeks and weeks.'

'Well, Red,' said I, but on he plunged into the imagined joys and dangers of the life unfettered. What could I do but watch him talk? We'd named him for the vigorous passerines so plentiful in the yard the day he was born, but there was never a songbird as energetic as Redstart.

One evening he returned from a long ride on Chief, his oversized gelding. He'd been gone since morning – not unusual for that boy. He strolled into the house hungry and self-important with a whippy weal on one cheek from galloping through the trees.

'Well, I found the old boatman,' he announced, as though it had been Livingstone. 'I went down to the river so Chief could drink and I could swim, and here he came rowing. Standing up like before. He almost fell over. His name is Glendon and he lives in a barn.'

'You talked to him?'

'Yes sir I did.'

'Was Glendon sober?' asked Susannah. She was at work on a painting – we never thought she was listening while standing intent at her easel, but she always was.

'He might of been,' said Redstart, in a vague way.

His mother looked at him. 'You kept your distance, I expect.'

I said, 'Well, let's have it. Is he a tramp, as you believed?'

'No. He makes boats. He made that boat he's always standing up in. He lived in Texas and Oklahoma and Kansas and in Mexico by the Sea of Cortez. He's coming here for breakfast tomorrow.'

It was a fair haul of information. I was proud of Redstart.

'Breakfast?' said Susannah.

'That's right,' said Redstart, 'so you both get to meet him. I guess it's a good thing I went riding today!'

Susannah set down her brush and came around the easel. She had a little stab of burgundy on one cheek like a warning. 'Did he agree to come for breakfast, Red? Did he *say* he's coming?'

'No,' said Redstart, who ignored warnings of all kinds. 'But I told him to come, so I expect he will.'

'Unless he resists being ordered about by fractious infants,' I suggested.

But Redstart was adamant. 'He told me his name. He didn't want to say it, but I tricked him and out it came. You know what happens, once you get a person's name.'

'Nope,' I replied. 'You'll have to tell me.'

'Why, then you have power over him,' said Redstart.

It's an old business, it turns out, this notion that learning a person's true name gives you leverage; I have since found it in Indian and Nordic tales and I suppose it goes back like so many good ideas all the way to the Tigris and Euphrates. Nothing is new under the sun. Anyhow Glendon appeared in his white dory next morning about an hour past sunup. Our pug Bert saw him first and stood on the dock barking and slobbering. Bert doesn't truly bark but says *oof, oof,* like a disappointed farmer. Glendon drifted up, putting his oars to rights while I went down to greet him.

'Monte Becket,' I said, holding out my hand. He grasped it and stepped up out of his dory and immediately let go like a nervous child. He was a short one, trim as a leprechaun and not as old as his white hair had led me to assume. He wore a long split-back jacket such as dressy horsemen used to wear, and he had vivid green eyes that might believe anything at all. I'd rather not say I smelled whiskey so early in the morning; nevertheless, there was an evaporating haze around our visitor. He nodded to me but said nothing and kept glancing toward the house as though it were a place of dread.

I said, 'I'm glad you've come, and I surely beg your pardon if Redstart overstepped his bounds – he can be bossy. Come on up. Susannah's made rolls.'

Glendon said, 'What did you call that son of yours?'

'Redstart.'

'Aha, Redstart. Thank you, Mr. Becket.' And up we went, his anxiety flown off with the breeze.

The first thing Redstart did was lay claim on him – yes, it was Sit by Me Glendon, Pass the Rolls Glendon, Tell About Mexico Glendon! Both Susannah and I began to stop our imperious child, but the old fellow shook off these attempts and weathered Redstart with dogged grace. People ask, *what was he like?* Had I invented Glendon myself I could not have introduced a more puzzling guest to our table. He was formal in the way of men grown apart, yet energy teemed behind his eyes and in some ways he seemed a boy himself. He might laugh abruptly at one of Redstart's childish jokes; he was pleased by the simplest plays on language; and, like a boy, he kept eating rolls as long as there were rolls to be eaten. To Susannah he gave all possible deference, rising whenever she got up for more coffee or frosting, saying thank you in reverent tones and with averted eyes. These manners endeared him to Susannah straight-away, so that she looked round the table to make sure Redstart and I were noticing how a gentleman acts. He gave his story in bright shards. Raised in Michigan, he had traveled west to become a cowboy, a memory that still excited him. He had been twice up the Chisholm Trail with herds of steers, had sung to them and swum rivers in their midst, and had a horse gored from under him during a stampede. Once in the Montana Rockies he had stumbled on a shady cleft where fifty hapless livestock had bunched up in a blizzard. The snow was still melting when Glendon found the place in July and he beheld a shrunken grimy snowfield with dozens of hooked tapers slanting up from it, the horns of steers growing rapidly into the sunshine like Satan's idea of horticulture.

'Redstart says you built that boat of yours,' I said, wanting to get him off cowboying. He'd left home at twelve – already Redstart was realigning his own future.

'Yes, I love a boat,' Glendon said. No one made comment and he seemed quite willing to leave it at that, but then he abruptly added, 'My wife loved them too. She believed they were alive in some ways.'

'Your wife?' Susannah inquired.

'Yes, my Blue,' Glendon said. 'Arāndano's her name – that's blueberry, in the Mexican tongue.'

'But you are alone now,' said Susannah tenderly.

'Yes, we have been apart more than twenty years. She has another man, I understand.' Glendon looked suddenly as downhearted as if the estrangement had happened hours ago, instead of decades.

'Why, I'm sorry,' said Susannah, and we fell into one of those spreading defeated moments from which there is no right recovery.

'Well, I'll be going, thank you for breakfast,' Glendon said, and this time he did not wait for Susannah to rise but was up and gone glimmering. Redstart scooted after him and there we sat, Susannah and I, perplexed.

'He's like Peter Pan,' she whispered, which happened to be the stage play we'd attended on that first heady trip to New York City.

'Then I'd better go see him off,' I replied, 'lest he fly away with our son.'

I followed them to the river, not really trying to catch

up because Glendon appeared lighthearted again away from the house and the breakfast table and Susannah; he walked with his hands in his pockets, Bert rolling about his ankles, and he said something that made Redstart laugh and look at me over his shoulder.

'Tell one more western tale,' said Redstart, as I came up with them at the dock. 'Just one more, Glendon, before you go.'

Glendon thought a moment, then with a quiet spark said, 'I have been four different times on trains that got robbed, yet never lost a dime,' offering this tidbit as though it were a riddle.

'You were a train detective,' said Redstart. 'You foiled the robberies!'

'Shan't tell you,' said Glendon.

'You were a Pinkerton man!'

Glendon laughed aloud, saying, 'I'm telling you nothing!'

Redstart frowned, then said darkly, 'Why, you've got to tell me, if I say so – I know your name, remember.'

'Nope,' quoth the old sprite, raising his brows, 'for you know me by first name only, while I have both of yours, Redstart Becket!' And stepping to his boat, he danced a short hornpipe of victory. Truly Susannah had it right, for he was Peter Pan before my eyes – shifting, magnetic, a neat invitation to the curious and the lost and the needy. He twirled a line and was adrift, and we waved and shouted as he seized his oars. The captivating imp! How could I know he was indeed to take flight, and very soon, and that it would be I, and not Redstart, who went with him?

5

Back to the thousand words for a moment: How easily they came at first! I always liked mornings and it was a simple matter to rise at five and scratch down my daily measure. Giddily I wrote a long manuscript about an epicurean shipping tycoon who goes witless like Nebuchadnezzar and tears off his clothes to gallop apeknuckle through the countryside, eating the long-stemmed grasses beside the railroad tracks. I thought it both moral and comedic and even, occasionally, daring; if it rambled a little, Susannah and the boys didn't mind. A funny story! Yet when I mailed it away to Hackle & Banks, a young editor named Bat Richards wrote back to me with polite candor that this might not be a proper follow-up to *Martin Bligh*. He believed it was discursive, aimless – *maundering* was his admirable word. Bat hinted that Grace Hackle, too, had been disappointed in my Nebuchadnezzar tale; he wondered what other romantic, thrilling, and (he added) concise adventures were trotting through my mind. Meantime he had some good news: *Bligh* was into its seventh printing. Rights had been purchased for publication in England! A bank draft would soon follow!

I burned Nebuchadnezzar in a milk pail, stirring the pages with a driftwood staff, and congratulated myself on enduring pain in the service of art. Soon Bert trotted up, and I tossed a stick, and Bert chugged away and brought it back. In this way we played for some time; afterward I felt decently propped up. I had a new story idea and went in the house to write it down.

This one was about a boy who shoots two intruders in the dead of night and straightaway flees the law. I had it in mind that the boy become a dangerous western hero along the pattern of Tom Horn. His would be a life of wild horses, of slender escapes, of comrades laid in shallow graves! Then would come his arrest, his days of sorrow and despair; in the weeks before his hanging he would write his memoir as a lesson to youngsters everywhere who thought it romantic to 'don the red bandanna.' I dashed off the first hundred pages of this project and sent them with a personal appeal to Grace, as I was still smarting over the snub from her subordinate Richards.

Yet Grace was not enthralled. Her reply agreed to 'work with me' on the book though she believed it would take much editing. Frankly, the letter was a little terse. She confessed to having 'flung pages about the room.' She said it was no *Martin Bligh*. If I was determined to continue 'this undertaking' she would naysay it no further. There was a postscript, no doubt written later, in a softer mood. It contained a bit of news about the hallowed *Bligh*: Eleven printings and still rushing forward! Translations underway in Germany and France! Also, the eminent director D. W. Griffith was eyeing it for a moving picture! A bank draft would soon follow.

Well, I never finished the outlaw tale either – next to Susannah, there was no one I was more determined to please than Grace Hackle. She was a refined woman. It was disturbing to imagine her slinging my manuscript, goaded by my weak idioms.

I then wrote a breathless opening chapter about a man whose skin began to turn more transparent day by day. First he was merely pale, then indistinct at the edges. Gradually he could make out bones beneath his lucent hide. No one else could see this condition, which was both relief and misery; his wife loved him still, his children ran about with their noisy passions, but the man was vanishing, and his memory with him. He forgot his friends and his work and began to sit all day, aware of his bones and teeth and his gurgling organs. Poor Susannah! She wept reading this harrowing attempt, and then I went and got mad at her for it.

By now I had left the post office and spent a little money. Bad judgment, oh, yes, but Mr. Bligh apparently had 'legs' and I was certain another story would come along, and the words to tell it with. We sold our unpretentious bungalow and took a big foursquare beside the Cannon River. I bought a horse for Redstart, Queen Anne chairs for Susannah, and a painted rowboat for myself. It was flat-bottomed and homely with leaky seams, and I loved it so much I would creep out past midnight and go down to the river to scull and bail and blink at the stars. Some believed the boat a mere trinket I desired having purchased a house on the Cannon. The truth, though I didn't know it at the time, was opposite. I bought that house to get the boat. You are no failure, on a river. The water moves regardless – for all it cares, you might be a minnow or a tadpole, a turtle on a beavered log. You might be nothing at all.

6

A week after Glendon came to breakfast I rose before dawn and launched my porous skiff.

I was curious about him, that's all.

It was a calm morning with no wind and a comforting primordial smell; a sizable fish swirled beside the boat, a tetchy bittern shuddered up out of the reeds. No one heard me leave except Chief who trotted whickering to the fence.

Some miles downriver Glendon's barn appeared in the first rays of daylight. I knew it from his description: a plain Mennonite barn thirty feet from the river. No house on the place. No shack or corn-crib. It had sooty little windows and smoke trickling out its tin chimney and a black fat-bellied pot slung over cold ashes in the yard. Two hard-wood rails were set in the ground like train tracks from doorway to water's edge. The square door was slid open and there sat Glendon inside, leaning against a stack of lumber. I nearly called to him but noted his tilted head and slack limbs – he was asleep. I beached the skiff on a patch of sand and tied up to a willow.

Normally a person wouldn't presume to enter a man's house with the man draped unconscious just inside the threshold, nonetheless I stepped in and slid the door shut. I nearly fell over Glendon's stipply ankles but he didn't wake or come close to it. There was a bottle beside him with an inch of smoky business in the bottom, yet there was something innocent in the way he slept. Maybe it was his big easy lungs, for his chest rose and fell with barely a sound. I leaned down to shoo away a mosquito on his cheek. He reminded me of Redstart, who could drop asleep on a flint pile.

Now you are asking, *What were you doing in there?* I wasn't sure either but sat on a sawhorse and gazed around. A rowboat lay in progress before me, graduated half-moon frames on a timber strong-back. There was a black cook-stove, a porcelainized Hoosier cupboard wiped clean. No table or chairs, no food lying around – the drinking bachelor is often a renowned pig, but Glendon's barn could accurately be called tidy. Even fastidious. The floor was of unpainted planks over sand, swept bare except for drawknife shavings under the rowboat.

The craft itself was beamy with a square undercut stern. Its planks were red cedar. From its shallow rocker this was a boat you could stand up in to row or to cast a fly across a stream. I bent down and put shavings to my nose.

When I looked at Glendon he was looking back. His eyes were yellow at the edges. A small-caliber revolver lay on the floor next to the bottle. I hadn't noticed that before.

'Glendon, hello, it's Becket,' I said.

And he said, in that mild voice of his, 'Hello, Becket. I expect you're here to help me work.'

He had me build a fire under the iron pot, filling it by bucketfuls from the river. Meantime he set up a long tin trough and stacked inside it a dozen lengths of milled cedar. He removed the blades from two block planes and shined them on a pumice stone and rinsed the blades under a hand pump. By the time he'd dried and replaced the blades I had so much wood on the fire he laughed and looked away.

While the water heated he handed me a block plane and showed me how to remove, by long angled strokes, curls of wood from the bow's rough stem. Paying no heed to my apprehension he set me working downward on the left edge, himself working upward on the right; stroke by stroke the bow grew more fluid and proportionate while curls slid down like ringlets and dropped in aromatic heaps. I could have shouted, could have wept, but Glendon was all business and wanted that stem just so. There was no talking for many minutes. When we finished my forearms were covered with shavings and I felt the weariness of a better man.

'I am glad to have company, it has been a long while,' he said.

'My son wanted me to invite you back.'

He smiled at the floor. 'That Redstart, I suspect there's only one of him.'

'Thank you. Do you have any children?'

He said, 'No, I never. I am told things happen for the best.' He turned away and peered at an upended block plane in the light of the window. Loosening the set screw he slid the blade up into the body of the tool and tightened it and ran his fingers along the bottom to make sure the edge wasn't exposed.

I said, 'Oh, a family is plenty of work.'

'That's what I hear,' he replied.

Eventually we took the cedar planks out of the steaming trough and laid them up one at a time and bent them round the frames with jaw clamps. At this the shape of the boat began to be visible to my landsman's eyes and I said, 'What graceful lines.'

'They are decent lines,' Glendon remarked. 'You can see the sheer now, the curve. A line only gets grace when it curves, you know.'

We boiled and bent planks until we ran out of clamps. 'There are never enough of those,' Glendon remarked, as though this fact had long ago ceased to irritate. His eyes had lost their yellow cast. He poked around his shadowed workbench until he found a knob of bread wrapped in burlap. This he broke in two and gave me half. It was old bread of a coarse texture and I ate it with the happy feeling I had earned a meal for once. Brushing crumbs from our hands we stepped down to the river.

He said, 'You'd best know I am unreliable, that I am a poor friend.'

'A poor friend is better than none,' I replied. It is strange to realize you have no friends outside your own family – in fact I hadn't realized it until that moment.

'I have not always obeyed the law,' Glendon stated.

'Nor I my conscience.'

He considered me. 'I have seen the inside of more than one jail cell. It is nothing I am proud of nor would mention except you have a fine family. Also, I take a drink of whiskey now and again.'

I said, 'I am a fraud and impostor and for at least two years have lied regularly to many people, including my wife. Very soon now I will be found out and lose what small reputation I have managed to acquire.'

Glendon seemed taken aback. Though my confession was

24

perhaps too specific for the occasion, I could've gone on and on. I had the urge to laugh.

He said, 'Do you drink?'

'Not yet.'

'A fellow like you would find it inconvenient. With a boy around, and so on. It ain't all that convenient even for me.'

'You could quit.'

'Yes I could, but I probably won't. Goodbye, Becket.'

'Goodbye, Glendon.'

'Hale,' he replied. 'It's Glendon Hale.'

7

I didn't want to lie to Susannah – I tried to be honest any number of times. In fact the very next evening I strode into the parlor intent on unburdening. When I opened the door she said, 'Come see this, love.'

She was painting daffodils on a wide field, a handsome thousand or so yellow daubs. Susannah's work was well thought of in Northfield – this one had been commissioned by a local college president.

'Howser offered me my job back today,' I said.

So help me this was the honest truth.

'Howser doesn't deserve you.' Her paintbrush darted and stabbed like a hummingbird. 'Here, look at my flowers.'

There are times with Susannah when it's better to come back later, but my conscience had me, as Redstart liked to say, *by the windpipe*. 'I saw him at the hardware store. I was looking at some rope and he came over and said hello.'

'Oh, for goodness' sake,' said my wife.

'Two of his people have left in the past month.'

'You told him no, I assume.' Susannah cultivated a firm dislike of my former employer, who had told me several times I 'didn't tally well' with the vaunted postal efficiencies.

'I said we would talk it over. He seems rather harried.'

'He should be harried, to solicit a man he treated first

with disdain and later with envy. A little harrying might improve him – in fact I am certain it will.' Though elegant as lace, Susannah was ever keen to set bridges alight on my behalf.

'I thought it gracious of him to ask.'

'Did you tell Mr. Howser your new book is nearly done?'

'No,' I admitted, and stopped there. You should know this about my wife: colors are as strong spirits to her. Yellow makes her insouciant, reckless, caustic. The brighter tints of orange render her nearly dangerous. If it's a quiet, confiding talk you're after, by all means wait until her palette is stocked with cooler, more seafaring shades. I said, 'After all, it isn't what you'd call *nearly done.*'

'Well. Soon it will be.' She looked at me, the brush hovering over daffodils. 'You haven't read to me in some time. How is that rogue Mr. Dan faring?'

That's right – I hadn't yet told her Dan Roscoe had been shelved. Nor that I'd begun a new tale about a pirate with a glaring birthmark and a strange halfheartedness about his career. I was forty pages in. Already there were signs of decay.

She set the brush down. 'Monte, is the work going slowly?'

'Yes.'

'But there's progress, isn't there?'

'A thousand words a day.'

She took my hands in hers. 'As you love me, there is progress?'

There is no excuse for lying, but that very morning I'd read over her shoulder while she wrote to her mother: *My darling is still at work on his second book, which none can doubt will exceed his first in reach and power.*

'Oh, good progress,' I assured her, and leaned down for a kiss, and then, as if to seal my deception, peered in at her daffodils. I was amazed to see not only yellow and orange in those petals but also blue and violet and a spicy russet that somehow fit. 'Why, sweet, that's exactly right. That's better than real.'

'Then I will finish it,' she said, clearly pleased, 'and you will finish Mr. Dan, and we'll throw ourselves a party.' With that she let go of me, and her brush took flight again.

Do you see how it was that I could not bear to fail in front of her? Do you see why I deflected?

And so I rose each day and dipped my nib. I filled my hopeless quota. I was the Dickensian halfwit who composes letters by the hour, only to make them into kites and fly them up to God.

Glendon began taking supper with us once or twice a week. He kept an orderly greenplot and never arrived minus chard or kale or chives in wet burlap. At first he was a quiet and somewhat formal visitor, yet the whole house lightened with him there. I admired his plain language and courtesy and the way he found everything interesting but himself. Redstart of course was polite as a pry bar.

'Tell about the lightning strike when all your buttons liquefied,' he'd say, or 'How about the boy you met tossing knives in the street,' and Glendon would push himself back from the table and yield up a trail drive or desperado or other narrow shave. Truly if not for Redstart I doubt he'd have come so often.

But it was Susannah who seemed in some ways to best understand Glendon. Halfway through another cow-oriented narrative she saw an opening and interposed gently, 'How did you meet your Blue, then, if I may ask it?'

He gave her a look both stricken and grateful. 'Why, I met her on the seaside, ma'am. On the Gulf of California.'

'The Sea of Cortez,' Redstart quietly amended. It is the Gulf of California on most maps, but for poetry's sake Redstart preferred to credit the brazen conquistador.

'That's where I met her, anyway,' said Glendon.

'Please tell about that, if you will,' said my audacious wife.

Glendon blew through his nose, reached in his vest pocket and withdrew a briar pipe. He would never build a cigarette in the house but a pipe is a courtly smoke. He packed it and scraped a kitchen match against the stovetop.

'Well, I was fresh out of work, ma'am. I had a gelding named Ribbon and fifty biscuits in a saddlebag. We were drifting west from the rancho country. One day we climbed a hill and there was the sea. My goodness – did you ever go to the ocean, Redstart?'

'Nope.'

'There ain't any preparation for it. It was so pretty I lost my head and galloped Ribbon into a state of resentment. The sea is always farther than it looks. We didn't get there till the next night. When I took his saddle off he reached down and bit me on the knee.'

'Chief wouldn't of bit *me*,' said Redstart.

'I camped by a spring and watched the sea until a little sail hove up from the south. A fishing rig, an old man working a net and a youngster bailing water off the bottom. I hailed them and they come ashore. "You are lucky to have that horse, brother," the boy says to me.'

'Honest? He was the one with the sailboat,' Redstart pointed out.

'Oh, but Ribbon was impressive,' Glendon replied. 'One of the faster geldings in that part of Mexico. Not quite the fastest,' he added. 'Anyway they lived up the shore a ways and asked me to supper. I let the boy ride Ribbon home and I went in the boat with the old man. That's where I met Blue,' he said to Susannah. 'She was his great-niece.'

Susannah said, 'What was she like?'

'Oh, a quick step, lively eyes, you know the things that

30

draw a young man. But awfully quiet,' Glendon said. 'I had some Spanish, you know – I'd say something to her and she'd only nod. I wanted to hear her voice but she didn't let me, not at first.'

'How old was she then?'

'Sixteen or thereabouts. She lived with her mother in the town of Oscuro and walked over every day to look in on the old man. Air out his rooms, make supper. I don't think I heard her voice for a week.'

Susannah smiled. 'Monte wasn't such a patient suitor as yourself.'

'Maybe I was too patient,' Glendon replied. 'Once I knew her voice, you see, I couldn't leave. No, then I had to hear her laugh. Another long wait. She'd come watch me work on the old man's boat. It was coming apart, you could poke your thumb through it in places. He was too stiff to do the repairs himself, but he was a good teacher. I bent new planks and pounded oakum in the seams while Blue came and watched. Every day I tried to make her laugh. I told jokes, made faces – but no, I didn't get to hear that particular music till I finished the boat and took her out in it. Up went the sail in a rowdy breeze and away we flew. Then she laughed, all right!'

'I don't wonder that she fell for you,' said Susannah, her cheeks bright as poppies. She'd fallen for Glendon herself. We all had.

'Oh, now, it wasn't entirely me that got to her,' said Glendon, abashed. 'A sailboat's a terrible advantage – everyone knows that, I guess.'

9

At last I commenced to cheat. I slashed my goal to 500 words a day, then 300. Some days I didn't reach even that; when the sun was high I would stack my pages in a drawer and head downriver. Like a boy I began to hang around Glendon's barn, sometimes trimming or steaming planks but more often sweeping up or just watching. Mainly he built two designs: an elfin peapod and the longer vessel he called the Dobie Swift. They were only rowboats, it is true, yet Glendon was a master: He never worked from a drawing but eyeballed lines and measured with a waxed thread.

'You should ask more money for these boats,' I told him. He had confided to me his price for the Swift now under construction. He was building it for a dairy farmer whose world, I suppose, wanted a little splendor.

'Why is that?'

'You must be barely meeting expenses.'

'Look at this copper, ain't it glad?' He held up a bright sheet. It pleased Glendon to make shiny inlaid sections in the small foredeck of his Dobie Swifts. He generally shaped copper or bronze to the profile of a bird in flight – aglow with polish, they were pretty and simple as sonnets.

'You might be able to produce more boats,' I remarked, 'if you cared to take on some help.' I said this cautiously – it won't surprise you I had begun to imagine myself in such a role. Not that I was any sort of hand with the work as yet, but it's true the contours of Glendon's rowboats had begun to settle and sing in my mind. I pictured sheerlines and tumblehome, rocker and lift; I woke from dreams where my hands shaped gunwales instead of sentences. Who doesn't long for the door in the air?

I said, again, 'Did you ever think of that, Glendon? Did you ever think you might want an associate?'

'A partner? I don't know, Becket.' He ran the back of his hand over the hardwood keel of the upturned Swift. 'Boats are a solitary enterprise, generally. They don't care to be hurried.'

10

'What do you think of visions, Becket?' Glendon inquired one night. He'd come to dinner preoccupied, agreed to a few hands of whist at which Redstart was almost unbearably competitive, and stayed later than usual – Susannah had left the porch and gone off to bed, freeing Glendon, I saw now, to lower his voice and ask his unsettling question.

'Visions,' I said, my heart sinking.

'Dreams, apparitions. Do you reckon them credible?'

I did not tell him no. I did not say to him, Visions are a writer's stock-in-trade but that cupboard is bare for me.

'I keep picturing my girl Blue, on a horse, on the other side of the river.' He brightened. 'Maybe it's just my grubby conscience.'

'What's she doing on the horse?'

'Trotting to and fro. I seen her several times now. She's got a muslin dress on and my black coat over it. Horse is a little Tobiano.'

'That's precise, for a dream.'

'Seems like she's looking for a place to ford. The horse won't cross over. She rides knee-deep into the river and looks across at the barn.' He reached in his pocket for cigarette makings and rolled one on his knee, watching me wonder what to say next. Gently he said, 'You think I am

34

simple, Becket? Think I've got one wheel in the sand?' He scratched a light for his cigarette – his eyes were firefly green and nearly merry.

'You might,' I replied.

He laughed softly. 'She's still pretty. Got a rifle in a scabbard. I ain't sure whether she's come to forgive me or shoot me.'

'What do you mean to do, Glendon?'

He shrugged. 'I'm nervous she'll get that mare to swim across, next time. Blue always knew how to talk to a horse.'

We sat quiet while he smoked the tobacco down and stubbed it out on his boot heel. He said, 'Monte, I didn't ever ask her forgiveness. I was a stupid youngster, you understand. My reasons for leaving seemed good, but they weren't. They were poor and selfish.'

My insides shrank. I sensed a bad ending on the way.

'I am shortly bound for Mexico,' he said.

'But she is remarried, you said.'

'I don't aim to win her back. No – to try would be another wrong against her.'

'After so many years, does it matter if she forgives you?'

'It matters that I ask.'

Do you remember my forlorn mood when Glendon first rowed past in the fog, the time he didn't stop to visit? It returned to me now, with a bitter flavor.

'Well, I'll be sorry to see you go.' I tried not to sound petulant but certainly failed. 'When will you leave?'

'Saturday. I'd go sooner but there is a boat to deliver.'

I didn't reply. His mention of boats brought back to me the idea I'd begun to nurture, the notion of us as partners in trade. I saw it now for foolishness, for a nonsensical flight from all I could not do. Yet I hated to give it up.

He said, 'You want to come along, Becket?'

'What's that?'

'Come along to Mexico.'

My throat lumped straightaway. I was pleased, you see; of course I couldn't go, but didn't say so straight off.

He said, 'I'd be glad of the company. You would be back in six weeks. I understand if you can't do it, though – why, you've got Susannah to think of, and Redstart. I hate to leave them myself, and that's a fact.' There was a little hiatus while both of us thought it out. He may have been having doubts, as he added, 'Also, you got them thousand words a day to perform.'

Shame climbed my face. In my thoughts I drifted through what Susannah might say to this offer. Why is it our failures only show us more clearly the people we are failing? For I saw Redstart laughing at some sparkly fact added to his hoard of knowledge; I saw him on Chief, turning tight circles, raising dust from the grass.

I said, 'I'd like to go, Glendon, but you've hit it exactly – my responsibility's at home.'

He nodded, rose and slapped his legs awake, and picked his way to the river. He had more than a touch of night blindness, so it took him awhile to get there. Then I heard his footsteps on the dock, then for a while his oars thumping in the locks. Then quiet. Far off on the river a match flared briefly.

11

Susannah was still awake when I went in. It had to be done. I said, 'Love, I'm going back to the post office. I've done my best. I can't write a book anyone will want to read.'

She sat up in the darkened room. 'Monte, you can. I've never doubted you.'

'I tried and can't. I'll talk to Howser tomorrow.'

'What about Mr. Dan?'

'Dead alas and his grave unmarked.'

She lit the lamp and we sat together on the bed. If anything is harder to watch than the face of the person you have deceived, please tell me what that is.

She said, 'What about your thousand a day?'

'Not worth much, as it turns out.'

She was quiet.

'I didn't know for a long time, but now I do.' I touched her shoulder, which did not give.

Her serenity was commendable, given I had spent five years telling her all would be well.

She said, 'Let me be a minute, please.'

I left the room, left the house. It was a cool, strange, expectant night. The mosquitoes had withdrawn for a time and I went down and sat on the dock with my feet in the river. I didn't think about much – didn't think, for example, about my wife or the words we had just had, or about the future, or the desolate end of my short career. I thought about block planes, about wood peeling away until just right.

The door closed softly back at the house. Susannah's robe swept with a sound like grass. She came to the dock and went to her knees behind me and clasped her hands around my chest.

'Don't go back to the post office,' she said.

'I don't know what else to do.'

'Go to Mexico with Glendon,' said this arresting woman I had married.

She had been listening through our open bedroom window.

'But why, love?'

'Because he dreamed of his wife,' she replied.

There we stayed in the breathless night. Love is a strange fact — it hopes all things, believes all things, endures all things. It makes no sense at all.

'I will be home in six weeks,' I said.

'You had better be.'

'You're too good for me, Susannah.'

'Yes, I am.' She pulled away from me and became formidable. 'I'll expect letters. A man who can write a thousand words a day can spare his wife a hundred now and then.'

THE OLD DESPERATE

We boarded the Great Northern in the desolate hours. Susannah and I didn't go to bed at all but stacked trousers and shirts into a grip along with razor and books and folding money in a brass clip. At one o'clock we sat silent in the kitchen holding hands on the tabletop. Susannah didn't want to show me her eyes but I saw them anyway. At last we rose and she rolled sandwiches into waxed paper while I woke Redstart. He kicked off sleep with lawless exuberance only to recall I was going away on a train and he was not. I felt him slump. None of us had heart or words.

Glendon met us at the depot. He'd ridden his durable sorrel to town the previous day and boarded her at the livery and himself at a hotel. For Susannah's sake he wore a somber face but anyone could tell he was keen to leave – when the train heaved up he bounced on his toes as if he were nine. He gave Susannah's hand an awkward shake, then grasped Redstart's.

'Farewell, amigo. Is there anything I can bring you from Mexico?'

'A rattlesnake skin,' was Redstart's instant reply. Glendon nodded and was gone into the sleepy train with my son gazing after him.

My own goodbye fizzled. I'd written a short and perhaps

overly rueful verse on the back of a scalloped photograph. The picture was one Susannah loved, of the two of us laughing by the shore of Lake Superior. I imagined her reading my verse there on the platform, her eyes brimming; I conceived a send-off rich with absolution. As it turned out, though, the light was dreadful – she turned the card this way and that and couldn't discern the words and gave up at last and poked it in her handbag. Why was I a slave to sentiment when it failed me so reliably? Meantime Redstart had disappeared somewhere. The train groaned forward; finally there was nothing to do but step aboard and fix Susannah there in her tawny linen coat and pumps. Bareheaded and pale she stood watching my face and didn't wave or blow a kiss, though Redstart did pop up beside her with a jolly look and pantomime to me that he had laid pennies on the tracks, to be rolled out like dough at our departure.

Rocking south I found Glendon and sat beside him. The coach was half full of nodding passengers. At the rear a small group of young men sang in near whispers. They were practicing harmonies – en route to some gospel tent, I suppose, for their repertoire found the present world intolerable.

'Becket,' Glendon said softly.

'Yes.'

'You're generous to come along.'

'No. I'm glad to come.'

He shut his eyes and slept. The young men whispered their salvation songs. They worked until dawn on voicings and rhythms, rewarding themselves at last with a stealthy foray into ragtime. They tapped their knees and snickered, a hopeful sound that made me realize I'd told Glendon the truth – despite my unsatisfactory parting from Susannah, I was glad to be on that train. When first light showed pockets of fog I even imagined it was smoke instead, and ourselves charging pell-mell for danger – an unfussy childhood sensation I'd forgotten all about. It seems strange, looking back, that I ever believed I would soon be home again.

In the strong sunlight a wattled conductor moved through the coach, informing us the dining car was open, the barbershop soon to follow.

'Barbershop,' Glendon said. 'Becket, ain't this transport? A barber on a train!'

'It's plush,' I replied.

'And fast – we are already in Missouri.'

We rose and smacked and patted down our corrugated sleeves.

Few things lift spirits like a boisterous dining coach – this one smelled of bacon, coal oil, citrus, scorched porridge. Racks of limes and pale oranges hung behind the counter. We took a booth just being vacated by a police detective with a handcuffed lout in his custody; the gospel fellows were there, laughing to draw the attention of two blondes eating pancakes; plus a tribe of Mormons engaged in shrewd debate about the great Giants pitcher Christy Mathewson, who refused to pitch on Sundays. Say what you like about their doctrine, these elders knew their baseball.

Before we had a chance to order, a young man asked to join us. 'Sorry to intrude, there are no other seats,' he said, sliding in by Glendon. 'I'm Samuel Cobb of the *Globe;* look there, I've lost a cuff link, not that I'll need it where I'm going. With whom am I about to enjoy breakfast?'

Glendon supplied our first names and asked Cobb where he was going that cuff links were not compulsory.

'Mexico,' Cobb replied. He was flushed, with schoolboy cheeks and a pleasant cynicism that made you want to pay for his coffee. He was heading for Chihuahua to interview the famous *insurrecto* Pancho Villa.

'The brass wanted a piece about President Carranza,' he informed us, 'but Carranza's a bureaucrat. Who cares? Villa's the real story in Mexico. I told them one sharp page about Villa is worth the King James Bible about President Carranza.'

He pronounced it *Mehico* as though he'd been born there, though of course he was only an affable East Coast young-ster marked by race-horse ambition.

'I am writing a travelogue en route,' he informed us, setting out paper and a fountain pen. 'Maybe you fellows would enrich my narrative. Where are you bound, and on what errand?'

'Oh, your narrative will be rich enough without us,' said Glendon mildly, just as a regal colored waiter arrived at his elbow. I'd been observing the waiter right along; though old and eroded, he never lurched with the train but moved among the tables steady as a ghost. He took orders with his hands clasped behind his back and didn't write a thing down.

'Ham and eggs,' Glendon told the waiter, an instant before meeting his eye.

'Yes, sir.'

Cobb and I ordered the hash. The waiter nodded to us but didn't move on. Glendon looked up at him and said, 'Hello, Franco.'

'Mr. Dobie,' the waiter answered.

I had a tilting sensation, as on a carnival ride.

'You were a young fellow last time, Franco.'

'Not anymore, Mr. Dobie.'

'Nope – no, look at us now,' Glendon said.

The train swayed and the waiter remained with us in silence.

Glendon said, 'Franco, this is my friend Mr. Becket, and here is Mr. Cobb.'

'Pleased to meet the gentlemen.'

Rarely have I been more fully at sea. Cobb half rose from his seat, saying, 'Well, a chance reunion, isn't this a propitious turn,' but he might as well have been outside the train, in Missouri, talking to himself.

Glendon said, 'I knew you right away, Franco.'

The waiter said, 'You're aware there is a policeman on the train?'

'Yes, we saw him.' After a moment Glendon added, 'Do you know what I am now?'

'Honest, I expect, sir.'

'So much as I am able, yes.'

Another little silence.

'I still got to say something to that policeman, Mr. Dobie,' said Franco.

'Of course,' Glendon replied.

3

Back in the coach Glendon sat with his bedroll and grip across his knees – he'd paid a porter to retrieve them from the baggage car. He looked at me expectantly and I did not disappoint.

'What are you fleeing from? What have you done?'

Unruffled he replied, 'I oughtn't have asked you to come, Becket.'

'What is this Dobie business?'

In saying the name aloud I remembered what he called his rowboat, the Dobie Swift.

'How much do I need to tell you, Becket?' he inquired sadly. 'Is it enough to say boatbuilding was not my first career?'

'What was, then?'

'You would make me say it,' was his pained comment.

'I am owed the truth.'

He drooped a little. 'I did say I was unreliable. A poor friend – those were my very words.'

'I was obtuse not to see it. You robbed trains, didn't you? You robbed this train! That's how Franco knows you.'

'Not this one, no. Franco was on the Union Pacific in those days.' He looked at me miserably. 'Maybe someday I'll have the leisure to tell you about it, if you still care to know.'

'You have the leisure now.'

'That's not so. If I stay much longer, I'll end up having to speak with that policeman, and then the road gets narrow in a hurry.'

'You told Redstart you were a detective. A Pinkerton.'

'No, he conjured that belief all by himself.'

'You allowed him to sustain it.'

The door of the coach whistled open and Samuel Cobb arrived.

'You will forgive me for asking,' said he, out of breath.

'Asking what?'

To Cobb's credit, his manner was apologetic. He dropped his voice and said, 'For your story, sir. Won't you tell me what this is about?'

'Didn't you get my story already, from Franco? You're a quick lad, it's easy to see,' said Glendon kindly. 'I thought you'd have it in your hip pocket by now.'

'I'm afraid Franco is taciturn.'

'Well, disappointment comes to us all.' Glendon stood and took note of the countryside – we had swung alongside the Missouri River.

'This is bitter luck,' said the doleful Cobb. 'Here's a bracing story happening right in front of me, and you fellows won't tell me what it is.'

I said, 'Mr. Cobb, we need a few moments here.'

He gripped my sleeve. 'Take me into your confidence. Please! I may even be of service somehow.'

'I'm sorry, Cobb,' said Glendon. 'You're very decent and I wish you well.'

The newspaperman decided against further pleading and adopted a flat tone. 'I don't want to be indelicate, but if you won't speak to me I'll approach that detective myself.'

'That's probably the right course,' Glendon replied. 'That's what I'd do, were it me.'

'Give me a reason not to,' Cobb urged. 'Don't you see I'd rather write your story than watch it end?'

'I appreciate that. You go on, now, and do what your conscience suggests. Good luck, Mr. Cobb.'

When the scribe had left in a state of agitation, Glendon hoisted his baggage and I followed him out onto the smoking platform where the wind batted in our ears.

'And where are you going now?'

'You know where.'

'This is a mistake,' I said. 'You needn't run. Stay and let me find you legal counsel.'

But he only shook his head and looked off toward the Missouri, as if waiting for something particular to appear. The gradient flattened and turned upward, the train slowed and labored. I felt sudden pity toward Glendon; under such strain, his civility to the journalist Cobb remains impressive to me.

'It isn't as bad as you believe,' I said. 'Whatever happened was long ago. You have lived honest a long while – you've built a business, and friendships. That is certain to mitigate any charges that might be brought.'

'The charges are bigger than you imagine,' he replied. 'Moreover, they are true. There is no forgiveness for me under the law. Goodbye, Becket, you were a steadfast friend, go home to your wife and boy.' And so saying, he threw his bedroll and grip into the long-stem beside the tracks and followed them off with a leap. I saw him disappear and the grasses thrash; then he stood and raised a hand to me before collecting his kit and starting away.

49

4

I returned to the dining car and took a table. In moments the waiter Franco stood beside me.

'Mr. Franco, how do you know my friend?'

He said, 'How may I serve the gentleman?'

'You may answer my question. What has he done?'

Franco didn't answer but stood waiting for my order.

'Please, Franco.'

He was carved of stone, and the train swayed round him.

'I beseech you,' I hissed, and the sound fit, for it was my dignity escaping.

Franco said, 'May I bring the gentleman a cup of coffee?'

I nodded. He brought the coffee. Presently my mope was disrupted by the weary-looking officer we had seen earlier. 'Good morning, sir, my name is Davies. I'm a detective with the Kansas City police. Royal Davies.'

'Good morning, Detective – join me,' I said, gesturing at the seat.

'Thank you. I've been up and down this train,' said Royal Davies mildly, catching Franco's eye and raising a finger, 'and your companion is no longer aboard.'

'No?'

'No, he has vanished. I am not surprised. What can you tell me about him?'

I tried my hand at deadpan. 'We both embarked from

Northfield. I am getting off at Kansas City. He intended to continue on, I thought.'

Royal Davies withdrew a small notebook. 'And I intended to relax on this little excursion.'

I was too jumpy to keep quiet and asked where he had traveled.

'To Chicago to see my sister. It wasn't meant to be a working trip. I'll write down your name, if you don't mind.'

'Monte Becket.'

'And his was Glen Dobie?'

'I knew him as Hale,' I said, and was immediately appalled to have given away so freely my friend's true name.

'Did you know he was a wanted man and felon?'

'No,' I said, aware of my neck hairs.

Royal wrote a moment in his notebook. He drew up his eyebrows and said, 'Becket, did I ever arrest you?'

'I would remember it, Mr. Davies.'

'And yet I know your name,' said he.

From his granddaughter, as it turned out: she was fourteen, a reader of wide-eyed tales. She'd gotten *Martin Bligh* for Christmas from a favorite teacher. How about that? But if I hoped this unlikely connection would be of use to me somehow, it was not to be. Royal Davies was a little more cheerful, but that was all.

'She loved that story, you know. Talked about it at dinner until it frankly got in the way. I wonder if you would inscribe her copy. Would you do that?'

'You mean you have it with you?'

'Oh, no — no, Mr. Becket. I mean, maybe you would inscribe it tonight.'

With coldness in my guts I said this would depend on

my business in Kansas City. That I was come to research my next book. That I would be busy in municipal records and library stacks.

'How long will this research take, do you suppose?'

'No more than a few days – then I'll be traveling home.'

'I'm afraid you'll have to extend,' said Royal Davies.

'That is not my intention,' said I.

'More intentions,' he waved. 'Relax, Mr. Becket. Be my guest for a day – well, maybe two.'

'I'd rather not extend! What is this about?'

'Nothing at all, I suspect. It's a matter of checking on your association with the nimble Mr. Dobie.' He put his elbows on the table and looked me over. 'He's rather the old desperate, you know – been out of view for some time.'

It does not flatter me that my skin took a peppery chill at his words, nor that I bridled, saying, 'I told you, I barely know the man.'

He gave me a kind look. 'And yet you confirmed to that newspaper fellow, Mr. Cobb, that the two of you were traveling together. Now, here comes the station. Don't worry, I pledge you a comfortable stay.'

'Are you arresting me, Mr. Davies?'

'I am inviting you to my home,' said he, 'until a sharper detective than myself can ask you this and that. It may take half an hour; it may slow you down a day. In the meantime, it would please my Emma if you would come write your name in her book. Don't make more of this than it is, Mr. Becket.'

His small speech set me at ease again and made me remember something important, that is, my own innocence. I thought of Glendon's hazy identity – his duplicity, it began to appear, toward me, his friend. I suppose my feelings were injured. In any case this Royal looked steady and responsible with his trim whiskers and weary gaze. I said, 'Where is your other charge?'

'Sleeping, chained to his seat. If he had got more sleep to begin with, he mightn't have robbed the till. Tired people assess their chances unwisely.'

I smiled at that and Royal Davies nodded. 'You're doing these youngsters no service, you know,' he said, looking tired himself. He got to his feet and braced as the train huffed to a sooty platform. 'You authors, I mean – this world ain't no romance, in case you didn't notice.'

'So I am discovering,' I replied. It was, I suppose, the expected wry answer, and made my host chuckle, but now I am taking it back. I take issue with Royal, much as I came to like him; violent and doomed as this world might be, a romance it certainly is.

5

Royal Davies's brave wife suffered with a brutal arthritis, so much of the labor in that house fell to Emma, the grand-daughter. Her parents had moved to San Diego and she was to join them in a few weeks; it was plain to me her grandparents viewed her approaching departure with dismay. I can testify she roasted a beautiful mallard hen that night, with stuffing and candied yams, and cleaned up afterward – an obliging girl.

As for Mrs. Davies, she kept me under the reptile eye while listening to her husband's presentation of contemporary Chicago, of his sister's health, and of the bothersome train ride home. He was a bright observer, and I soon saw he had to be, for Mrs. Davies asked him a chain of incisive questions which built one upon the other until she had in her mind a satisfactory portrait of her husband's absence. You'd think it might abrade, to be probed that way by your spouse, but Royal Davies seemed to shine and grow younger under her spotlight, and he leaned toward her, his language and whole manner becoming honed and precise.

She then turned to me and said, 'Very well, Mr. Author, it is your turn.'

'I am at your service, Mrs. Davies.'

'You are a man of letters,' said she. 'Tell me, what do you think of Boyd Singleton Ample?'

I said, 'I think he is very good, yes, a very important writer.'

There are any number of reasons to tell this sort of lie. As a well-treated guest, I didn't wish to seem critical of her taste. Worse, I didn't wish to appear jealous – every one of Mr. Ample's books sold much more briskly than *Martin Bligh* had.

'Go on,' she said, nodding.

'Well, his insights on human miseries are salient,' I ventured. It didn't seem like a weak limb to climb out on – it was a common opinion among people who were serious about Literature and the phase it was in, whether of ascent or decline, and What It All Meant for Society. In his most recent novel he had sallied out with a number of momentous ideas, namely that war is difficult, and that poverty is difficult too; in fact, that much of human experience is marked by difficulty. I don't remember who is at fault.

'Horse puckey,' said Mrs. Davies, an excellent glint in her gaze.

'Pardon?'

'He is boresome. Humorless as a mole. Tell me, are you familiar with *The Pestilence of Man*?'

'Yes. Yes, I am.' I was mortified, because in my politic reply I'd set myself to defend a novel I hadn't even finished. I tried! But it's a long book.

'And did you laugh much, reading it?' she asked.

'I'm afraid not, Mrs. Davies.'

'Call me Celia, please. Did you get much good from it?' she persisted.

'Why, I think so – Celia.'

'And what particular good would that be?' said my rigorous hostess.

'Well, a broader understanding of human darkness, I suppose,' I said, seizing a trite phrase from a review I'd seen somewhere. Oh, I was on thin and melting ice now!

Celia Davies said, 'At this minute many people are reading books by that man; I will tell you how to identify them. They own a furtive brow, men and women alike; they bend their slight shoulders, they tug their lips and fret. Mr. Becket, do you find yourself improved for your new understanding of human darkness?'

I adjusted my own shoulders. I had a new admiration for Royal Davies, that he could be a match for her. 'Few things have managed to improve me, Celia,' I admitted, 'although a day or two of your company might.'

Then she laughed, which was the youngest thing about her; Royal took her hand with an expression of delight, and I was released from that table.

6

I think often of Celia Davies. She could squeeze a conversation to its rind, leap it east to west, or change its axis wholly. Her wits were as supple as her fingers were rigid. I don't know her story, for she was an adept evader of questions, but her life would be a giddy crossword, working down from some clues and across from others.

By dusk I felt in the home of friends. I had ceased to dread my forthcoming interrogation, and Royal suggested with some pride that I go down to his dock and enjoy a little evening on the river.

People who live on riverbanks understand one another. If you can't be on a boat, a dock will do. Royal Davies's dock was wide with a bench on the end where you might sit in contentment with the ponderous Kaw slipping under you, and beside the bench Royal had bolted an iron post on which you could hang flowers or a kerosene lantern.

'What are you writing, Mr. Becket?'

It was the granddaughter, Emma, holding a slip of paper and her copy of *Bligh*.

'A letter to my wife.' Though a poor one, awkwardly composed.

She blushed brightly at this and said, 'Is it a love letter?'

'Yes,' I replied, which renewed the blush. She had an ungainly gallantry – I found myself thinking of Redstart, who would've ignored her even as he stood on his hands to catch her eye.

'Is Mr. Davies coming down?' I asked, for she seemed out of words.

'No, he is rubbing Grandma Celia's hands. He has a balm he uses every night.'

'They're going to miss you when you move to California,' I said.

'Oh, no!' she replied, dismissing the notion.

I scratched away at my letter in the dying light.

'Mr. Becket?'

'Yes?'

'Did you love writing *Martin Bligh*?'

'I did, yes.'

'I wanted to show you my bookshelf, but Grandpa said not to trouble you,' she said, then with disarming practicality, 'I like you better than Spearman, but not so well as Alcott. Here.'

She had taken the time to copy down the titles of all her books, some two dozen of them, and she handed me this inventory; thus I was given a peep into her life, which was a rich one, for there was *Lorna Doone,* and *The White Company,* and *Last of the Mohicans,* and *Life on the Mississippi,* and *Kidnapped*. Of course there were also lesser titles, such as *Her Prairie Knight* and *Nevada Juliette.*

'It's a winsome collection, Emma,' I said, squinting down the list. And it was — a most gaudy parade, and she loved it all. I said, 'Have you a favorite character among all these?'

Without delay she answered. 'Alan Breck, who kills his enemies in the roundhouse and writes a song about it before the bodies cool.'

It is a recurring sorrow to me never to have raised a daughter.

She said, 'Will you read to me from your book?'

'It'll be getting dark,' I observed, and she fled in her skirt for the lantern.

There is a scene where Martin is being pursued by Chiricahuas – his horse has run itself to death and Martin has strapped the mailbags to his own back and is running full claw through a mesquite thicket. Probably such a thing is not possible – I'd never seen a mesquite thicket to know. Martin anyway dives and scuttles and is a clever jackrabbit, but these are the scheming Apaches so you would have to say the outlook is bad. It's a tense scene, if I say so, and Emma drew her knees up and hugged them, and I bent to the page in the yellow light and gave Emma my best production, because I had no daughter, and because even as I read I recognized the coming time when Emma would laugh at my little story and take up with Mr. B. S. Ample or a similar concerned citizen.

'Oh, read some more!' Emma cried, when Martin had got safely away.

'No, not now. You go up to the house.'

'Thanks, Mr. Becket,' she said, and went.

I set down my notebook and watched a johnboat move down the Kaw toward its confluence with the great Missouri. The johnboat had no lantern at its bow and was a flat graceless box like a wagon bed.

It bothered me that I hadn't been able to talk better sense to Glendon. I kept seeing him heave his gear and then himself off that Great Northern train. Why had I not persuaded him to try the law? Certainly I could've worked on him, chipped away, swayed him from folly.

Susannah could've done so, had she been along.

Well, I'd be back in Northfield in three days. Perhaps it would be easier to tell these things to Susannah in our own sunny kitchen over cinnamon rolls.

I stood and doused the lantern and was startled to hear a chuckle nearby, out on the river. The chuckle came from the johnboat, which had drifted quite near. Staring out I saw a silver waterline, a dab of silver above it.

A man in a boat, standing up.

JACK WAITS

Read the confessions, the memoirs, the courtroom transcripts: There is always a line the scoundrel steps across and becomes a wanted thing. Sometimes the line is theater and robbery and kicking the fellow off the bridge; sometimes it's simply a signed sheet of paper.

Perhaps it is fitting that my own line was merely the end of a dock.

'Becket, again,' said Glendon in a low voice, tossing me a rope. 'What do you suppose are the chances?'

'Glendon!'

'You were reading to a little girl as I went past. I knew your voice, you see.'

I looked up at the lit windows. 'This is Royal Davies's place. A police detective and a kind host.'

'Are you in trouble on my account?'

'I don't think so.'

He nodded. He looked small and exhausted and melancholy, and hope awoke in me.

The porch door opened and Emma came out and shouted into the dark, 'Mr. Becket? Come up for pie!'

'I'll be there in a minute,' I called. To Glendon I said, 'Come with me.'

'If I do that, I will miss Blue.'

'It is what's right,' I told him.

'Imagine it were Susannah, and you twenty years gone.'

He looked away and grasped the dock post as if to shove off.

I said, 'Glendon, it might be your final chance to give up on easy terms. Davies is a good man; you will get fair treatment.' For you see, the moment he appeared there arose a picture of the skilled lawyer, the kindly judge, the life restored. Suddenly it seemed clear – Providence had given us this opportunity. 'Don't you see? We have met again here for exactly this purpose!'

Glendon replied, in his blunt fashion, 'Nope, that ain't it.' He squinted out at the water. 'Fog is coming in, I feel it on my face. Can you see far in this? What can you make out?'

'I see a bow wake where that barge is passing,' I said. Fom the shuffling and lowing there were cattle on the barge, heading down to the Kansas City stockyards, I expect. It was a great long barge.

'I don't see it, I hear it only,' he replied. He went quiet; fatigue lay on him like blown dirt. Then 'Becket,' he said, 'I'm sorry to ask, but I'm going to anyway. Won't you come along? It's shabby of me, and there's not a thing in it for yourself, or your sweetheart, or your cunning lad. In fact I suppose it will prove the most expensive thing you ever do, and you are bound to live with regrets and have no kind forgiving thoughts for Glendon Hale; still Blue comes before me, and I am asking you to come along and help me see this through.'

Sighing I replied, 'Davies says you're an old rogue. A bandit of tolerable rank. "Nimble Mr. Dobie," he called you.'

'I was obliged for a while to use names besides my own. I am sorry to have deceived you, Becket.'

'He claims you kept outlaw company for a long span of time.'

'Almost a decade.'

'Did you kill anyone?'

He turned from me and looked into the southern sky. 'You have every right to be a hard customer, Becket. Will you come, or no?'

'Glendon,' I said, 'what I am supposed to think of you? I wish you'd tell me that.'

I heard the porch door open again, and this time it was Royal. He called out, like an old friend, 'Say, Monte, are you coming?'

Glendon said nothing. He stood relaxed and balanced – *contrapposto*, my artist wife would say, a hand on a hip. I could feel the draw of his silence, the draw of his naïve and weak-eyed quest for atonement; no doubt even his shifty past was a draw, for his life seemed a curving line, capricious, moment by moment inviting grace.

'Monte?' Royal called again.

'Of course,' I replied. 'Of course, I'm on my way.' And off the dock I stepped, into that heartbroken vessel.

In this way I crossed over. In this way I slid apart from all that was easy and comfortable and lawful; and so tired was my bandit friend that I took the oars myself and rowed facing forward. You just see better, standing up, and I enjoyed the feel and sound of the sweeps, and not until we were miles upriver did I remember my clothes and grip, back at Royal Davies's house, and my unfinished letter to Susannah, abandoned on his dock.

2

He slept several hours while I rowed upstream – my hands and forearms were aching when he woke and sat up in the johnboat.

'We're short of food,' he stated.

I'd been wondering about that. Swing heavy oars all night, and you are likely to want breakfast in the morning.

He said, 'I haven't much: corn biscuits, salt, a water jar. About two mouthfuls of whiskey. We need to replenish.'

'Couldn't we catch a fish?'

'I've got no hook and line,' he said. 'We'll try to find that too. Meantime, let me know if you see any turtles. A turtle is first rate.'

'This business doesn't pay too well, does it?'

He gave a worn laugh, sighed, adjusted himself on the boat's soggy floor, and pondered his dubious origins.

'I don't even recall how I started,' he said. 'I was a poor learner in most ways but you know what, I made a quick little bandit. It come to me like speech. I'd walk to town and back home to discover things in my pockets. Pulleys, bolts. Shiny stuff.'

'Like a crow,' I said.

'Yes, I suppose. I'd haunt the docks or the Odd Fellows Lodge. Or the doctor's office – oh, but he had bright tools, scissors, tiny round mirrors for peering down your mysteries.'

He laughed softly. 'I had a fine collection of sparkly bits.'

'What about your parents? Didn't they see what you were doing?'

'They missed quite a bit, for we were never acquainted,' he replied, which made me forget the oars until we lost headway and began a slow arc backward.

'Who raised you, Glendon?'

'A number of people. I remember most of their names. There was a hardheaded churchgoing couple who could see down the road and tried to iron me out, and a schoolteacher, never mind her, and there was a stumpy old duff who made toast and jam every day of the week, but by then it was late in the game. I was adept at slipping off.'

It took some time to absorb – this revealed black crow of a child. It cut from me the stubborn assumption that we all start alike, and made a larger achievement of Glendon's everyday goodwill and decorum.

I pushed us upstream while the moon fell and was buried in the southwest horizon. When dawn touched the river I saw a large fish swimming beside the boat, a broad-backed fish with a pointy tail fin. In the chalky light that fish accompanied us upstream just beyond the radius of the oar; its knobby spine against the current made a creamy nimbus of foam.

'Glendon,' I said, 'what made that waiter Franco recognize you, after so much time had passed?'

He didn't answer. When I looked round, his head was laid back against the transom and his mouth had fallen open. He was still the boy adept at slipping off.

3

I woke to the ruthless sun – it pierced my eyelids, it smoked against my face. My back and shoulders were a rigored snarl, but my hands were the worst of it. Those oars! Their paint was worn off a thousand years ago; the grips were cracked and splintered. Though I never thought my hands were soft a horde of blisters had arisen and these boys were fat and toadlike.

I got to my knees. Glendon stood on the riverbank skipping stones across the water. He called, 'Good morning, Becket, how do you fare?'

I held up my hands with a croak. Immediately his face darkened. He trotted to the boat, which we'd pulled up into tall weeds, and emerged with a wood bucket and a flat brown bottle. Overturning the bucket on a level patch, he told me to sit down.

'Let me see your hands.'

I held them out. They were half-open and immobile. Placing his own hands underneath mine, Glendon with sudden force squeezed them shut. Blisters split, water ran down my wrists. 'Hold them out again,' he ordered – I'd jerked them to my solar plexus.

'What's in the bottle?'

'Whiskey.'

'No thanks,' I replied, even as he uncorked the bottle

with his teeth. Grasping my flayed left he doused it with the whiskey, then did the same to the right while I hissed a few rough syllables questioning his method.

He said, 'I got feet like this once in Oaxaca. They went septic and bloated like death, everything purple right up to my knees. Would you like that?'

While the sting evaporated from my hands, Glendon dug out his half jar of clean water and his corn biscuits. The biscuits were old and collapsing but smelled so good I soon forgave him the whiskey. We ate them quickly without talking, listening to a persistent cow bellow upwind goodness knew how far away. Tossing the last crumbs in his mouth Glendon looked at the sky, then put his palm to my forehead.

'You're fevered and it's getting hot. You need some shade.'

He returned to the johnboat, emptied it and dragged it to a sandy place. While I watched he leaned the boat up and over so its bottom faced the sun, propping it with a driftwood crutch.

'Crawl under,' he said. 'There's a farmstead somewhere close. I'm going for provisions,' and with that he climbed the shallow riverbank and was gone.

The shade failed to soothe, however. As the sun climbed all breeze vanished. The johnboat accrued heat instead of deflecting it. Also there were tiny holes in the packed sand – I dreaded insects, though none came out to pester me. Eventually I rolled out from under and gimped up the shore. It was all hot sand, mudwhorl and boulders; redwing blackbirds fought in clumps of dwarf willow. I was so thirsty the murky Kaw River looked clear. Abruptly faint, I sat in the lee of a tall rock and shut my eyes.

I dreamed Susannah was there and laughing. In the dream I'd made some appalling error and kept confessing and confessing, yet she refused to recriminate and would only laugh and suggest we go enjoy a nice picnic.

When I opened my eyes a massive snapping turtle lay relaxing not twenty feet away. Redstart would've been impressed – this brute was six times the size of our Cannon River painted turtles, with a ridged head and moss sprouting on his shell. He was also fearless to the point of disinterest. Recalling Glendon's advocacy of turtles I found a decaying perch in the shallows and offered it to the snapper on a willow rod. He didn't move. I flung the perch away and prodded the turtle's snout with the rod. Nothing, though his round eye was upon me, his patient and calculating gaze. I backed away – I had no experience catching snappers, plus my hands hurt. As I headed back to the johnboat my dream of Susannah returned and I ached with remorse and grief that I was not with her.

When Glendon strode in he had a calico bundle under his arm. He said, 'Here we are then – go ahead, open her up,' and immediately set about making a driftwood fire.

The sack contained half a loaf of wheat bread, molasses, butter, a brick of castile soap in white paper, and a jar of turpentine. Two pale squash and a glossy orange also rolled out at my feet.

I said, 'Someone was kind to you.'

He didn't reply but tore off a chunk of bread and opened the tin of molasses. His demeanor was businesslike and I thought he must regret my presence, a concern that faded when he poured molasses on the bread and handed it to me. It's a better meal than you might think. By the time

70

we finished, the driftwood had caught into a hot low fire and Glendon set a skillet over the flames. He sliced in butter and shavings from the soap. Seeing my look he said, 'Don't fret, this ain't dessert I'm making,' stirring until the castile melted into the butter. When the skillet smoked he moved it onto the mud and poured in a little turpentine, stirring this mess until it thickened and cooled.

'Now bring me those poor soldiers,' Glendon said, nodding at my hands. I wanted none of his reeking homebrew but what could I do? Dipping it up in his palm he spread that combustible on my weeping blisters.

'Hey,' I said. Despite being warm from the fire, its effect was cooling. I flexed my cautious fingers – a few blisters did split, but the ensuing pain was clean and a sort of icy reprieve. 'Hey!'

'Yes, what about that,' he replied. He picked up the calico and tore it in strips and wound it smooth over my hands, leaving the fingertips free.

'We'll leave now,' he said, 'but look, we can fish on the way,' pulling a coil of braided line from his shirt pocket, then a folded paper containing two fishhooks.

'Wait, Glendon – there's a turtle up the shore,' I said. 'A big one. He was there an hour ago, anyway. I didn't know how to bring him in.'

'Whereabouts?'

I motioned upriver. There was a boulder on the sand shaped like a knee and the turtle was just beyond it.

'Thank you, Becket, good spotting, a turtle would serve us well.' He stooped to his pack and found a small sheath knife and a whetting stone. Whisking the dark steel back and forth over the stone he said, 'You know, I'd lost track of the years since I took a thing not mine. Even that john-boat I bought off a youngster, the shrewd little customer. But this supper of ours, that medicine, these fishhooks – I am a thief again today.'

'I'm sorry. It's on my account.'

'No, it's what I always was.' With a pained smile he added, 'It just weighs more, this time around.'

4

How much do you know of snapping turtles? Redstart knew a lot. They might reach a hundred pounds and a hundred years old. Their beaks and their wills are adamant: Once clamped on something, such as your heel, not even death will pry them loose. Redstart's friend Clive Hawkins once killed a snapper by removing its head with a crosscut saw, and it still walked away and made it nearly half a mile to the river before it stopped. Butchering that stubborn pilgrim they found a Chippewa arrowhead embedded in its shell – a scrawny Hawkins boy must've seemed like no adversary at all, at least until that saw blade appeared.

So I was impressed when Glendon staggered into our tatty camp with the snapper alive and profoundly offended. He had it upside down by the tail. The turtle bent its neck this way and that to get its bearings. I'm sure the brute weighed sixty pounds.

'I thought you were going to kill it,' I said, when he dropped the snapper on the sand by the johnboat.

'I was, but it's hot,' he pointed out. 'As soon as we kill it we have to eat it; otherwise it'll turn.'

The turtle poked its head up, sighted the river, and made three or four inches of getaway before Glendon stepped on its tail. He said, 'Where do you think you're going, uncle?'

That's how we ended up sharing our slight johnboat with a snapper as broad as a barrel. Glendon heaved him up front and barricaded him there with half a dozen melon-sized stones. The turtle slewed around and tried getting up the sides, finally backing his tail into the bow and watching us resentfully.

'I'll row,' said Glendon.

It was good of him to spare my hands, but the new arrangement wasn't comfortable. The snapper forward meant I had to share the stern of the boat with Glendon's pack and bedroll. Also there was a small leak; I had to keep repositioning the gear to keep it dry. By moonrise I was sitting in an inch of brown water, despite dedicated bailing with a tin cup.

I said, 'We are not getting quickly to Mexico this way.'

'I was thinking that,' Glendon replied.

'At the next town we might find a car,' I suggested.

'That's enticing, but I don't drive, Becket. I never learned.'

'Why, driving's a pleasure,' I said. 'Everyone should drive.' Susannah had taught herself; she had an instinctive feel for the shifting mechanism and loved to accelerate through gut-tickling lifts and hollows.

I said, 'I could teach you in ten minutes — think how impressed Blue will be when we show up and there you are, behind the wheel of a car.'

'I don't imagine that would impress Blue,' he replied. 'No, I don't imagine she'd be too much impressed if I landed a Curtiss airplane in her yard.'

It was hard to hear his voice so downcast. 'How long were you with her, Glendon?'

'Two years, a little more.'

'You never told me why you left.'

'I wasn't a very good citizen down in Mexico – not till I met Blue, at least. After we married I built her a swift dory. That girl loved water. Then a neighbor liked the boat and wanted one too, so I made another and traded him for a couple of cows. That's how it went. Two happy years, Becket.'

He'd been sculling steadily along but now missed the water with his right sweep and stopped a moment to recover. He said, 'One day a man rode up and looked at our little casita. He sat on his horse a long time, looking. Then he rode away. Next day he was back knocking on the door. I stayed in the hall. He told Blue he had a job for me, but she said I wasn't home. When the man left, I told her he worked for the provincial or even the central government and when he came back the conversation would not be about a job.'

'So you took off? You just left?'

He said, 'I was afraid.'

'I bet she'd have gone with you.'

'Yes, she would've,' he agreed. 'She wanted to go – we had quite a battle over it. Of course I couldn't jeopardize her that way.'

'Didn't you jeopardize her by leaving?'

'Either course was evil. I judged things would go easier for an abandoned wife than a complicit one.' Glendon picked up his pace with the oars. 'I promised I'd send for her. She let me take her little dory, and I left in the middle of the night.'

'Was that the last time you saw her?'

He didn't answer for a moment, then said, 'Now you

75

bring it up, Becket, it seems I am still in the jeopardizing business. Witness yourself, innocent as a tot, yet fleeing the law with me.'

He had a point, though I was somewhat affronted by his *tot* comparison. I was about to take issue when there came a forceful scraping sound. Glendon flailed and we heeled badly – my neck hit the transom and my feet were in the stars.

'Did we hit bottom?' I cried.

'No, it's the turtle.' It had managed to crawl up over its rock fence and had tumbled into the midsection of the boat, where it scuffed about as if to bash the planks loose. 'Where is he? I can't see him!'

'Put him over the side and be done with him,' I shouted, over the thumping turtle.

'No – he'll feed us for days.' Glendon had found the snapper with his oar and now, night-blind as he was, reached down and got it by the tail. 'Here, help me block him up.'

Quite gently he set the turtle back in the bow while I crawled forward and rebuilt the barrier.

'Poor bugger,' Glendon said. 'Poor old uncle. Listen how quiet he's got, Becket. How awful he feels. You were never in jail, I suppose.'

'Not yet.'

'Well, it ain't any good. You don't ever wake up and say to yourself, What a pretty day, I feel good today. No,' he reflected, 'a jail ain't nothing but a collection of corners.'

5

We struck no town that night and laid up at dawn on a sandy shore under a cottonwood tree. The tree would've provided superior shade, but by noon the sky turned to funeral wool and November came hissing through the grass. There are people who 'predict' the weather, but on the Great Plains these are a fragile and disappointed little group. Glendon opened his kit and threw me a knitted sweater and donned an oilskin himself. We dragged the boat to high ground and knocked a few dead limbs off the cottonwood.

'Becket, I'm hungry. Go kill the turtle.'

I must've looked blank.

'Stick this branch in front of his nose. When he takes hold, pull him out of the boat. Pull his head as far out as you can and cut it off.' He handed me his knife.

'My hands are still pretty bad,' I said, despising my faint heart.

'I rowed us all night, I guess you can kill an old turtle,' he replied. His voice had a grouchy rasp I hadn't heard before.

I returned to the johnboat. The snapper appeared relaxed. Warily I held out the stick, which he refused to notice.

'He won't bite,' I called out.

'Tap his beak, that'll fetch him.'

I tapped away but the turtle just blinked and drew his head into his cave.

'He isn't coming out.'

Glendon came over and gave the snapper an admiring look. He said, 'You been reading our mail.' To me he added, 'Good luck, Becket,' then off he went and started digging an earthen pit under the cottonwood tree. He had in mind to build a fire in the pit and drop in the turtle and roast him slowly in the shell, along with the squash. We'd had nothing since the bread and molasses – in this cold breeze a roasted turtle sounded like Christmas dinner.

I laid the tip of the stick against its beak and tried to pry it open but nothing. You don't expect restraint from these beasts, you expect reflexive violence. Instead this snapper refused to snap and in fact looked canny and patient.

Soon enough Glendon had the pit dug and a vigorous fire inside it. He came over to watch my futile coaxings.

'You sound impatient. Look at his face – he doesn't like your tone,' Glendon said, amused.

'If that was my toe instead of a stick, he wouldn't show such control,' I complained. 'Why don't we just put him in the fire and cook him alive? That's what they do with lobsters.'

But Glendon was displeased. 'Cook him alive? Look at him. He's probably older than me. It would be impertinent.'

'Well, you kill him then. I tried, and he won't come out.'

'Cook him alive – for shame, Becket.'

This attitude of Glendon's struck me as impractical and possibly priggish. We were hungry. It was cold. Nobody ever thought it was impertinent to steam a lobster.

Climbing the riverbank I walked out onto the meadow where an upstart wind whipped the grasses into confusion. I didn't look at the sky until a cold gust struck my face – only then did I see the black storm front riding in from the west. It rolled forth in a toppling motion. Even over the wind I could hear the sizzling noise of water striking earth.

I turned and bolted, reaching the river with the first raindrops. They spanked the weeds, tore leaves off the cottonwood. Determined to cook something, Glendon had thrown the squash on the coals and covered the pit with dirt; without a word between us we turned the boat upside down and crawled under. The turtle was in there too, and together the three of us watched the rain turn to hail. It began as fingertips but changed to knuckles and fists. Amid this deafening rumpus the turtle decided to escape. Forward he plowed – the gunwale lifted against his ridged back, hailstones thumped his mossy shell plates. I caught Glendon's eye as the snapper moved out into the storm. Neither of us tried to stop him.

6

Luckily for the boat, it only hailed about ten minutes. Not many vessels could've stood up to more than that – some of those hailstones were as broad as my hand, and they fell in bunches. Peering out from under, all the land we could see turned white in a hurry. Even the river was lathered in the churn inflicted by that storm; the turtle left a dirty track through the ice as it shambled away, but that was quickly covered.

When the hail ended the rain resumed, a soothing noise after that unseemly pounding. I actually dozed awhile. When I crept out later, the smaller hailstones had all melted and the large ones lay shrinking in their craters.

Glendon sat under the cottonwood on the only dry patch in sight. Pale smoke drifted up from the mound where he had covered the fire. I could smell the squash cooking in the earth – my stomach lurched with desire.

'Look here, Becket,' said my friend.

Next to the mound, almost on top of it, lay the snapper. His feet were withdrawn but his head was extended and he looked curious and stately.

'What's he still doing here?'

'I guess he likes the warmth,' Glendon replied. He took his knife and uncovered the two squash. They were ruddy from cooking and steamed when he pierced their skins. We still had a little butter and Glendon produced the salt in a milk-glass shaker. He said grace in an apologetic voice, given he had stolen the entire meal; my fingers shook while I ate, and my eyes watered, and it was a remarkable supper right down to the seeds and the ropy core. I even considered eating the rind, but noticed Glendon laying his rind on the earth in front of the turtle. Instantly its beak flashed out – it wasn't faster than sight, as people will say, but it was certainly quick as a flinch, and the report of that beak popping was impressive. In seconds our snapper bolted the squash rind, then retracted his head as if to contemplate its effects.

'Goodness,' Glendon said – we were both a little shaken. 'What do you suppose he's thinking about in there?'

'Fingers.'

'I had the same theory,' he replied. 'Look at him, he's disenchanted. Well, go on and feed him that rind, Becket – let's see if he'll do it again.'

Glendon changed my bandages before we left and was pleased to see no infection; my fever had disappeared as well, and I didn't protest when he suggested I take a short stint at the oars. The only protest I did make was on behalf of the turtle, who, I argued, had earned a reprieve. Also, I confessed to a growing feeling it might be ill luck to kill the brute, even if I proved clever enough to do the job. But Glendon only laughed, saying, 'Nonsense, he was lucky today. We'll eat him tomorrow.' So we made a bed of sand in the bow for the turtle to sit on and poured water on the sand so he would be cool and content. At dusk we shoved off under emerging stars.

Rowing went better this time. I'd gotten used to the motion of the johnboat and the length of the oars, and the bandages guarded my palms from further damage; after an hour or so Glendon said I'd done enough and we switched places. I straightaway fell asleep in the stern.

I woke to Glendon's voice. He was talking – praying, it turned out, though I couldn't tell at first since he didn't speak in the fraught inflections common to prayers, at least my own. It was more as if he were relating to a good listener the details of his day. He told in brief about the farmhouse he had robbed for our supper, its drafty construction and air of paucity. He told of peering round a corner to see the farmer close by in the field, encouraging his draft horses in a clay-dust haze. In Glendon's tone were sadness, acceptance, and finally humor – this as he told about the snapping turtle escaping in the hailstorm, only to take warmth and comfort from the very fire on which we'd planned to roast him. The irony made me chuckle.

'Monte, you're awake.'

This may have been the first time he used my Christian name.

'Yes. I'm sorry to eavesdrop. I didn't know you were devout,' I said.

'Oh, no.' He was much entertained. 'Devout, ha! Nope, I got no such claim. Though I did get myself baptized, once upon a time.'

'As a boy, I suppose.'

'No, later, when I was staying at Hole in the Wall,' he said, so offhandedly you might've thought it was a colorfully named hotel and not the infamous lair of Cassidy and

Longabaugh plus dozens of less likable bandits. 'I know what you're thinking,' he added, eyeing me.

'Hardly a spot for church doings,' I admitted.

'That's true, and the fellow who dipped me was hardly church material. Crealock was his name; he'd been a thief, then a preacher, then came back around to thief again. But he'd preach sometimes at the Hole. He had a firm grip on Hell, yes he did.'

It was a serene night on the river, and Glendon told me of his salvation in some detail. Crealock had described Hell in upsetting similes until Glendon asked what he must do to keep from its torturous flames. There was a grassy stream flowing through the Hole and there Crealock baptized the young penitent, asking his name and receiving Glen Dobie; and Glen Dobie wept along with the preacher, who thanked him for his amenable heart and gave him a paperboard copy of Proverbs, although he could not read. Then the preacher instructed him to rest awhile and implore with God and taught him a short prayer to say. The new convert went to his bedroll rejoicing. He uttered the prayer a number of times and cried several times, feeling the mercy of God pour out like cleansing oil upon his limbs, and late in the day he arose and ate a sustaining meal of frijoles with side pork and rode out from the Hole with his friends and robbed the Union Pacific as it climbed the Wyoming foothills.

Then 'Hold on, Becket,' he said. 'Do you hear a noise?'

He held the oars still in the water for maybe a minute. There came a faint yawp or roar — an alarming, abrasive sound. As we listened it resolved to coarse laughter.

'Is there a boat?' Glendon asked. 'Can you see anyone?'

The clouds had moved off the waxing moon. It was

bright enough that dips in the land appeared as shadows. Looking upriver I saw a yellow light I had moments earlier taken for someone's cabin window – now I could see it was an oil lamp hung on a black line sliding swiftly down-river.

'It's a barge or raft,' I said. 'See that light?'

'I'm afraid I don't,' he replied, though between our progress upstream and theirs down, the distance was shutting dramatically.

'Look more to the left.' It was a big raft carrying the shapes of men. I couldn't tell how many. They were laughing again, though with more reserve – some new note had entered their revelry.

Glendon said, 'Hang these eyes of mine, what a disappointment they are.'

'There. Right there. See how close they're getting?' Because now in the moonlight I could make out three or four men squatting at the near edge of the raft. Another was standing aft – from his motions I judged he was steering with a pole or long oar. 'Look,' I said, 'there must be a strong crosscurrent. They're coming straight this way.'

But even at close range Glendon couldn't see them, for abruptly their lantern was extinguished. Onward they came. There was no laughing now aboard that raft, nor talking either. The man astern poled hard across the current, and the others crouched at the waterline.

7

Violence seldom issues a warning – I saw that raft sweeping down, yet it still didn't seem possible the men aboard intended us ill. 'Hello the boat!' I shouted, only a little wary, when they were perhaps forty yards away, but received no answer. Not until they were within twenty yards and still silent did I comprehend our trouble, though Glendon did – he couldn't see the raft but, guessing its position, dug in an oar and sent us surging away at an angle.

His maneuver saved us a ruinous collision. The man at the helm roared a vulgarism and bent viciously to his staff, aiming again to transect our course; the river brought them nearer and the men crabbed forward, one shirtless looking wild as Lear with his hair lashing his chest. Another was bristly and squat as a boar – the others I can't recall, but with these two I own details because just before the raft swept downstream, missing us by perhaps fifteen feet, Lear and the boarlike fellow gathered themselves and sprang. In disbelief I shouted *Glendon, pull!* but they were robust swimmers and reached us in seconds. The bristly man clutched the gunwale and the johnboat heeled so that Glendon sprawled in the bottom. That brought cheers from the raft, then more as the bristly man got a leg over the rail – his face was chaos: mucky nostrils, warped lip. I stuck my foot on his eyes and shoved even as Lear came swarming up the opposite side. On his knees Glendon swung an oar but missed and Lear tumbled into the boat, getting a fistful of my shirt. We tilted steeply and something skidded down hard on my ankle. It was the snapper. A claw flailed, there came a blunt report like the one we'd heard at supper, then Lear began to shriek. Where the turtle took hold we will never know but I can tell you Lear dragged himself over the side in the grip of a living bear trap and down they went the two of them, a final shriek burbling up out of the river like the sound of Hell established. The bristly fellow surely heard it too, for in his rush to escape he gave the johnboat a shove that carried us yards upstream. His companions on that wretched raft had drifted down a considerable distance, but I suppose he made it safely back. That devil was strong in the water.

8

From first to last the raft incident used fewer than ten minutes of our lives, yet every day I see the faces of those men – the one who went down with the turtle and the feral witless one who escaped. In the minutes afterward I was so glad to be living I could only tremble, but there was no sleep for either of us that night, nor much talk until just before sunup.

'Glendon, do you suppose he could have got to shore, somehow?'

As I said it the hinge of my jaw made a gristly cracking sound; I'd been unwittingly clenching it for hours.

'Now, don't you waste dismay on that fellow. He invited what he got.'

'Nobody invites that,' I replied.

'Well, at least he was bad,' Glendon said. 'If a man's got to die, let him be a bad man.'

'Good or bad, I'm not sure it matters.' You'll excuse my dark mood – it seemed I could still hear that last, sodden, faraway scream. I felt culpable and exposed.

'It matters,' Glendon stated.

I had no reply. Susannah appeared in my mind – she was probably just coming awake, my nightgowned wife looking out at the sunrise, at caddis flies lifting off the river and Chief grazing in the mist. This idyllic and distant picture heightened my grief. Belatedly it seemed my finest virtue was the distance I had maintained from death; now I had this freight to carry and no place to lay it down.

On we went upriver. The sun eased up off the eastern prairie and still he kept rowing. He said, 'I killed a man once, but he was a good man. God grant he'd been wicked.'

I didn't ask but he told me anyway.

'It was a train job – my last, it turned out. I came through the cars and this stout laddie stood up behind his seat pointing a gun. Handsome, a nice turn of speech. He offered to accept my surrender.' Glendon's voice tightened. 'I guess he worked up at the California legislature. You don't think of politicians having any spine but this one did. He had a wife, too, it seems.'

'What did you do?'

'I shot him. Monte, I shot that brave fellow three times, including once in the face. Yes, I did.'

He looked at me and I turned away.

'When the boys asked what happened, I made it out he'd shot first. It was easier to think of it in that way. I tore it down and rebuilt it in my mind, you see.'

I said, 'He would've shot you, I suppose,' guessing it was little comfort.

'I wasn't scared to die,' he replied. 'Truly I wasn't. It was incarceration that scared me.'

'Avoiding jail is poor reason for killing a man, Glendon.'

'Yes, it's as you say.'

He rowed on while the sun climbed and the river began to stink of heat.

'I got incarcerated once,' he said. 'It wasn't a week after leaving Blue. I rowed around the point of Silena and there were six Porfirian guards waiting for me in their epaulets. They broke up my boat and put me in a wood box in a place called La Bestia. Twenty months I spent in that box, before I slipped away. But you don't need to hear about that, no sir, you don't.'

Now we heard a train whistle and the passage of its wheels west to east. We heard the high moan of a steer. It seemed likely a town was around the next bend or two, so we pulled up on a spot where cattle had nibbled the lower branches off some poplar trees. It was cool and mossy under the trees. We rested against their trunks.

Glendon said, 'I ain't paid for that politician yet. After the wood box I got real hard to catch.' Mournfully he added, 'You see how it is, Becket.'

We sat a long time in the mossy grass. Lost, that's how I felt. A page had turned and the story was a new one filled with doubtful creatures. I got up and walked away by myself but no solace came, and I drifted back to the shade of the poplars. Glendon hadn't moved. From time to time he'd sigh like a dandy. He was tender that way; he couldn't bear discomfort between himself and a companion. Finally he sat himself up and said, 'Becket, this won't do. You have got to go back home.'

'I came of my own will, you know that,' I said, but grudgingly.

'Rubbish, you came under a deceit. I oughtn't have begged your help. It was weak of me and I rue it.'

A picture of Susannah arose like a breeze in my face, and excitement at returning to my known world, followed by a bewildering sorrow that my guilty friend no longer wished my company.

I said, 'What would you have me do?'

'You've been good to me. I won't forget. Go back to Minnesota. Kiss your wife, raise your boy. Why, you can be home in a few days.'

How the blood beat in my fingertips at that! 'But the police,' I said. 'Royal Davies. I'll have to get square with them first.'

'Of course,' he agreed. He was so amenable I could only picture him as he had always been with Redstart. Yielding, indulgent. Despite everything it reached to my heart.

'I'd rather not put them onto you.'

He replied, 'If your conscience allows it, I would appreciate if you neglect to mention Blue. Other than that it makes small difference. They won't get me, Becket.'

'You seem awfully confident of that.'

'I'm fairly sure of it. I'm a gifted sidestepper. It's natural as walking, I'm afraid.' He'd gotten out his briar pipe; packing it fully he leaned back with a match. Now that he'd done right by me and told me to go home, he seemed lonesome and resigned. He said, 'What do you dream of, Becket, at night?'

'That I am at sea, or in a snowstorm.'

'When I was young I used to dream of escapes, and wake up sweating,' Glendon replied. 'Now I mostly dream of captures, and you know what? I wake up calm.'

9

The town upstream was confidently named Revival, which fit my mood as we clattered up its boardwalks. Glendon was subdued, but I was thinking of home and Susannah's embrace. I'd even begun to imagine myself a better individual, one tempered by experience and loss. Talk about your quick recoveries!

Revival had wide earth streets and a sense of deferred prosperity. The single avenue between water and rail was occupied by livery and grocer and hardware and fine dirt whisking along the ground. I washed at an outside pump, entered the mercantile, and came out wearing a new denim shirt and carrying another in a tied parcel. A mob of boys was flocked by the tracks and I asked them about a barber.

'Behind the café.' One pointed. The mob was in merry form – a couple of them had a twisting bullsnake between them and were pinning it down head and tail with forked sticks.

I thanked the boys and Glendon tossed some pennies on the ground. They forgot the bullsnake instantly.

'It's a shave for me,' I said.

'I'll walk up to the depot.'

The barber was a cheery gossip boasting two chairs side-by-side before a wide mirror. Entering the shop I was jarred by my reflection in that glass. It was just barely me. I was used to resembling what I was – a well-meaning failure, a pallid disappointer of persons, a man fading. This fellow looked tired and rough, but – if I may say it – capable. Wary, I would say, and of dubious intent. It hit with a thump that people seeing this personage would not guess me for anything but a stranger with a firm grip. It was almost a pleasure to squint at the glass. What would Grace Hackle say, if she happened by and saw me? Nothing at all – but she'd think, *The strenuous life!*

'Step up,' said the barber, and I did.

As he soaped my jaws an old fellow swung into the shop. A straight-up, handsome, slender, leathery brute, he swept off his hat and took the other chair like he'd bought it off the showroom floor.

'In from Kay Cee?' asked the barber, for the train had rumbled in some minutes earlier; we could hear it panting still.

'California, by way of Kay Cee,' said the old strap, lifting his chin.

'You come through the big rains?'

'Hail on the tracks we had to get out and shovel.'

The barber wrapped a steaming towel on that gritty face and asked was he here on business.

'Yes, I'm looking for a man.'

'You're with the police, then.'

'Pinkertons,' was the disdainful reply.

Now the blood sang in my brain, it hummed in my hands. I felt unaccountably fearful.

'I guess you're after the brigands who came off the river,' remarked the barber.

'What brigands are those?'

'Bunch of no-accounts – came in on a raft, broke into Lilly Bale's tavern. She says they took two hundred dollars, but that's Lilly talking.'

'Your brigands will have to wait. I am after bigger quarry,' said the Pinkerton, through his towel.

'Whatever you say,' said the barber.

'I don't suppose you've shaved a short reprobate with white hair and mustache,' said the old strap. 'Demeanor I would describe as tranquil.'

'Be still,' the barber told me, for I had twitched as the blade approached. And to the other he said, 'Does your reprobate have a name?'

'It may be Dobie or Tracy or Hale, though he has others as well.'

At this all strength drained from me. I peered over at the man's hands on his knees, hands like rope and harness.

The barber began to take off my whiskers in long swipes. When he paused I craned out the window, but no Glendon did I see.

'Have you a photograph of this person?' inquired the barber.

'I wish I did; the bugger has managed to avoid all Kodaks.'

A few more swipes and my face emerged in the mirror. My customary face. I was sorry to see it.

'There you are,' said the barber, swabbing my neck.

I stood from the chair and put some coins on a shelf. Out I rushed to find Glendon coming up the boardwalk. Taking his arm I said, 'There's a man looking for you.'

'Who?'

'I didn't hear his name. Tall older man, dark, getting a shave. A Pinkerton agent.'

'Well, as I live and breathe,' said Glendon.

'Do you know him? Where are we going?' For we had changed course and were crossing over toward the café.

'To get some dinner,' Glendon said. 'If I have to become scarce why do it hungry?'

The place was almost empty and we took a table in front with a view of the barbershop. We ordered soup and coffee and had a short wait, during which I was confronted again by myself in the window. Oh, it was the old Monte in that glass. It was who I had been before I left Northfield; who I would be again when I returned. As we waited a kind of illness entered my limbs and guts. The window both reflected me and rendered me transparent. My clothes and skin rippled like the surface of water. There was my shaved and thwarted face, which I looked straight through to the street beyond. Here was my morbid thought: What if I am forgotten already? Suppose I go home, and she does not notice?

Before our meal arrived the leathery customer came out of the shop and stood a moment blinking in the sun.

'There is the man,' I said.

'I don't see so good from this distance,' said Glendon.

'Hold on,' I said, for the old man adjusted his fedora and came straight across toward us. I was some thirty years his junior but could only envy the resolve in his carriage, his easy step, his peregrine eye.

'Well, what about that,' said Glendon, with admiration.

'Who is he?'

'It's Charlie Siringo, the old badger. I didn't know he was still working. Maybe the Devil takes care of his own at that. He looks good, wouldn't you say?'

He did look good. At that age it's hard to do better than

fire and sinew. He came up the steps at a vault and entered the café. He nodded to me in recognition from the barber's and I nodded back, wondering that he did not come over to scrutinize Glendon.

'Doesn't he—' I whispered, turning to my friend, but Glendon was gone without a sound, like a dived water-bird, like a coyote vanishing into the brush.

10

Charles Siringo sat at the counter and ordered a slice of dark bread, no butter, cup of coffee. He took a piece of black chocolate from his pocket and laid it on the counter – he liked it unsweetened, I was to learn. He looked like a stork or Trappist. You would expect a Pinkerton to be inspecting the faces of everyone in the café, but Siringo merely unfolded a newspaper and bent himself over it. I laid a bill on the table and left by the front door.

Round the building I found Glendon in the alley. He had a loaf of brown bread in one hand and a pie in the other. A cinnamon dog with a big square head was sitting in front of him, tapping its tail and whining.

'I went out through the kitchen, look what the pleasant cook had on hand,' Glendon said. 'Let's eat. Behave, you,' he told the dog.

We came out of the alley with the loping dog and went up the street by the post office and seed merchant and blacksmith and finally crossed a dirt lot to a board church signed Revival Baptist. It was the last building on the west edge of town, the usual little white church except they'd run out of paint; half the church was white, the other half plain darkened pine. Also the steeple had never been mounted but was sitting in the yard like an obelisk. You could tilt it back and forth in the weeds. The church door was open and it was cool in there with gray light entering the windows.

We had no table but a modest altar and Glendon laid the food on it saying, 'Here we are, God, and grateful for the bread.' He opened the brown loaf and we fell to. The patient dog sat watching us and sometimes Glendon threw it a chunk which it snapped skillfully from the air.

'I'd planned to see you off, Becket,' he said. 'Things being what they are, however—'

'I'll go along,' I said.

'No. We agreed on this.'

I didn't want to explain; it would sound senseless. Yet at last I knew my mind on the matter. If I went home now I would be the living failure scribbling on the porch. The alien in the mirror with his bones below the surface. In short: not much use in this world.

'If I go home, I will disappear,' I said.

Glendon gave me a narrow look. 'I think Susannah won't forgive me.'

But I knew she would forgive him, and me as well. 'I told her six weeks. We have been gone only two.'

We finished the bread and embarked on the pie. 'Charlie Siringo, think of that,' he mused. 'You'll get a kick out of this, Becket – Siringo's an author. He wrote his life story, I think. There's hardly a felon he ain't chased. Never read it myself, but I knew a young man who carried that book around like the Bible.'

'He called you a "short reprobate."'

Glendon smiled shyly. 'What about that? Somebody must still be interested.'

'You're the gifted sidestepper, isn't that correct?' I inquired, with an eye to the windows.

'Oh, I'm light on my feet,' he said, 'but Siringo's no deficient. We know each other well, which complicates the matter. Moreover, I dealt him a slight once.' Glendon fed the dog a handful of pie. 'Of course it's been years, but I doubt forgiveness is the sort of fruit he cultivates.'

Revival's livery had three horses in clean stalls, then several empty stalls, and in back of the building two Ford A coupes on their tidy springs and a Packard with twisted green fenders. The Packard's front lid was propped wide and a boy was scrambling over its vast innards.

'We'd like to buy an auto,' I told the boy.

He was a grimy handsome child of sixteen or so – blond curls, girlish cheeks that must've vexed him no end. He said, 'Those two Fords are new. My boss Lewis knows Mr. Ford himself.'

'What about this one,' I said, nodding at the Packard.

'I'm still fixing it. Dr. Burke fell asleep and drove it smack into a grain bin.' The boy smiled at the ground and when he looked back at us his eyes were full of private comedy.

'How much for a Ford?' I asked.

'I don't know exactly,' he said. I suppose neither Glendon nor I looked like new-car prospects.

'What about the Packard?'

He looked it over. 'Lewis wants forty dollars for it. Don't those fenders look dumb? I can make it run, though.'

'Thirty sounds fair,' I said.

''Course it might bust a axle or a fuel line,' the boy added. 'Where are you gentlemen off to?'

'Why do you ask?'

'You wouldn't be going south by any stretch?'

'What's your name, son?' Glendon inquired.

'Hood Roberts.' He stood arranging feet and shoulders as if to make himself taller. His hands were black and he wore two different boots. He had a puffy lip. He said, 'I could ride along as far as Oklahoma. I'm full grown and a good mechanic.'

'How come you want to go?'

'Sick of Kansas,' Hood replied.

'Are you in trouble?'

The boy gave a dimpled grin. 'Down in Ponca City they got a ranch called the Hundred and One. They run western shows. They got Russian Hassocks and camel riders and gorillas in a cage. They buy horses by the trainload and sometimes they buy the train too. You drop me off at the Hundred and One I'll be just fine.'

I had to smile. In his certainty, his tumbleforth speech, was a trace of my own Redstart.

Glendon said, 'I know what the Hundred and One is. I asked were you in trouble.'

'No sir.'

Glendon shook his head. 'Cowboy days are finished, Hood. You need to be thinking along other lines.'

'Over nuts,' said Hood Roberts, his cheeks pinking with disappointment.

'Look, you know how to fix this automobile,' said Glendon gently. 'That's worth ten times knowing how to rope cows. There are a thousand automobiles in Kansas City and half of them need fixing. You got a good start, son.'

'You think cowboying's done you don't know the

Hundred and One,' said the boy in a small voice, looking away from us.

In no way did I believe Glendon would venture to give that boy a lift to Oklahoma. It was foolish, for we were truly absconders now – wanted men, sought not just by polite officers like Royal Davies but by the fiery Siringo, who happened to be within two hundred yards of us at that moment.

'I'll drive you there, if the Packard busts I'll fix it,' Hood declared in a burst. 'I'll work through the night. We can leave tomorrow. I'm a capable traveler.'

Glendon was quiet. Who hasn't had it happen? You see your blundering self in another, and your instincts turn to powder. For that matter, looking at the Packard, the idea of an included mechanic had its allure. The boy stood before us in his mismatched boots. Glendon said, 'Is that what you really want, son?'

'That and that's all,' Hood answered.

12

We slept in the tall grass by the river. It wasn't bad except I woke in the night to the sound of pigs rooting up a yard. A livid rending of sod a few yards from our campsite – when they finally moved off and I got back to sleep it was only to dream their eyes and tusks.

But it dawned at last, a shimmery morning. We emptied the johnboat and set her adrift. Lugging our gear we stumbled across a pocket of ripped earth twenty feet across.

'Gracious, what's this?' Glendon asked.

'Some pigs tore it up in the night, the noisy brutes,' I replied.

Glendon paled slightly. 'You heard the pigs?'

'You didn't?'

'No, I didn't. You'll laugh, Becket, but I dread those animals. A pig's a devilish creature – I'm just as glad I slept through it.'

We walked up toward the town. It was a cool day but not for long; already the sun was drawing misty coils from the grass.

'*I* didn't sleep through it,' I said.

Hood Roberts had worked all night, as promised. The Packard ran, though noisily, and I handed thirty-five dollars to a sandy-haired man named Lewis, who walked me round the car with its torn spokes and mauled fenders before handing me a bill of sale. Here is one of those moments a man remembers. Should you be considering the use of an alias, let me advise you not to pass too much time in choosing it; just reach in the old hat and pick one out rapidly. That's what I did. *Jack Waits,* I wrote, with a salty flourish, and handed back the paper.

'Traveling mercies, Mr. Waits,' said the courteous Lewis, and we were on our way.

Glendon, as mentioned, did not drive, so that part was up to me. Oh yes, Hood could drive, but I rarely allowed it – he was too distractible. He might cruise along evenly for twenty or thirty minutes, but say he observed something interesting off to the right: a Canada goose flaring in to land or an appealing horse throwing its mane about. Such spectacles made Hood forget about steering the Packard, and off the road we'd drift into whatever pasture or plowed field or other lumpy piece of Kansas was at hand. We had some dire flights! After the first day I drove all the time. Hood sulked a little, but he couldn't stay blue for long – his spirits were just too high.

'Did you see the way that farmer looked us over?' he would ask. 'Did you see that girl beating out the rugs? She wanted to come with us, I bet – she had a funny look.'

Everything looked funny to Hood in those early days. He talked and he laughed; he talked himself hoarse; he talked like a former mute distrustful of the cure. He told how he'd been to see the doctor – Burke, who'd wrecked the car – and how Burke cut a prodigious wart off the thumb of his right hand. Hood spoke proudly of that wart; he said it was dark and fuzzy like a small mammal. A mouse.

A vole. Once he forgot it and reached for a girl's hand and she screamed and ran down the road. He told us this story our first night out, camped beside the riverbank.

'Let's see the thumb now,' said Glendon, and Hood held up his hand; there was a dishy place where the skin was glazed shellac.

'It's a fine job,' Glendon remarked.

'Yes, he's a good doctor, but a sorry driver – this was the third car he spoiled in two years,' Hood said, adding, 'Doctors oughtn't be allowed to drive!'

It seemed fitting, having the boy along. I was glad for his company, his lifted soul. He laughed about the doctor, laughed about the wart; later, curled by the little pile of coals, he laughed in his sleep. Glendon sometimes did that too. In my whole life I have known just two people to laugh in their sleep. On that short trip from Revival to the Hundred and One, I was kept awake by both of them.

13

What can be said for Kansas? *Plain* describes it nicely, both as grassy tableland and unadorned prospect. It's wide and there you have it. To one born amid forest and bluff on the upper Mississippi, Kansas is so wide and its sky so flat it's disturbing.

'Aren't there any hills at all?' I asked Hood Roberts as we built up the fire in the morning. We were camped by the road and in that rosy sunrise could see miles of plain at every point of compass.

'Supposed to be some not far to the south, the Flint Hills, they're called. You don't seem happy,' he added, to me.

'I would be happier if there were a few hills,' I said, though I couldn't have explained why this was so. It wasn't just being out in the open that troubled me – though it's true a pursuer like Charles Siringo could see us from far away, it's also true we would see him coming. No, my anxiety was of another order. I felt laden. Air itself has weight and mass, and Kansas had the most air of anywhere I'd ever been.

'Even one hill,' I muttered.

But Hood only looked at me as though I were past understanding, and as for Glendon, he was almost merry. We'd bought a few pounds of bacon in Revival and he had some snapping in a skillet. A tin pot sat on the coals, jetting steam.

'Here now, be useful — pour us some coffee,' Glendon said.

'Oughtn't we get going, pretty soon?' I asked.

'Settle down,' he replied.

I handed him a smoky cup. 'I just can't seem to feel at ease.'

'You will.' He stood and nodded at the great whitening sky. 'We're sure small, wouldn't you say? Takes the onus off, somehow.'

Later, after I'd crossed hundreds of similar miles — after I'd slept on my share of plains — I would begin to see what Glendon meant. The time would arrive when I too exulted in something as slight as fresh bacon under big skies. But that morning there was little exultation for me. The rosy sunrise that lifted Glendon only made me think of Susannah and my poor judgment in leaving her — not just once, now, but several times. My various exits, my reluctance to go home, seemed expressions of abandonment. Even the hissing bacon made me glum, for bacon was Redstart's favorite breakfast. Deep in remorse I thought how poorly I'd repaid my family's trust. I cast my eyes about but found no comfort, only the fixed flat horizon, the limitless sky.

'Mr. Waits,' Hood said.

He may have said it more than once — I wasn't used to the name.

'What is it?'

'You ain't had but one chunk of bacon. Are you ailing?'

I gave him the rest and told him I missed my wife.

'Your *wife*. Is she pretty?'

'Pretty and smart – am I right, Glendon?'

'Those things, plus she paints like a Frenchman,' he replied.

Hood gave me a skewed smile. I said, 'You'd like her, Hood. She's got a feel for the road. You ought to see her drive.'

Hood said, 'Come on, Mr. Waits. You do the driving, I guess.'

'We trade off. She drives faster than me though it isn't really a contest. Once we drove all night up toward Lake Superior – we had three gasoline cans in back but still ran the tank dry and had to walk a few miles. The moon was so bright we could see wolf tracks by the road. She sang every song we could think of until we saw the harbor lights, and then we knew where we were.'

'Does she make good pastries?' Hood wanted to know.

'Orange rolls every Saturday morning.'

Glendon said, 'Do we have to talk about the rolls? A minute ago I was glad to be here.'

'I had a Danish one time, that Lewis give me,' Hood said. 'He called it a Danish, and there's a widow makes doughnuts for people she likes.' He regarded me a moment. 'If she's pretty, and good at pastries, then how come you're here instead of back home?'

I said, 'Would you like to answer that one, Glendon?'

'Not right now.'

Hood remarked, 'When I get a wife, you can bet I won't be off without her. I'll take her with me on a sorrel mare, or we'll drive someplace. Go to the city, go see the pictures.'

'She'll like that,' I said.

'Yes, she will, only she won't be driving. I'm the driver. I ain't having none of that.' Drawn by something, Hood got to his feet. 'Say, look – somebody's coming.'

The automobile was a glinting dot pulling a train of dust. It might have been six miles away. It was the only bright bit on the brown curved earth.

'Could be anybody,' I said.

'Could be,' said Glendon, but it seemed to me a little of the burden had grown on him again.

We kicked down the fire and tucked the bedrolls into the Packard. We didn't act like men in a hurry, though we surely were. All the while the strange automobile crept closer, dragging its dust like a comet.

14

The auto did not catch up with us that day, or the next. I drove faster than I cared to. We bought cornmeal and frijoles in dustbound villages, petroleum from a farmer who had a scaffolded tank and whose wife came out with fresh cold water. We bought a floury loaf of brown bread and a ripe cheese that made no friends. Glendon stayed out of view while we ran these errands. I was unaware Hood noticed this until we were stretching our legs at a vacant crossroads and he said, 'Do you gentlemen want to tell me who you're running from?'

Glendon spoke up. 'An old acquaintance of mine.'

'He got a grudge against you, Mr. Dobie?'

'Yes, he does.'

'What kind of grudge?'

But Glendon felt he'd given enough. 'I assume it's the angry kind. We'd rather not see him, that's all.'

'What happens if he sees you?' Hood asked – he did tend to persist.

With a glance at me Glendon said, 'You're a clever lad, Hood, but there's a confidence or two you ain't properly earned. The man has a complaint against me. Now you can fret about it or not as you like, but that's all you get. A child's ears shouldn't hear these things.'

Hood said nothing to this, but I was watching his face,

something like excitement building in his eyes and the trim of his mouth right up until Glendon made that comment about a child's ears. I never met a child who liked being called one; sure enough it turned a switch, and Hood nodded *all right then* and climbed back in the car.

Kansas continued flat. I still hungered for a hillside or building to break the tedium. Sculptors call this *relief* and they are right. I learned to take pleasure in the windmills spinning bravely along the route, announcing farms. Hood also loved the windmills and named the brands by heart: there's a Dempster, he'd say. There's a Aermotor. There's a Monitor. He knew them by profile and the action of their blades in flight. Some rose thirty or more feet into the sky and to me seemed grand signals of optimism or defiance; many were mounted only on stubby legs reaching nine or ten feet in the air. I asked Hood what Kansas did for water before the windmill came – he replied, Before the windmill there wasn't no Kansas.

All this time the Packard performed heroically. Time to time we'd stop and wait for our dust to settle and look back for the strange auto. Sometimes it was there, other times not. Once a brown cloud came between us and the shining automobile, a large cloud tumbling in from the west comprising Heaven knows what magnitude of topsoil. When it had passed the auto was still there but shiny no longer and had also lost its tail of dust. Hood suggested it had broken down and the driver was underneath it, working, and that might have been the truth.

On the third day the plains gave out to hills. They were green and dusty and creeks ran out of them, and the road curved up and round and felt natural **again**. I could have leapt from the Packard and kissed the earth. As for Hood, he had never before seen anything but plains. 'Look up there,' he kept saying – he believed us to have reached the mountains, though they were only the Flint Hills he himself had told us to expect.

We had gone some way into these pretty knobs when the Packard made a loud noise and quit. The noise was of something large knocking about loose inside the motor. At this time we were climbing a slight gradient and the Packard stopped and began to roll backward. Jumping out Hood threw a wedge of firewood behind a tire, then opened the lid and scouted the sighing motor.

'All right, mechanic,' Glendon said.

'I can fix it,' Hood replied. He didn't look sure. He horsed his greasewood toolbox from the car and rattled through implements like a wizard through his totems.

'Would you like some assistance?' I asked, as Hood wormed on his back under the Packard.

'Don't take it wrong but you ain't going to be no help to me.'

As it was evening we lit a fire and cut pieces off a loaf of bread and toasted them on sticks.

'So these are the Flint Hills,' said Glendon.

'I gather.'

'I believe Mr. Crealock had people in the Flint Hills,' he remarked.

'Who's Crealock?' Hood asked.

'Preacher I knew once. Not a regular preacher – he had no church, is what I'm saying. He'd had two or three but kept losing them. He'd drink too much, or forget himself and go to a dance, or play cards. I owe a lot to Crealock,' Glendon added.

'Sounds messed up,' came Hood's voice from under the car.

'I suppose he was,' said Glendon. 'He was kind to me, though, and taught me to read – that's worth something, I think.'

'Worth a pain in the backside,' Hood said, in a grouchy mood for the first time since he'd joined us. He was having a terrible go of it, to judge from his twisting legs.

'What happened to Crealock, did you ever hear?' I asked, for Glendon's face was pained at Hood's disrespectful tone.

'Yes, George Parrot shot him,' Glendon answered. 'I wasn't there when it happened, and I feel ill to this day when I think of it. George was big and powerful and in all ways a stupid person. I always felt someone must've put him up to it, although it may have been his idea. He was sufficiently mean all by himself.'

At this we heard a sharp metallic lurch and Hood roared a string of impolite adjectives. He might even have cried a little. It wasn't his fault. I've looked under a car or two myself, since then – it's bedlam down there, no beginning no end, and a consequence for everything you touch.

15

Poor Hood – the Packard, so dependable on the flats, went all balky confronted with rise and fall. We couldn't go ten miles without some new problem putting us out of commission. The car would cough and stall, or bang like gunfire, or run down like a clock. We had so many stops it was no surprise when, in the evening shadows, the silver auto crested a rise and came down into the valley of our latest trial and pulled up behind us. The door sagged open and Charles Siringo hove out and stretched. Without shame I admit to a case of cold horrors, though Siringo did not look especially intimidating. He looked like any man does who has been driving too long. He rotated his neck and swung his arms back and forth and even touched his toes, the limber old screw.

'Hello,' I said. Glendon was nowhere in sight. All afternoon he'd been tipping the flask. I was worried he might stroll unawares right into this nervous gathering.

'Hello, we shared a barber,' said our visitor. 'I am Charles Siringo of the Pinkerton Agency and you are Jack Waits, I happen to know. I have been trotting after you these several days.'

'Well, and here you are. What can I do for you?' I managed to utter.

Siringo looked me over. 'Do you recall from the barber-shop, Mr. Waits, that I am seeking a man?'

'Remind me,' I said. Stricken, fuddled, mine sounded like a stranger's voice.

Siringo hesitated and said in clipped fashion, 'Man of fifty or so. Might be using the name of Dobie. White hair. Green eyes.'

'If you are looking for this Dobie,' I croaked, in my new voice, 'why follow me?'

'Some youngsters up in Revival mentioned a fellow of that description,' Siringo said. He nodded at my clothes. 'They said his companion was younger, dark, had a denim shirt on.'

My palms itched like a thief's. 'That was certainly me,' I allowed.

'Then where is he, Mr. Waits?'

'I'm sorry for your effort. It's true we crossed paths there by the railroad, but I don't know the man.' I wondered at the ease with which this tale emerged. The simple telling of it calmed me. I went on, 'He seemed a friendly old sort, though. Soft-spoken, as you say. What has he done to gain the Pinkertons' attention?'

Siringo squatted and examined the ground at his feet, saying gently, 'Oh, Mr. Waits, his felonies would make a long book.' He peered up at my face and I won't soon forget his coiled intent, his buttery tone. 'It was those boys' guess the two of you were traveling together.'

'No, it's only me and Hood, here,' came my distant reply.

Siringo nodded. 'You wouldn't know a man named Becket, would you? Monte Becket?'

This shook me terribly, as you may imagine; but by now

Jack Waits had climbed aboard, so I said, 'Is he another of your felons?'

'No,' Siringo replied, as though resigned. 'No, he ain't.' Then he seemed to perk up and said, 'What's that sound, fellows? Is there a creek nearby?'

I felt better when he said that – *fellows*.

'Yes, sir,' said Hood, pointing down the grassy draw.

'Excuse me then,' said Siringo, brightening. He stood upright and slapped the dust from his pants and strode to his automobile and leaned deep into it. Out he came with two long bamboo tapers which he fit together to make a fly rod. He whipped it to and fro a few times until it felt right and said, 'Gentlemen, it's nearly dark. Don't think me rude, but a man must take the chance that's offered. Why don't you two build a fire, I mean to bring back supper.'

And with that he set off through the brush like any eager sportsman out for the finned quarry. Can you credit this? From suspicion to camaraderie, like a man changing clothes!

Of course we tore all round that little campsite the moment he disappeared, looking for Glendon. Hood checked the rear seat of the Packard, just in case, while I poked through the heavy grasses, but no luck, and the thought occurred that my friend might be at the creek himself and about to get surprised. Hood Roberts had the same idea – he was at my elbow and I saw his eyes shine as he cupped his hands to his mouth.

'Wait, Hood, what are you up to?'

He said, 'Hooting like a owl!'

I saw it straightaway – he wanted to warn Glendon via desperate owl noise. Every boy knows that's what the Indians always did. To say Hood was excited doesn't approach it.

He was aiding a fugitive! Fixing the car of a desperado whose felonies would make a long book! Even when I talked him out of hooting and got him to help me build a fire, he was almost out of his skin.

'Suppose we hear gunshots, what'll we do then?' he said.

'Sprint down that gully and see who is standing.'

'Suppose Glendon overcomes him by guile and brings him back hogtied and blindfold,' said Hood, ashine with joy. 'What'll we do then?'

'Untie him and let him go. What do you mean, blindfold? Why would he blindfold him?'

Hood ignored my question, saying, 'If they shoot each other to death, what will happen to that silver automobile?'

But none of Hood's scenarios transpired. In fact quite some time went by before Mr. Siringo returned to the fire. He was alone. He walked up into the ruddy light and his pant legs shone wet to the knee.

'Here we go,' he said, laying four striped fish beside the coals. They were decent little bass like those we used to take in the spring spawn up in Minnesota.

'Success,' I remarked, with fraudulent gusto.

He looked at me closely. 'There are men who claim they fish just to stand in a creek, you know. They say the fish are not the point of it.'

'A creek is a pleasant spot to be, even if you catch nothing,' I said.

'That is asinine. A man fishes because he is hungry. Now get these ladies on the fire, and we'll call it supper.'

16

In the accounting of debts there are few bigger or less compensated than those I owe to young Hood Roberts. There was his work on the Packard, of course, and we all know a good mechanic is worth his weight in precious metals; that aside, Hood was the purest liar I ever knew. He lied for profit as many do but he also lied for joy, which is less common – it may even be he lied for beauty, by some deeply buried rationale.

We rolled the four bass in cornmeal and fried them in a big warped skillet Siringo hauled out of his silver car. He was not a terrible host, though he acted like the place was his own by private arrangement. At one point he leapt up and went to his car and brought out two bound copies of his memoirs. These he inscribed for us *with deep regards* then propped himself into the position of Visiting Bard and told stories. They were good stories, full of posses and stolen mustangs and strayed payrolls, and all led back to this Glen Dobie. It was a captivating narrative and Siringo was so magnetic in the telling that even I found myself drawn toward confession.

'I saw your man,' said Hood Roberts all at once – I felt my throat pull shut.

'Is that right,' said Charles Siringo.

'Well, the white hair you mention. Mustache. I wouldn't of thought he was a bandit, a fellow that short.'

Siringo straightened ever so slightly. 'You didn't tell me this before.'

'You didn't ask me – you only asked him.' Hood sounded offended.

'All right, I'm asking you.'

Hood smiled. 'He came in looking to buy a car.'

'Your boss Lewis didn't mention him.'

'Lewis didn't see him. Lewis was gone,' Hood said, unhurriedly – he had a fish bone stuck in his teeth and was trying to get it out.

Siringo said nothing but relaxed back onto one elbow.

Hood worked the bone a minute or two, got it finally, and pitched it in the fire. 'Look at that – I'm bleeding,' he said, touching his gums.

'Did you sell him a car?' Siringo seemed annoyed that he had to press Hood for details.

'Nope.'

'Where was he going, did he say?'

Hood said, 'Is that side of fish spoke for?'

Siringo had his own eye on the fish, but nodded sourly at Hood to help himself.

'Thanks.'

'Did he say where he was headed?' Siringo repeated.

'Well, he mentioned Sioux Falls. I suppose that's in Kansas.'

'No, it's not,' Siringo said, annoyed.

'Oh,' said Hood, settling into the last piece of fish. I felt bad for Glendon, out lying in the brush somewhere, smelling fried bass. Siringo seemed intent on camping here with us – it looked like no supper for our outlaw friend tonight.

Siringo brooded. The evening stretched before us. He said, 'Sioux Falls is in South Dakota. Did he mention South Dakota?'

'He might of. What's the matter?' Hood said.

'Did he mention it or not?'

Hood stared at Siringo. 'Well, I don't remember. I would of paid closer attention, but I didn't know a bully old Pinkerton was going to come along and badger it out of me. How about that?'

The boy had a streak of insolence I feared would make us trouble.

Siringo appeared to retreat a little, though, and took a calmer tone. 'You say you didn't sell him an automobile.'

'He hadn't the money,' Hood replied, his mouth full. 'Also I can't sell 'em, only Lewis can. He would've fired me. Of course, I was leaving anyhow,' he added thoughtfully.

Siringo got to his feet. When agitated he wove back and forth like a charmed snake. It must have been confusing – he would've known, probably from Royal Davies, that Glendon had boarded the train from Minnesota to Kansas City. Why would he spin around now and head for South Dakota? Siringo said, 'Boy, are you dead-on certain he said Sioux Falls?'

And Hood replied, 'How come you ask me something anyhow, if you won't listen to the answer?'

It wasn't twenty minutes before Siringo announced, 'I'm leaving, you gentlemen may have this rocky paradise to yourselves.' His voice was distracted and upset. He stomped around getting his kit together and generally acted like a man disabused of a pet idea. As I would learn, Charles

Siringo wasn't used to this. For forty years his pet ideas had turned out to be correct – they'd made him a good living, even made him famous. Now his hunch about Glen Dobie appeared to have jumped the tracks. He didn't even wash the fish skillet but tucked it in the car all scaly and slick.

'Goodbye, Mr. Siringo,' I called – he had the silver car running and its big headlamps lit and was turning it round in the road with some difficulty. I don't know where he got that automobile. We certainly didn't see anything like it during our brief hours in Revival. Hood informed me with relaxed contempt that it was known as a Cord. 'A Cord ain't no Ford,' he said, which I guess was true, as the Cords were never to throng roadways like their cheaper cousins. Still the Cord was a thing of beauty, and terribly long, and getting it turned around took Siringo many tries. When he did finally leave us it was to head back north, toward Revival again and toward South Dakota.

17

'You ate all those bass,' Glendon complained, appearing at the fire as Siringo's elegant auto vanished into the Flint Hills.

'Where were you all this time?' I said, not without some heat.

'I took a small siesta,' he said. His hair was pushed awry and poked about like any drunkard's. For some reason the sight of him this way filled me with trouble. I could not imagine what I was doing in this place and again began to blame Glendon in my heart.

'He asked me about Monte Becket,' I groused.

'Who's Becket?' Hood wanted to know.

'Waits is Becket,' Glendon replied.

Hood gaped until his dimple appeared – his day just kept improving.

Glendon said, 'You could have been yourself, Monte. You could've owned up. It would have been all right.'

'I'm sure it would've. I'm sure Siringo would've seen nothing suspicious in my use of a counterfeit name.'

He said nothing to that. He ran his hands through his sweaty hair.

'Say, did you hear my story?' Hood said to Glendon. 'I sure headed that old man in the wrong direction! What did you think of my story?'

'I think you've had a little practice,' Glendon replied.

Hood fell quiet while I found Glendon a lump of bread and the last rank cheese.

'And you're Jack Waits for certain now,' Glendon said. 'I'm sorry, I know how it feels. If it helps any, I thought Jack handled himself fairly well.'

I had fallen into something of a wallow – I suppose Glendon felt bad about it. Clearly he wanted to lift the mood. He said, 'What about it, Monte? Did you ever use an alias before?'

'No, I never thought of it,' I said – although I *had* thought of it; in fact Susannah had suggested I use a nom de plume on *Martin Bligh*. The vain truth is I wanted to use my real name just in case it was a success. This, however, seemed off the subject. Also I was enjoying a spot of petulance. 'What about you, Glendon? You've lied about your name for years. Give me your wisdom on the matter.'

He had eaten the bread and offered the cheese to us and after our refusal flung it into the brush with obvious relief. Now he was packing his little briar. He said, 'The thing is to get a name that tallies with how you are inside. A name is like the shirt you pull on in the morning. Take Siringo. I didn't know his name back then; he went by Jip Fingers or Dull Knife. A flashy name always pleased him. The shirt that feels most like your own skin is the one you want for the long trip.'

Hood said, 'So your name ain't Dobie.'

'No.' Glendon lit his tobacco with a flaming twig from the fire. 'I used John Bartle for a time. It was easy to remember when you woke in the morning. But some of the fellows would tease and call me John Bottle, which hurt my feelings.

So I thought it over and lit on Solomon, but there was no living up to that. Let's see, I went through a little spate. I tried out Mike Dugan and William Fast and then Harry Tracy, and here's a funny thing. Harry Tracy seemed to fit. I liked the name. Here was the cotton shirt you might say. I was Harry Tracy for better than a year and then, don't you know, a man arrived at the Hole who was also Harry Tracy, only that was his actual name.'

'I heard of Harry Tracy!' Hood exclaimed.

'A dangerous person,' said Glendon. 'An awful boy. Soul rot, that's what he had. The only specimen I ever knew who liked shooting people and would look for reasons. You want no association with a boy like Harry Tracy.'

'I got a alias,' said Hood Roberts suddenly.

'What is it?' Glendon asked.

'Hood Roberts,' was the grinning reply.

'Come on,' said I.

'No, it's true,' he replied.

'What's your real name, then?' I persisted.

'Well, never you mind!' said Hood. He was plainly injured. Glendon also was looking at me in a way that confirmed my question was bad form.

'It ain't Hood Roberts, is all,' said Hood.

'So what about you, Jack Waits,' Glendon said, deflecting talk from the suddenly moody boy. 'Why select that name, of so many available?'

'I don't know. I just reached down and up it came.'

'Well, it's about perfect, anyway,' Glendon observed.

'Why perfect?'

He drew on his pipe and regarded me across the fire. He seemed to feel some sadness about my new acquisition, yet it was sadness alloyed with humor. 'Well, because Jack waits, don't he? He always waits,' Glendon mused. 'Then one day you write down his name instead of your own and lo, Jack is free unto the world.'

There is one more thing you should know about that last night in the Flint Hills, and that is how Glendon, as the fire weakened, took his bedroll and walked some distance into the brush and slept apart from Hood and me. I didn't question this but in the night I was awakened by footfalls. So stealthy were they that I did not speak but tensed and peered out under my eyelids. Glendon was kneeling at Hood's side, lifting the blanket to get a better view of the boy's face. For his part Hood was sleeping like one does at sixteen. He was ruddy from the settling coals. I watched Glendon with curiosity then noticed something, a humped profile to his shoulders. His boots were wrong also. My guts liquefied. It wasn't Glendon. It was Charles Siringo.

He looked at Hood, was apparently satisfied, rose silent as a hare and stepped across the fire to kneel beside me.

I feigned sleep as if born for that very purpose. I don't know how long he looked into my face. Despite close listening I did not hear him walk away. Sometime later I did hear, very distantly, the ignition of an automobile and its diminishing hum to the north.

In cold relief I fell asleep, only to wake before dawn with Glendon himself this time squatting beside the dead fire.

'He came back,' I told him, while Hood slept on.

'Yes, he did.'

'What did he expect to find? Does he know you're with us?'

124

'He doesn't know.'

'But he came back,' I repeated.

'If he hadn't come back, he'd be a fool,' Glendon said. 'That's something Charlie never was.'

THE HUNDRED AND ONE

I

Now a cloud appeared in the south and east. We didn't understand what it was right away – coming out of the Flint Hills we saw a dark line scribed over that horizon as though the land itself were an inky color there – and we drove toward the Hundred and One raising dust over the abruptly windless plain, each of us glancing left now and then without knowing why. I can tell you we didn't talk much that day, though Hood kept bringing up his artful misdirection of Charles Siringo. He loved praise and pursued it with as much delicacy as any five-year-old. It's true we enjoyed the prospect of the old predator moving quickly in the wrong direction – we congratulated Hood until he began to seem a little too large, whereon we changed the subject.

The Packard functioned smoothly and we stacked up eighty miles in one day while the cloud remained a nearly imaginary presence to the far southeast, like an army or a rumored sea. In this way we traveled several more days while the heat rose in the afternoons along with the spectral dust of the road.

The horizon meanwhile grew darker.

Nearing the Oklahoma line we encountered a cool breeze – the cloud's advance guard, its annunciation. The wind was a relief after the heat but we looked askance at the approaching weather, which seemed to crawl over the continent with calculated stealth. We passed towns where people leaned from their windows or stood in the streets looking into the eastern sky, ranches where children hurried to empty clotheslines and penned remudas nickered and tossed their manes. My own fear registered as a tendency to run the Packard at high speeds. Hood buttoned his shirtsleeves and hunched in the auto. Glendon alone seemed unafraid of the fetid yellows and violets atwist in that appalling cloud. Attaining a height of land we stopped the car and stood in the noontime sun to watch it come. Only miles away fields lay under nightfall. Trees caught the sunlight then were extinguished. It was as though we looked across at another country and it was night there.

Hood asked Glendon whether he'd seen any such thing in nature and Glendon stretched and told, in a bemused voice, of a dark fog that swallowed his boat for four days. This was immediately after he fled capture and left Blue standing in the surf of the Sea of Cortez. The fog next morning was so heavy he could stand at the tiller and not see the mast. He tied the dripping sail along the boom and so flat was the sea that the dripping was all the sound he had in those four days. Hood wanted to know if the porpoises came and kept him company – he had heard of porpoises and their famous goodwill toward men – but Glendon said no, it was just him and God, and God not saying a word. The story didn't do much for me, but Hood seemed to feel more cheerful. In times of dread it's good to have an old man along. An old man has seen worse.

Hours later we drove out of sunshine into cold and stagnant gloom. It seemed impossible there was no rain.

Immediately Hood began singing to himself, simple school-yard tunes along the lines of 'The Bear Went Over the Mountain.' He was apt to hum when he was ruminating or couldn't sleep; it did no harm. The country under the cloud smelled of damp lime and the colors were dark and mossy. We were all of us uneasy – I'd have sung too, if it would've helped. As it was, the only helpful thing I could do was drive, so I turned on the Packard's headlights, which seemed naïve and petite against this occupying night, and I drove. We seemed the only thing moving. Hood moodily produced the penciled directions to the Hundred and One his former employer Lewis had given him. We went through the silent town of Ponca City in which bats dropped out of eaves everyplace you looked. We crossed a bridge over the Salt Fork of the Arkansas River. Hood called out to me to turn at this barn, at that painted house; one of the landmarks was a bison ranch and we glimpsed their arcane humped profiles behind a fence built against giants. Now the Salt Fork appeared on our right, bending close then turning away. Ahead were lights – and now a familiar weighty shape reared up suddenly; I braked hard and Hood Roberts threw himself with a yelp to the floor of the Packard.

'I guess we're at the ranch,' said I, for the fearsome shape was exactly one African elephant strolling beside the road. The elephant bellowed and stamped; its ears rippled like laundry, its weedy tail slashed about. Poor Hood, he moaned like a sylph, but Glendon wore a bewildered smile. An elephant! I knew right then he was glad we'd come.

2

For all Hood's faith in the Hundred and One, there was no question that storied place had entered a slow fade. I'm sorry to have missed its prime, for it was once the jewel of western showbiz. Hood knew all about it. The ranch was owned by three brothers named Miller who through luck and audacity had amassed more acres and beasts and renown than any six ranches on the Great Plains. For two decades the Hundred and One held every ace. Wild horses bought by the Millers inevitably became the finest cow ponies working; newly purchased land tracts seemed always to reveal deep pockets of oil barely under the clay. Proud entertainers, these brothers built a circus kingdom with its own streets and cafés, with film stages and trick riders, with Arabian camels and lions in cages and gorillas returning the stares of patrons. People traveled from neighboring states to glimpse these exotics and to witness action scenarios from the Vanishing West. The Millers erected a grandstand they boasted would be visible from the moon. At its peak a thousand cowboys and Indians worked at the Hundred and One, and every night at six they had a war.

In recent years, though, attendance was down. Popular whimsy was in motion and apparently away from cowboys; some people had begun to think if the West was going to Vanish it should probably get on with it. Also, certain favorite performers had departed or died, such as Cyclops Mike, and the Siamese Twins who rode with a binary saddle and could rope two steers at a time.

'So this is the mighty Hundred and One. I didn't expect it to look so down at the mouth,' Glendon remarked, as we drove between leaning storefronts under the liver-spotted cloud.

'It don't look bad, that's an effect of the weather,' Hood mumbled – I could barely hear him.

Still it didn't rain. Painted signboards stood around advertising that night's Wild West performance on the parade grounds – the show was canceled, I am sorry to say, so I missed my chance to see a Wagon Train of Brave Settlers, Savage Indians Taking Scalps, Flaming Arrows, and so forth. It would have been nice to have seen that show just once. I talked with a youngster who'd been in the crowd the night a gristly old Mimbreño, aroused by raiding again after long hiatus, forgot himself, scalped a fellow performer, and stood shaking the trophy at the roaring spectators as the cavalry rode in tooting their horns.

But as I say, the performance was shut down by the ominous and apparently endless cloud. What is more forlorn than an empty carnival? Where does everyone go? We left the Packard on the street and took two rooms at a boardinghouse where the wallpaper slumped and the lightbulbs buzzed and browned.

'Look, they're making a picture,' said Hood, peering out our window – I shared a room with him on the second floor. He was looking across the street at a foursquare clapboard with light pouring out the open door. Its windows were bright rectangles past which vivid characters spun. A

camera wheeled by on spidery legs pushed by a beefy youngster in a backward golf cap, and a girl stepped out the door
lighting a cigarette. A Mexican girl in a dress the color of
sunsets. She stood in the street holding the cigarette in her
fingers and looking up at the cloud. Hood leaned down
so intently his head struck the window glass, then pulled
away lest she look up and catch him watching.

'Oh, gee,' he remarked.

'Gee what?'

'Gee, she is awful pretty,' Hood elaborated. I might've
expected him to blush with this admission but the opposite happened; his face looked bare and bloodless, as though
the mere sight of this señorita had stopped his life and set
it in some form of reverse.

The girl took a few twirling steps down the boardwalk
like someone accustomed to an audience. She examined
the hostile sky and made, I believe, a face at it — she gave
the old cloud an insouciant sneer. She dropped the cigarette on the boardwalk, set her toe on it, and spun round
before running back into the building. It was a small but
beautiful display.

'You think she's a actress?' he wondered, when he found
speech possible. 'You think they let you stroll in and watch
while they run the camera?'

'Go ask.'

He rose and went down the hall to the bathroom and
returned twice to request my razor and comb.

'You don't need to shave,' I said.

'Sure I do — look here.' And leaning up to a lightbulb
he pointed out a few dozen brown feelers exploring along
his jaw. It occurred to me once again that Hood Roberts

134

wasn't all that much older than Redstart – neither his face nor his judgment were fully formed, an apprehension that would keep me soft toward him in the coming days, when so many others were howling for his life.

3

That evening I asked Glendon whether he believed the fog
that encapsuled his boat on the Sea of Cortez was a maneuver
of God Almighty to pursue him into the arms of justice.
We'd purchased a bag of sugared pastries for Hood and
were walking in the twilight toward the vacant parade
grounds of the Hundred and One. I thought my question
might be a dangerous one – who doesn't dread what God
might be up to in our pivotal moments? – but he answered
with a straight yes and we walked on.

'Do you fear justice, Glendon?'

'Yes, I do,' he replied, so simply that I realized I feared
it too.

'Do you wish you had gone back, then? Back to Blue?'

'Yes, but I didn't do it,' he said, adding, with a wry glance,
'fear seems my bedrock principle, wouldn't you say?' His
regret was strong enough he wrote Blue a repentant letter
with the help of ruined Crealock, whose Spanish in the
heartfelt regions surpassed Glendon's, yet it must not have
been a satisfactory letter since Blue never replied. 'One day
you will have to go back in person,' Crealock told him, yet
Glendon knew that to return anytime soon would likely
cost him his liberty. His crimes in the country of Mexico
were a horde memorized by authorities. Cattle were only
the beginning; trains in those provinces were creaky affairs

open to an inventive bandit who took joy in his craft. The performance of theft came to Glendon with such little difficulty he considered it a kind of gift. He was a fastidious bad man who scarcely touched his victims. Spoils appeared as though conjured in his pockets. This talent plus his aptitude for deflection made him nearly untouchable by *policia,* though he proved quite human the day the Porfirian officers blew his boat out from under him on the Sea of Cortez.

'They had a short cannon set up on the beach,' he said. 'I came around that point not fifty yards from shore and there they were – I gave them a laugh, that's for sure.'

'A cannon? For one American bandit?'

'Well, there was a sporting element to it. They were betting how many shots it would take to hit the boat.'

'How many did it take?'

'Seven or eight. When they started finding the range I jumped and swam for it, but they kept firing till they sunk her. That was a little mean, I thought.'

Reaching the edge of the parade field, we beheld a puzzling sight. Before us stood half a dozen slim wood pedestals. They were elegant, carved like the Doric columns outside libraries, but what caught the eye were the orange glass spheres resting on them. The size of large citrus, they seemed to gather what light there was in that doleful setting.

'What are these, Monte – are they fine art?' Glendon asked.

'No idea,' I confessed. Strangely, the spheres didn't seem out of place, but then the whole ranch under that alien cloud resembled one of Goya's mesmeric notions.

137

'Well, they're pretty little moons,' said my friend. Something about the unlikely ornaments seemed to touch a disconsolate note, and he added, 'I'll admit something to you, Becket: I am sick of being chased.'

'Siringo has gone to South Dakota,' I reminded him.

Glendon laughed as though Siringo were the least of it.

We stood quietly before the row of globes. I wanted to raise one in my palm. As in a storybook I reached for the nearest bauble, only to have it vaporize before me like an enchanted thing.

The slap of a gunshot arrived a second later.

The shock of that sound is with me still – it smacked and prickled as I stood confused, watching an orange cloudlet rain over the grass.

'Why, they're targets,' Glendon mused, as another of the little globes turned to a column of steam. In panic I threw myself to the ground. *Slap* came the sound of the shot.

'Drat my eyes,' said Glendon; he couldn't see who was shooting. Neither could I, once I'd gained the courage to poke my head up and look around. As we crouched, the remaining four spheres burst and drifted over the lawn, each followed by its tardy black-powder concussion. Then a distant slack shape I'd taken for a sleeping dog rose and stretched and became our confident marksman.

Despite a fast gait it took him a long time to reach us. I'll admit to some nerves at his approach. Among noted riflemen there is reputed to be a predatory quality – the great Crockett is said to have moved like a panther even when going out to get the mail. That's what this fellow reminded me of, all buckskinned and moccasined, though there was something un-Crockettlike about him too.

'Why, it's a woman!' I said.

Yes, she heard me, for I received a wounded glance.

'Good day, miss, you are most impressive,' said Glendon.

The woman stopped where she was – a big supple woman. She said, 'Saints above, tell me it ain't Glen Dobie!'

'I guess it's me, all right,' said Glendon, though he was fidgety and plainly had no idea who this woman was now trotting forward in a state of high emotion.

'Glen, it's me! Darlys DeFoe,' she declared.

'Darlys?' he said, as wonder and relief settled on him.

Darlys DeFoe dropped her long buffalo gun to the turf like a willow stick and leapt upon Glendon forthwith.

He was staggered a moment by her attention and heft – she was kissing his cheeks and his forehead and mouth. Getting hold of her arms he removed her gently saying, 'Darlys, meet my friend—'

'Jack,' I put in.

Glendon's eyes rolled. 'Jack was about to lay hands on that globe when you shot it. You gave us a scare, Darlys.'

'I'm Darla now,' said she, and so she was, on the handbills and circulars we'd seen pasted up or blowing the streets: Deep Breath Darla, Queen of the Long Shot. She was at that time the Hundred and One's beauteous lady sharpshooter; since Annie Oakley, every Wild West Show in the world had one.

'I ain't seen you since the train stopped in Marquez,' said Glendon, as kindly as possible, holding Darlys DeFoe at arm's length. 'All this time I kind of pictured you in Virginia or Alabama – someplace genteel.'

'Things went otherwise for me, Glen.'

'Well, you've got a job and are famous good at it,' Glendon

replied. 'Don't you think I saw the handbills? Darlys, you're an attraction!'

Darlys DeFoe blushed, the tragic old moonbeam; seeing that blush I had an urge to pull Glendon aside and warn him somehow, but it would've done little good. Glendon was already walking with Darlys toward a lit tavern at the edge of the grounds. The old girl was waltzing along like an ingenue, if you can picture an ingenue with a large-bore buffalo gun in her knuckly hand; but Glendon, I noticed, had his hands in his pockets and was talking with easy rapport, as though she'd been a man.

4

'I married Rory – that's what tripped me up so bad,' she told us. 'Rory Day. I met him in Kansas City just a few days after you put me on that train, Glen. I thought he would be nice to me, but no. The only nice thing about Rory was his teeth.'

'Well, I don't blame you – you'd just come from Hole in the Wall,' said Glendon. We sat in a beer-stained booth in what was called the President's Tavern and overlooked the parade grounds and prairie beyond. 'Nice teeth must've seemed like enough,' he added.

She looked gratefully at my friend.

'On the other hand,' he said, 'didn't I pay for you to go all the way home?'

'I didn't go, Glen, I'm sorry. My papa had that cheese shop, you know. If I had gone home it would've been a long life of wrapping cheese. Rory swept me up and we got married in a week. He had ideas. He taught me to shoot baubles from half a mile away. It's harder than it looks.'

'Where's Rory these days?' asked Glendon.

'He got drunk and fell in the river.'

'Darlys, I'm sorry.'

'Oh, he was drunk most of the time by then. It ain't like I wanted him to die, but he thumped me around enough.

When he turned up in the river I found I could bear the pain.'

Sudden disclosures of a private nature embarrassed Glendon – he looked so awkward Darlys hurried to change the subject. 'There's another old friend of yours here, Joe Barrera. Have you seen him?'

'José? Truly?'

'He's always down at the stables – you should go look in on him.'

'He won't be glad to see me, though,' said Glendon.

'Why not?' I asked. 'Is he a relic from your days in the train business?'

Glendon smiled. 'Far from it. José is a cousin of Blue's. He had a concertina and could play it like an orchestra. He brought it to our wedding, in fact.'

Darlys said, 'Did you marry again, Glen? Where have you spent all these years?'

'I build rowboats; it's pleasant work. I don't pine for those old days,' he said. 'No, I didn't marry.'

'Do you ever see anybody? Do you see Cawley or Jip?'

'No one from that time,' said Glendon.

'You never much cared for Jip,' she said, with a teasing inflection.

'I did like him, but Darlys, he was bad to you.'

'I remember his smile. He was awfully funny – I never had another man who made me laugh like Jippie.'

'Well, that's all right,' Glendon reflected. 'It's proper to remember what was good. But look, you've turned things to your advantage now. Tell us about your act here.'

She was, as the handbills claimed, a long-shot artist. She could hit a grapefruit at a thousand yards – 'Well, you saw,' she said to me, pleased at having shot that target from under my hand.

'What's this Deep Breath business?' Glendon asked.

'That!' She waved her hand. 'Jos Miller gave me the name – he used to carry out a chair and watch me practice. Lord, I enjoyed it. I couldn't hardly miss when Jos was there. He'd watch the targets with a spyglass. He always said that once I pulled the trigger there was time to take a deep breath before the bullet struck.'

'That's a top-quality talent, Darlys,' said Glendon.

She reached into her jacket for a pair of brawny spectacles. 'I got to use these, now. Sometimes I miss even so. Last month I missed four times in a row. I got laughed at, and Jos Miller heard about it. He already cut my pay. If it happens again I'm fired.'

We sat in the tavern watching heat lightning play above the earth.

Darlys said, 'How come you did that, anyway, Glen? Took me out of the Hole and put me on the train?'

The question surprised him. 'Why, because you asked me to, Darlys.'

'Did I?' She was disturbed, unable to recall this.

'Yes, you did.' Glendon smiled. 'You were such a sweet girl, what could I do but comply?'

Blushing, she replied, 'What would you do for me now, Glen? Any prettiness I had is gone. Were I to ask, what would you do for me now?'

'Whatever I could,' he answered, at which she got up and kissed the top of his head and strode out of the tavern.

'Poor Darlys,' said Glendon, as we watched her go. 'It's a shame about her eyes.'

'I suppose it is.'

He rounded up on me. 'You haven't much sympathy for her, I think.'

I replied, 'Her difficulties are of her own making. Maybe she ought've gone home to the cheese shop in the first place.' The truth is, I felt more than a little impatient with Darlys DeFoe. Glendon had already rescued her once – it seemed likely to me she was hoping he would now rescue her again. Aware of sounding coarse, I pressed on. 'She ought to start thinking about her next act.'

Glendon looked at me with reproach. 'Maybe she's tried that, Monte. Maybe she don't have a next act in her.' He rose from the table and laid down some coins. He said, 'Maybe you ought to have some understanding of this.'

It was as near as he ever came to reminding me of my own transitory moment as an attraction, featuring my own long shot, *Martin Bligh*. How hard I'd looked for the elusive next act! How hard I was looking still!

5

Well, Hood was in love. No doubt you guessed it the second he peered out the window at the agile señorita – I guessed it myself and had it confirmed when he wafted in late.

'Fellows, wish me well, I am in love,' he said, from his blowsy elevation.

'Is *she?*' asked Glendon.

'She will be,' Hood replied.

'What's her name?' I inquired.

'Alazon. Mr. Becket, you saw her – she's a rose, you got to admit.'

We got little sleep that night, at least Hood and I didn't. He was bursting with that girl and insisted on reporting his evening to me moment by moment. Down he went and sure enough they had the cameras running. The film was called *Sign of the Red Men*. It featured a young jawline of German extraction named Ern Swilling. He said it *Svilling*, and many at the Hundred and One were betting honest dollars on his future – that you never heard of Ern was fate's joke on Ern. Anyway Hood went down and crossed the street holding a china teacup in his right hand. I saw that with my own eyes, from the window. The teacup confused me until he admitted stealing it from a display in the tiny lobby of the boardinghouse; he was looking for flowers but found none. Entering the building he didn't see Alazon right away. A few people stood within a floodlit set of mock walls resembling the inside of a ranch cabin – the clever Ern, a pallid girl called Selma playing his beloved in the film, and a fellow Hood described as 'bitten and weaselly' who jabbed a forefinger into his palm for emphasis when speaking. This was the director of the movie and the butt of many gags among the cast, though when I spoke with him later he seemed like any craftsman pursuing distinction against large odds. Drawn by soft talk, Hood spotted the girl with a Mexican boy his own age. A handsome tall lad with an effortless laugh – yet Hood suffered less than one minute of excruciating jealousy because when the girl saw his tentative advance she left her caballero with his sentence unfinished and came and looked up into his face.

'She's so pretty, I just forgot how to talk,' Hood told me. I loved him for that. What man has not stood in lumpen torment before the face of beauty? Wordless, he stood sheltering the teacup in his two hands.

Her English was less complete than her understanding. She accepted the teacup with delight, though I suppose she knew exactly where it had come from. Not the leading actress Hood had supposed, she'd still managed to appear in several films as part of a mob or in church scenes. She laughed him into an easier mood and took him round, introducing him to her friends: her cousin LaJila, who worked in the kitchen and came daily to watch the filming and absorb the language; exhausted old Daniel, who painted wheeled backgrounds with mountains and skies of such genuine appearance that, when rolled outdoors, birds tried to fly through them and fluttered to the ground in confusion.

'Who's this now?' Hood asked Alazon, as her tall caballero approached. He was smiling, a terrifying expression to witness on the face of your rival.

'Ignacio, my brother,' Alazon replied, at which Hood's belly filled with such buoyancy his feet could no longer feel the floor. Grasping the offered hand he knew Ignacio for an ally and friend. It emerged that Ignacio was the reason for Alazon's presence at the Hundred and One. The first of his family to come north, he had worked several years as a bronc peeler in the Millers' breaking pens – painful employment he spoke of with humor and pride. The broncs had dealt him many fascinating scars, also eighteen broken bones 'that he *knows about*,' Hood told me. This line of work seemed to Hood so heroic that when Ignacio invited him to visit the pens next morning and ride for the foreman Hood felt the grip of destiny. 'You see? I told you cowboying wasn't over, Mr. Becket.'

It had taken Hood about ten minutes to adjust to my real name.

'It's what I came here for,' he added.

'And Alazon, also, I am guessing.'

'Of course.' Hood thought. 'I'd of come for Alazon even if there weren't no cowboy work to be done,' he declared.

'Yesterday you didn't know there was any such person as Alazon,' I said. He was so unbalanced, I couldn't resist chiding him a little.

'If there weren't no such person as Alazon,' Hood proclaimed, 'I would have made her up.'

There isn't much a fellow can reply to that, so I reminded him that broncos get up early and suggested he sleep.

'Sure, Mr. Becket,' he said.

But I was the one needing sleep that night, not Hood. Bunked under the open window I sighed and turned as Hood talked softly on, gesturing with his hands at the ceiling. 'I ain't ever going to forget this,' Hood said. 'I am meant to be here. So is Alazon. Maybe she don't love me yet, but she's going to. Didn't I tell you, Mr. Becket? Didn't I say this place was something?'

6

Sometime in the night the rain commenced. It didn't pelt or sheet down as it reasonably might after a hundred miles of black cloud, it was only a mild rain and people shrugged at it and went to work. Hood rose early to set off for the breaking pens, and I suppose no actor ever approached an audition with more passion. He cracked his neck and snorted through his nose. Because of his excitement and the damp-flannel feel of the boardinghouse I put on my slicker and walked along with him.

The pens were at the far end of the parade grounds, a mess in that weather. A handful of cowboys stood drinking coffee under the tin awning, Ignacio among them sporting a wide brim hat and a sash about his waist. He welcomed us both and introduced Hood Roberts to a stocky rooster who handed Hood a lariat and pointed at the knot of grumpy horses bunched against the rails. This was the foreman in charge of the Millers' vast remuda. He said some words to Ignacio who took another lariat and swung over the fence; his boots hitting the mud made his compadres laugh and elbow each other. 'Get that *malvado* horse,' one cried, setting up a chorus of disagreement. *Malvado* I under-stood to mean wicked, but these fellows had given names to every horse present. Therefore Ignacio, now aboard a slight mare prancing through the muck, darted with his lifted reata among Unsightly and Witch Eye and Robbie's Knee, a youthful bay stallion named for the cowboy he had lately crippled. I was told Robbie wished to come back and prove himself no quitter but had instead received a few alphabet lessons while still bedridden and was reemployed as a sign painter. In horse work you want two knees that bend.

For Hood, Ignacio chose a short-barreled mare called Espiritu, or Spook. To look at her you wouldn't have thought she was much – a little brown horse like any other – yet the cowboys cheered at this selection and Ignacio roped and led the mare into a round pen of green lumber nailed to railroad ties set deep in the ground. Here Hood waited with the rain trailing off the back of his derelict hat. He had a light saddle over his shoulder and a scared smile on his face. Among those weathered vaqueros Hood looked perhaps fourteen. Ignacio snubbed the bronc to a railroad tie and Hood stepped up and set the saddle on the quivering horse. She was not quivering with fear. I saw her bilious eye. She quivered with rage.

Here is my cheerful confession: Unlike many of my boyhood friends, I never wished to be a cowboy. A slim nearsighted child, to me every horse seemed a sinister creature apt to reply with hostility; it was only when I was a bored man in a post office that the notion of 'horse' gained allure, and this only on paper. Now, with Hood snugging a wide cinch against Spook's belly, I recalled the truth, which is that a horse has no need to traffic with people. You are a feeble and tenuous being; the only thing a horse wants from you is your absence. The mare sidestepped and twisted against the snub as Hood got up in the stirrups –

could I have stopped the whole thing like an anxious father I'd have done so, but the vaqueros were shouting and Hood was nodding at Ignacio, who reached over the upper rail and released the horse.

The mare reared back immediately, flailed high and slipped leftward with Hood's fist in her mane. She came down on four feet and crow-hopped tight circles while the cowboys hollered, then reared again so vertically she fell straight backward onto the fence which became a spout of magnificent splinters. This move was designed to ruin both Hood and the saddle, but Hood dropped off when the balance tipped and the saddlehorn snapped at the pommel. Alarmed shouts arose as two or three hands ran forward shaking out loops, but as the mare swiveled back onto her feet there was Hood Roberts coming up with her, his boots seeking the stirrups. Poor Spook! Throwing her head she bucked amid sprinting cowboys toward the outer fence. She knew it was her final border and she meant to clear or rupture it – forward she went, full on and her head down, cones of mud twisting behind, the wind driving rain in our faces. We saw her front quarters rise and clear the top and Hood's body straighten as her belly hit the rail. It shattered and fifty feet of fence swayed. The horse fell into free territory with a profound slap that made everyone look down or away and then she was up, dragging Hood Roberts by one stirruped foot. I thought he was dead or soon to be, for he bounced behind Spook like knotted straw as she stretched out toward the Salt Fork. Over a small rise went the two of them, and their sound vanished with them, so that all we could hear was rain hitting tin and dripping off in puddles.

How we ran, then! The cowboys grabbed what horses they could while the few visitors ran on two legs toward the breached fence. Ignacio saw me afoot and wheeled his delicate mare and gave me a hand up, so I was among the first to top the rise and see what had become of brave Hood Roberts. He was not in sight. Spook was a swimming horsehead angling up-current. The only honest guess was that Hood was under the water, and I can testify that time became a tedious waltz while the mare looked here and there and blew through her nose and considered the weather and perhaps enjoyed a number of choice memories before settling on a place to come ashore. Sure enough, when she came up out of the water there lay a mud boy at her heels.

I moaned in lament, but Ignacio said, 'Look there.'

'What? He is still hanging by the stirrup,' I pointed out.

'Yes,' agreed Ignacio, at which I saw what I had missed – when Hood had vanished over the rise, bouncing like straw, his foot had been locked in the stirrup. Now his *hand* was in the stirrup. His foot was free.

'What's happened?' I asked – I still thought he was dead, you see. I thought there had been some freak repositioning during his infinite drag under the water.

The mare, tired by her escape and her swim, was moving at a slow walk up the riverbank.

As we watched, the mud boy sliding beside her reached up with his free hand.

'Caballero,' Ignacio breathed.

Hood achieved his grip and with a swift heave stood abruptly onto the stirrup. It was as stunning an ascension as any I have seen. He weaved a moment before veering down into the saddle; and the cowboys watching from the rise, and others still coming on their snuffy mounts, began to bellow and hoot, and the spectators scrambling afoot picked up the glad cry even before they saw its cause.

In all I suppose no more than twenty people saw Hood Roberts's beautiful reappearance, yet twenty witnesses are plenty to make a legend. Moreover, twenty people in full throat can make quite a sound. Hood heard it even through mud earplugs, he told me later — he said it wasn't until he heard those cries that he knew he could stay on no matter what, that the fight was his and nearly over. No doubt Spook heard it too, because directly she picked up again and began to run; but she had exhausted all ready weapons now, the bucking and the river and the splintering fence. There was nothing for her to do *but* run, and it was suddenly plain that no mere running horse could shake Hood Roberts off. Indeed he held on, with his head tipping back in the wind, anticipating her sudden turns, and when Spook at last began to slow he spurred her flanks and made her continue full tilt until foam painted her neck; thereon he turned her with the reins, receiving small argument, and to and fro they went in full view of us all; at last he brought her back to the bank and forced her to dance in the tightest of circles, ten times in each direction — and only then did he give her rest.

It was the sort of deed people would have made songs about, once, or poetry; and though no one did so now, Hood's gaudy and dogged and certainly accidental ride sprawled straightaway into the talk of the Hundred and One. As events twirled forward, as Hood first attained grace then tipped away, I was to hear the tale refashioned in a dozen lively colors; how he stayed under the water for ten full minutes; how he leapt to her back on the other side and rode standing upright with his arms outstretched; how the sun itself pierced the great cloud long enough to strike Hood's shoulders as he swam the mare back across the swelling river. It is a fact that Ignacio took the orange sash from his own waist and tied it around Hood's as he rode Spook back to the stables; it is a fiction that even Spook herself was won over by her conqueror and would nicker lovingly to him and be ridden by no other.

A cowboy doesn't ask for much, that's my observation. A flashy ride, a pretty girl, momentary glory – for a day or two, I'm glad to say, Hood Roberts had them all.

7

The fourth day of rain I entered the President's Tavern to find Glendon uneasily drinking coffee with José Barrera. José was a trick rider at the ranch. He was at least sixty yet still managed, through a sanguine outlook on pain, to startle crowds by riding at full gallop standing on his head in the saddle. More importantly, he was Blue's cousin — that's why Glendon was uneasy.

'Hello, Monte, come join us. José, this is Monte,' said my friend, with marked relief.

Jack Waits, I noticed, was going by the wayside. In any case José paid me no mind but shook my hand while telling Glendon, as though I weren't there, 'The whole family thought well of you, and then you ran away.'

'Yes, it's true,' Glendon replied, gloomily realizing I was no shield against direct speech. 'I ain't had a day without remorse, José.'

'So now you are seeking her out again. What for?'

'To own up. Declare my regret.'

José drained his coffee and rose. Like many veteran riders he walked hitchingly as though unused to his own feet. He lurched to a tarnished urn on the counter, filled his cup and returned to the table. 'She waited for you a long time,' he remarked. 'Five years, or six. Her husband is named Soto. He has two fruit orchards and three or four languages. A decent man. I met him only the one time, at the wedding. People said he spent a lot of time thinking.'

'Thinking?'

'Yes, he enjoys thinking. He's a good man so far as I know. What I am saying is, don't go find her and expect anything to come of it.'

'I won't.'

José said, 'She might not forgive you. I wouldn't.'

'I got no expectations,' Glendon replied. 'I plan to say my piece and leave.'

The vaquero appraised him. 'If that's all you mean to do, I will tell you something. She is no longer in Mexico. She and her husband bought the orchards in California, on a river called the Rienda. Last I heard, that's where they were.'

Glendon was startled; he'd been set on Mexico, on the Blue of his memory. This seemed a large adjustment. 'How'd you happen to find that out?'

'From that friend of hers, Marcela. She came up here a few years ago and watched me ride. I bought her lemonade; we had a picnic,' said José, becoming wistful. 'I thought something might come of it, but nothing did. That Marcela was a cutie, though.'

'I remember Marcela,' said Glendon.

'There used to be lots of cuties coming through this place, but not anymore. Not for me, at least. I'm leaving here. Colonel Miller gave me the boot.'

'He fired you? How come?'

José shrugged. 'He isn't himself. The river is up to its banks. He's afraid the rain will be the end of him.'

'The lower pens are getting spongy,' Glendon agreed.

'Last night the colonel asked a few of us old ones up to

drink his whiskey. He asked us when it will stop. Who can say, but he's the boss. Everybody else predicted sun in two days. That's what I should've said too.'

'What did you say?' Glendon inquired.

'I said it looked like it might rain forever. Did you ever see a flood? It's uglier than fire and makes a worse smell. I didn't try to make him mad, but he said I should go, so I'm going.' José got up, pulling on a slicker. 'Are you going to pay for the coffee?'

'All right.'

'Good, thank you, I'm saving my pennies.' At the door José paused. 'If you find her, tell her you saw me. You should leave soon, though. That river is losing its patience.'

8

Now comes a distressing part of the story, and not just because Charlie Siringo shows up. As Glendon said later, Charlie *had* to show up; it was necessary for Charlie, for Glendon himself, and even, finally, for me, that Siringo wash into the Hundred and One on the edge of the coming deluge.

No, the distress was all Hood's. And the actor Ern Swilling's. And Alazon's. Certainly Alazon's! For she did fall swiftly in love with our Hood Roberts, just as he hoped. It seemed perfect to me, I'll admit, their sudden romance – the kind of story we all want in dispiriting weather. Hood's sensational ride made him briefly luminous. People reached for his shoulders as he passed, little boys ran at his legs; vaqueros touched their hat brims. Alazon too was entranced. Who can blame a girl for returning the affections of the sudden champion? Besides, hers was no fleeting regard. I'll remind you she liked Hood well enough pre-heroics, and she would like him still when the heroics were forgotten. As for Hood – this boy who claimed an alias, who laughed in his sleep – he was on the hilltop we all remember or believe we remember. He talked about Alazon until Glendon's ears pinked. Her little waist! Her fine wrists! Sometimes she sang him jubilant Mexican rhymes; when she held his hand, he thought he was going to fall down. She had called him her *paloma,* Hood said, asking Glendon what it meant. Glendon replied that it meant dove, an expression of true tenderness; Hood's expression revealed he knew this already but only asked because he wanted us to know his joy.

'Then I guess I'm her dove,' he said. 'What do you think of that?'

A few days after his famous ride Hood paid a visit to the movie set. Would he had not done it, but what else was there to do? Rain had put a stop to cowboy work and the Hundred and One was beginning to empty; Glendon and I would've left too, except that he seemed suddenly averse. I had the grating sense that Darlys DeFoe was the holdup.

In any case, here we sat. Where to go but toward the lights and the noise? I was at the set when Hood came in. Ignacio and several others were with him, happy for idleness, shaking their ponchos and laughing; but the movie set, like any foundering ship, was a perilous place. The cloud and the rain had bred an atmosphere of pestilence: Actors thrashed about in desolation; the weaselly director was out of sorts. They were shooting the scene where Ern Swilling strikes down the villain, a lecherous bank officer named Rance. Ern then kisses pale Selma and carries her out the door. A straightforward scene from every picture ever made; but they were having a miserable time getting it right, the kiss in particular. Ern would take a swing; Rance would stagger back, cracking his head on the wall; then Ern would sweep up old Selma and plant one on the lips while the director gnashed in torment.

'What's the matter?' Ern demanded, after three or four abortive embraces.

'You're kissing her wrong,' replied the director.

'She's kissing *me* wrong,' Ern complained, and though it sounds whiny, I must take his side. The girl kept moving her head in sly fashion: Though I am not the world's expert on kissing it was clear to me this Selma was a reluctant participant. Moreover, it wasn't hard to see why. Selma, Hood had informed me, was keeping company with Ignacio; well, Ignacio had just appeared with some of his damp compadres to watch the filming. If there was one thing Selma did not want Ignacio to think, it was that she was kissing Ern Swilling with anything like actual passion. Thus she thwarted Ern at every pass. That's how it looked to me: down would come his pooched lips, and Selma would tip her face at the tiniest angle. She'd stiffen, cheeks all waxy and pink, and Ern would just glance off. It didn't look like kissing at all. It looked like a girl deflecting a neighbor boy who had been carried away by *amor* and whose feelings she wished to salvage.

'Sel, kiss him right this time,' the director instructed, but by now Selma was habituated and again poor Ern slipped off to the side. Can you imagine the cowboys' delight at this development?

'Ach!' said Ern, missing again and dropping the girl's feet to the floor, at which the vaqueros cheered without restraint and Hood called through cupped hands, 'It's all right, Selma, pretend he's a cowboy,' transgressing the iron decree about quiet on the set. The vaqueros hooted for joy. Ern Swilling looked humid and confused. I saw Hood wink at Ignacio – Ern saw it too, I suspect.

'Ten minutes,' cried the director, shying from the lights like a crab.

Even now things might have righted themselves. The vaqueros climbed up to mingle with cast and crew; Alazon appeared from behind a partition, looking for Hood; to credit Ern Swilling, he straightened and nodded and seemed even to laugh at himself while Selma drifted toward Ignacio.

I had a tablet along and was content to stay on the bench – I was muddling around with a description of the place for Susannah. When the first shouts erupted I didn't even pay attention; I was trying to get the colors right. Then boots scuffed and I peered up to see Ignacio take a swing at Ern Swilling. He missed as Ern moved aside, knocking a chair off the raised set. The lights were still on, and as they jockeyed to and fro dust rose from the floor around them. I remember wondering if this was a real fight or a staged one for the entertainment of the cast; wondering, in the unattached way a mind has, how dust could rise anywhere after so many days of rain. I never learned what started their dispute; probably something indelicate got said.

'Fight!' yelped a glad cowboy. Ignacio was made of scrap iron and the smart money would've been on him, but nature had been ridiculously kind to Ern Swilling – besides his marquee appearance he was strong as a bear with the easy world-beater genetics we were all to encounter in coming years. His movements were fluid and abruptly Ignacio was down on his back. Oh, he popped up in a hurry, but Ern stepped forward all business and Ignacio's knob flipped back twice as though hinged and down he went again. The vaqueros stood perplexed – *an actor!* – while Ignacio rolled to his stomach and lay on his elbows. He seemed to be casting about for answers to critical questions. Ern watched a moment, then turned away only to be hit on the nose by Hood Roberts. Hood hit him once. Ern reeled backward and fell off the set. It wasn't the blow, it was the fall that got him — a mere three-foot drop. It testifies to our frailty how a specimen like that German boy could hurt himself in such a paltry mishap. The floor wasn't stone or cement, either; it was soft pine boards. You could bounce on the balls of your feet and feel them give.

Even so, Ern Swilling's neck broke so neatly he didn't know it right away. He lay on his side expecting any second to bound up and fight Hood Roberts fair and square.

'Come on, then,' he said, in a tone so awfully upbeat someone started to cry.

Hood stood looking down in bewilderment. Of course there was an instant gathering round the crumpled Ern, who gave no sign of understanding what had happened.

'Give a hand up here,' said Ern, but no one offered Ern a hand. It was a sight to unman the toughest witness. Even if someone had offered him a hand, Ern couldn't have reached for it.

'His head's on backward,' whispered a vaquero.

'I'll bust your rump, Roberts,' Ern said cheerfully. For a few seconds his good humor was so intact none spoke for fear of reality.

Then Ern fell quiet.

Then he said, 'Say, what's this?' which I suppose is a common question at moments of discovery.

The right thing for Hood Roberts to do would've been to leap down and reassure Ern Swilling; to shout for doctors; to exemplify comradeship and good form. He didn't, because he was frightened. Before us all lay the hopeful film star with his face turned east and his body west. Ern, whose voice abruptly lost hold of sensible words and became a choked howl as he got his first grip on the transformed world; on the fact that he was no longer a sought quantity or screen actor but a handsome young paralytic with no prospects whatever for fame or wealth or for that matter much of a lifespan.

I said, 'Where is a doctor on this place?'

'Right, and where's that Hood Roberts?' someone asked. I looked round, but Hood was gone: a full adult now, you see, and newly adept at the furtive departure.

9

So Hood fled in the rain with the girl who loved him. They stole two horses from the Hundred and One and set out southwest for the great fugitive destination of Mexico – that's what Glendon believed, at least. The going couldn't have been easy, either. Minutes after Ern's ghastly fall I stepped from the building into violent rain. Gone was the almost sleepy shower that had been constant nearly a week. This was a cascade, a monsoon. The street was a brown canal. I held out my hand and drops pounded it white in seconds.

'I can't bear thinking of those youngsters, on the run, in this,' Glendon grieved, back in his room.

'He shouldn't have run anyway,' I said. 'It was only a blow with a fist. He wasn't looking to break anyone's neck.'

Glendon stalked the room, running a hand back and forth over his hair. After some minutes he said, 'Well, now he's taken flight and taken those horses, which makes him a wanted article. You think I ought to go after those two, Monte, and bring them back?'

'That would be an irony, wouldn't it?'

He scowled at me. 'What's ironical about it?'

'Well, you're a wanted article yourself.' I shrugged. 'That's a fair irony.'

He wasn't amused. I shut my mouth, too late like always, and went back to my room to bed.

In the morning he knocked before it was light. I was glad to get up – I hadn't slept. Neither had Glendon, to judge from his pallor, but his voice was decided and strong.

'Well, I'm not going after them,' he announced. 'Much as I want to, I can't carry the boy.'

'Come in,' I said.

'Be awfully hard to follow them anyway,' he said, and a crack appeared in his tone.

We sat by the window with no light in the room, rain penny-striking the glass. It was impossible not to think about Hood and Alazon out on the oceanic plains, the two of them wayward and bone-sodden and lost. We didn't talk about them, though.

'I dare not be sidetracked,' Glendon said. 'There's Blue to see about.'

'Right.'

'Also, there's Darlys to look after,' he added.

I knew it. 'How much looking after do you intend to do?'

Glendon now revealed that Darlys had asked him for money – enough for a train ticket east.

'But you did that once before. She didn't go, if you'll remember.'

'Things have changed. She wants to go.'

I couldn't think of anything to say.

'I got to help her if I can, Monte.' He didn't actually have the money but had promised Darlys DeFoe he would try to get some.

I am guilty of chronic bad form in the matter of Darlys DeFoe. No doubt I rendered the weary put-upon sigh so despicable in other people.

'Don't fret – she won't take any money from you,' Glendon said. 'She heard what you said, about her looking like a man.'

I ignored that and asked Glendon how he meant to get the money.

'I'll talk to Jos Miller. He's in straits, you know. A lot of his help has gone. There might be something I can do.'

That reminded me that Darlys herself was employed by Jos Miller and had been for some time, so I asked the question that occurred to me: 'Why does she have no money?'

Glendon lifted his head and looked at me in wonder. 'That don't matter. Why don't matter. Isn't that clear to you yet?'

But it wasn't clear. I was not always a man to grasp the obvious. We sat together as the darkness thinned and became morning. Eventually a ragged line of kerosene torches appeared in the rain. 'Come on,' Glendon said. 'People are leaving – let's go down and help.'

Not everyone left the Hundred and One – in truth the boardinghouse soon brimmed with guests, as it was the only building besides the Millers' own residence that floodwaters did not reach. Oh, it was near – at high tide the basement was full and we had a quarter inch of mud slip where the floor sagged – but overall the boardinghouse stayed dry, and diehards appeared with blankets and bacon and mordant smiles, and people camped in the stairwells. The Salt Fork Flood was a horror for the animals; though the cowhands rode out and cut many fences, several hundred pigs and more than a thousand turkeys and a great number of cattle perished. Some were swept down the streets while we watched from the windows; dead cows wearing the Hundred and One brand were found bloating across the countryside for weeks afterward – it was said one Miller steer washed up on a reach of the Salt Fork more than fifty miles away. The rains dealt the mighty ranch a blow from which it was to make only fractional recovery; still, no people drowned, and none fell into despair beyond convalescence except for Ern Swilling – of course, in his case the flood was not to blame.

We helped all morning with the final exodus. Strangely, it was not depressing. The people leaving on the wagons had lost homes, possessions, wherewithal: most of them climbed up holding no more than a grubby blanket or two, yet there was endurance in their postures. Cowhands and journeymen, wrinkled and smooth, some with families, men and women stricken by loss which for many of them was neither the first nor the hardest. Trounced again! Yet their shoulders refused defeat. Among those assisting at the wagons were Darlys DeFoe and José Barrera – apparently he'd been forgiven by Jos Miller, who worked at his side, gallantly handing people their beloved wreckage. And away they went, some waving goodbye as the drafters bowed their heads and bent forward following the memory of a road. Out they rolled in a languid, soaking caravan: a sorrowful day but not a hopeless one. Glendon, checking harness and soothing the animals, seemed especially glad for the work. He stood in the street with the water eddying over his ankles; he hummed to the horses, and they calmed themselves.

10

A dozen men gathered that night in the narrow lobby of the boardinghouse; José was there, and a brilliant soak named Bodes who repaired engines, and an old Ponca Indian chief named Iron Tail whose face you may still see on what is called the Buffalo nickel. Those of us with booked rooms gave them up for the women and brought our things downstairs. There'd been some consternation over this arrangement because of the monkeys. Did I mention the monkeys? The ranch had a variety of these hairy fellows, large and small, chained here and there for the entertainment of visitors. When the waters began to rise it seemed only right that the monkeys be unchained to fend for themselves. But an unchained monkey will seek a high place; a number of them had ascended by rainspout and trellis and were sitting in misery on the boardinghouse roof. You could look out the upper windows and see them crouching in the lee of the dormers. They weren't chattering or performing, just climbing about slowly on their spidery hands. It was unnerving to the ladies, who locked the windows and shut the blinds.

Perhaps it shouldn't have surprised us to hear an anxious pitch issue from upstairs; the pitch rose quickly into a screech.

'That's Melva,' said a young ranch hand, popping to his feet in the dark — his name was Lehi, a boy in his early twenties. 'There's an attacker,' Lehi cried. I learned later that Melva had long suffered from dreams of attack; she would wake screaming if anything unusual happened, sometimes even if Lehi just rolled over in his sleep. Up those stairs he flew like a witch, with two or three young men right behind. Later, Melva herself admitted the truth: It was warm and damp up there. With so many women sharing the same air, she felt she could hardly breathe. While the others murmured in sleep, Melva rose and opened a window. That improved things; the sweet air helped her sleep. She was dreaming of a beautiful child, a perfect blond cupid who curled into her soft neck, when something went awry. Melva had handled many a clean baby and knew their smell to be of warm cinnamon or nutmeg – this baby didn't smell like any good spice, and it wasn't warm, either. The screech was already coming out when she opened her eyes and saw the terrified monkey retreating with its white fangs exposed.

'She's going to remember them fangs a long time,' mourned Lehi, back downstairs. He'd got hold of the twisting monkey, heaved it back out on the roof, and closed the window. 'There'll be no more sleep for Mel tonight,' he added.

Iron Tail said, 'You are lucky to have your wife here. I have a headache tonight. I wish my wife was alive.'

No one replied, so the old chief continued.

'She used to help me when I got a headache. She would rub my neck with her strong hands. Sometimes I couldn't bear the light, and then she would cover my eyes with cool mud. That was a good way to go to sleep. When I woke up, the headache was gone.'

'My wife never took away my headaches – she generally brought 'em on,' said a man sitting on the floor next to the door. He said it in the tone of someone going for the laugh, and he got one or two, but the truth is we weren't much in the mood for wife wringing. The monkey commotion had unsettled the men whose wives were upstairs; it made those of us without our wives miss them. We were a dozen weary men in a damp room with one smoky candle for light and no prospect of rest.

Iron Tail said, 'When the headache was bad she would rub grease into my neck. That was a good wife.'

Then Glendon said, 'My wife used to go sailing with me, down in Mexico. We had a little boat. She was a fine sailor. There wasn't anything on that boat she couldn't do as well as me.'

'I remember you two on that boat,' said José Barrera, without rancor.

'My wife got so she couldn't see me anymore,' said an old man propped in a corner. 'She could see everyone else. Just not me.'

'Say, now,' someone remonstrated.

The old man said, 'It's the truth. I walked into the house one day saying Darling it's me, and she couldn't hear nor see me. If I touched her she'd see me again, but pretty soon, out I'd fade.'

It froze me, hearing that old man. I said, 'What caused it, sir?'

But he didn't answer. He took a breath as though considering my question; then Iron Tail, who was standing nearest the candle and had been gazing into its flame, remarked, 'I don't know what kind of grease that was. It was strong grease.'

170

'Maybe 'twas bear grease,' offered Bodes, the mechanic, in a voice so nasal it seemed to arrive through a pinhole.

'Not bear grease,' said Iron Tail. He was a little impatient, as though he knew all about bear grease and didn't think much of it.

'Was it skunk grease?' asked Bodes. 'What did it look like?'

'I don't know,' Iron Tail admitted. 'I had that mud over my eyes.'

There was a silence during which I hoped the man in the corner would speak up. I wanted to know whether his wife had started to see him again, as time passed, or whether he had become invisible to other people as well. His children, for example – could they see him? This was my question: If you eventually become like a ghost to all who know you, how do you bear the loneliness?

The candle guttered along. It didn't throw much light. Except for Iron Tail, who stood right next to it, I couldn't tell one man from the next. A few were able to sleep sitting up, but the rest of us just murmured or dozed. I shut my eyes and fell into nostalgia. I remembered a couplet I'd written to Susannah. A painting she made for me of a lovely small house beside a river, a house she said we would one day occupy together. She was seventeen when she made that painting; she had a clean mature eye, even at that age. I wished I could see the painting again. Had we lost it somehow? Sitting in the dank boardinghouse, my head against my knees, I wondered where it had gone.

'Saints above, Jip – tell me it ain't you!' said a woman's voice.

At those oddly recognizable words I lifted my eyes. While

I dozed, someone had lit another candle; it was the old man from the corner, the invisible husband. He wore a brimmed hat that obscured his face. He'd fetched a candle and stuck it to the floor with wax and was playing a hand of solitaire. The woman who'd spoken was tall, trousered, and fringed – she'd been there all along, I suppose, and once again I'd assumed she was a man.

'Don't you know me, Jip?' said Darlys DeFoe, squatting beside the old cardplayer.

'Nope,' came the cool reply.

'Oh, you must. You must remember,' and prizing the candle off the floor she held it near her face. 'Look closer – see if you know me now.'

Annoyed at losing his light the old man raised his head. I was wholly unprepared to see Charles Siringo's face under that hatbrim, yet there it was – his pitted and dashing face. It was a fearsome sight to me.

'Very well, I don't know you,' he said. 'Give me back the candle.'

'We were sweethearts at Hole in the Wall, Jippie,' Darlys said. She was pleading and earnest; for the first time I felt honest compassion for her. 'It can't be that long ago; say you remember.'

'Why, I'll give you this much,' said Charles Siringo. 'I have been to the Hole on many occasions, and I did have a few sweethearts there.' Then his face turned wily and he said, 'None were as rugged as you, however. I have better-looking brothers! I'll take that candle now, goodbye.'

Had he contemplated a year I doubt he could've chosen more cutting words to say to Darlys DeFoe. I found myself hoping she'd douse that candle in one of his eyeballs, but she only handed it to him carefully. Maybe she was dazed by his cruelty. He didn't even watch her depart but dripped a mound of fresh wax on the floor, fixed the candle on it, and returned to his game.

And that is how Siringo reentered our lives. For the rest of that night I watched him at his solitaire, and I wondered when and how he had come to the ranch, when nearly everyone else was leaving it. Did Glendon know Siringo was in the room? When the deck of cards was finally put away and the old savage was at rest, I got up and crept about – it was a congested little crypt, that lobby – but I couldn't find my friend, and at last I went to the door and stood listening to the hard rain and the water flowing past at rising speed and sound.

In the charcoal dawn Glendon appeared with his bundle and we stepped out under the awning. I said, 'Charles Siringo is here.'

'Ain't he a bloodhound? I think he is better than he was. And now I have got to leave. Alone, this time.'

The rain came off the awning in endless strings.

He said, 'You see how it is, Monte.'

I nodded. We were both fatigued – by the flood, by Siringo in that very house, by many days lost and the vanishing of Hood and the bumping of barrels and drowned beasts against the flagging porch.

'I enjoyed our travels,' he said. 'At first chance, it's back to Susannah for you.'

To this I agreed without condition. Through the long night I had pondered Siringo's strange and familiar testimony – how his wife had ceased to see him. The conviction had taken hold that I must go home immediately.

Perhaps there was still time to keep my own hazy outline from becoming permanent.

'I feel sure we'll meet sometime again,' Glendon said.

It put a knot in my throat, that sentence. The knot returns as I mention it.

He said, 'Beware of Charlie. He'll want to use you. Stay out of his grasp. He has a strong grasp — it used to be strong, anyway. I've got no reason to think it's weak now.'

'Glendon. Did Siringo know Darlys DeFoe?'

'Yes, he did.'

'Were they sweethearts at Hole in the Wall?'

'Yes, they were.'

I said, 'Is there anything I can do for Darlys?'

It was so dark I couldn't see him smiling — I heard him, though. He said, 'No, I've taken care of that. Thank you, Monte.'

We shook hands and he stepped off the porch. 'Why, what about that,' he observed, 'it's near to my waist,' and hoisting the pack to his shoulder he melted into the rain.

II

As Glendon tested the surging water, Ern Swilling, on the cot upstairs, was about to test the infinite. His windpipe had sustained an awful kink; kept from collapse by a length of rubber tube akin to yard hose, the tube snaked free in the wee hours and Ern moved on without lifting a hand. The actor's meek death put us all on edge – we shouldn't have been surprised, yet we were. Two or three of the ladies came down to a cold breakfast still insisting poor Ern would rise in triumph; this is the prospect they were discussing when the doctor, name of Clary, entered in his tailed coat to explain with chagrin about the slipped hose.

'The fault is my own,' Clary said quietly. 'I fell asleep and was not watching. He died for my failure.' These remarks have little to do with the larger story, but I report them as a mark of that doctor's humility. The truth is he'd been awake nearly sixty hours before dropping off in a ladder-back chair at Ern's side. 'Regret is ever the physician's companion,' he told me later, sallow with weariness and burden.

Regret, regret: I felt it too. Regret for Ern Swilling, certainly, and his family; regret for the kind doctor and the upstairs girls in their theatrical despair; but chiefly I felt it for Hood Roberts, whose name was suddenly being whipped about with a fury reserved for the vilest reprobates. The malevolent thug! Murderer of the next screen Romeo! Of course Hood had only set out to defend his friend Ignacio. *How would you like a punch in the nose?* Any nine-year-old boy worth a dime says it every week.

Hoarse moans were still echoing round the boarding-house when a commotion of sorts broke out. 'Yonder comes a boat,' called an imp in a window, but he was too quick and got it half wrong: there was a boat, but it wasn't coming. It was going.

'It's got two men,' he added, missing again; it contained only one man, Glendon Hale, plus a pair of spotted pigs who were staying very still in the tiny craft. It was a rummy little coracle – a dishlike vessel of ancient design, prone to spin when paddled. Despite this Glendon seemed to handle it with ease, and it occurred to me that for the sake of ballast Glendon had overcome his dread of pigs. To my knowledge, pigs are no happier about a flood than monkeys; yet these seemed at peace, seated somewhat grandly upright and behaving themselves with their snouts in the air.

It was a charming sight, but looking round I saw Charles Siringo push through the little clutch of onlookers and lean out the window. Siringo wasn't charmed! It's fair to say he was aggravated – he shot me a dark look by which I understood his eye had been on me for some time, then pulled on his coat and waded down off the porch. Charging around in hip-deep water is no easy deed but Siringo leaned into it holding his gunbelt aloft and traversed the flooded street several times, looking for a vessel in which to give chase. In the end he settled for a tall horse, one of Jos Miller's gold-medal drafters. Mr. Miller favored black shires imported from the English midlands – his favorite, a gelding called Mammoth, was at rest high and dry on the Millers' covered portico. Climbing the steps, water streaming from his pockets, Siringo seized a handful of mane and tried to leap aboard Mammoth but slid off. A shire is two feet taller than your common nag and Siringo led the temperate beast down the steps and mounted from the porch rail. The water rose only to the horse's belly and Siringo rode it easily up the street while buckling his gunbelt in place. Few if any guessed his intention, for he smiled and seemed to enjoy the spectacle he made astride Mammoth – tipping his hat, for example, when the ladies waved to him.

What a strange, sluggish pursuit it made! Mammoth refused to giddyup but only picnicked along at a walk; even so, he gained on the bobbing coracle. I saw Glendon bend with effort, so that the craft half spun and the pigs dipped and scrabbled; then Siringo, seeing he was noticed, lifted his revolver and fired. I don't know how long a shot it was: too long apparently. Siringo holstered the revolver again and put Mammoth forward.

Well, the gunshot alerted all that a drama was under way. Soon everyone was leaning out the boardinghouse windows, the ladies agape, the men clamped, the children shoved to the rear. I was told later that two of the upstairs ladies had opera glasses that they employed without shame. Siringo urged the shire ahead with what seemed to me outrageous patience. He was beginning to disappear in the rain. I don't know how far off he was when he again lifted his arm and pointed in the direction of Glendon. A thousand yards? Twelve hundred? By now Mammoth seemed nearly atop the coracle. I want to say all shouting ceased as we waited for the report, but perhaps there was no shouting to begin with. Perhaps everyone was as numb as I was. Siringo sighted along his arm. When watching an execution, does anyone shout?

Then there was a report, at which I can reliably tell you several women began to cry; only it was wrong, the sound of that shot. It was close. As if fired from above us the report echoed off the water and decayed above the flood-plain; then, 'Lookit him, he's killed,' cried the imp, because Charles Siringo had drained down in the saddle and slumped forward against the neck of the shire. Relieved of direction, the horse made a half circle and began its slow return while Glendon, in the coracle, continued on.

I would love to tell you that Darlys DeFoe turned herself in. That she came down off the roof of Marland Oil across the street, where she had climbed unnoticed when all eyes were on Siringo and the big horse, and that she presented herself to the law and told her tale of misplaced affection. That would be romance! That would be opera! But the fact is she disappeared even more handily than Glendon himself had done. José Barrera said he saw 'a tall man wading toward Texas' while the rest of us were transfixed watching Mammoth's slow return, but who knows? Though a search turned up one fifty-caliber shell casing and a soaked sheepskin on the roof where she had rested her rifle, nothing suggested where Deep Breath Darla might be planning to go next or by what means. So far as I can tell, no one who was then at the Hundred and One ever saw her again.

Which, I suppose, is fairly romantic too.

Meantime Charles Siringo lay against the shire's neck like wet bedding. There was some debate among the boardinghouse audience whether he was alive or dead on that horse, but I hadn't any doubt of his living. Laugh all you like at the old perception of the fated existence; Siringo wore it like his own skin. You can't kill history. You can't shoot it with a bullet and watch it recede into whatever lies outside of memory. History is tougher than that — if it's going to die, it has to die on its own.

A new day appeared and I wrote Susannah. It wasn't a proper letter, but it was the longest thing I'd managed to put down since leaving home. I wrote about the treacherous brown flood, about the day of departing wagonloads with their sallow passengers. I wrote how it was to see the yellow sun again, but words were poor compared to the relief I felt, which was acute as bee stings.

In fact the old sun appeared the morning after Glendon's providential escape. The great cloud dissipated as though released from duty and the light came over a horizon that was no longer a ranch but a calm and littered sea. I suspected more days would pass before I was able to leave. José Barrera tried to drive a hayrack out behind two of the big shires; the rig made it fifty yards before the horses lost all footing and the harness had to be cut loose.

I was sitting on the ledge of an open window, groggy with sun, when Dr. Clary stepped into the lobby.

'Excuse me, are any of you gentlemen Monte Becket?'

No one but Glendon and Hood had used my real name in weeks. It was a strange and welcome sound that brought me to my feet.

'What do you need?'

He said, 'Mr. Siringo is repeating your name.'

Charles Siringo was in the ad hoc infirmary upstairs.

He had been shot in the ribcage though the bullet's route was still a mystery. Clary had ascertained one smashed rib and believed the lungs were whole but beyond that was unwilling to guess. Siringo had arrived unconscious aboard Mammoth and was carried upstairs in a state of escalating fever, but soon awoke and began to shout nonsensical language. Clary took his hand and was met with violence; he restrained him and was met with rage. At last for Siringo's own safety he dosed him with ether, only to have the old vulture wake hours later, still angry though with less noise.

'He's saying Monte Becket,' Clary told me. 'You might help him settle. What else he's saying doesn't make a lot of sense.'

'What else is he saying?'

Clary didn't answer so I followed him up the steps to the infirmary. It was no place you would choose to be sick but the doctor had made the best of it. He had waded to the small hospital maintained by the ranch and manhandled supplies to high ground: surgical implements, corked brown bottles, setting plaster and bandages by the roll. Amid this smart clutter lay Siringo in the bed vacated by Ern Swilling. Frankly, Siringo looked soon to follow Ern wherever. He was talking in a husky baritone like a man still in the tavern at sunup. He didn't look at me but breathed out a dragon of illogical syllables.

'Wait a little,' said Clary. Siringo bored on in his husky voice. Abruptly a few words spilled out. Names mostly. I remember he said Jip Fingers. He rolled to and fro in his ravings. He said Monte Becket, and I answered him yes.

'Who are you?'

'Becket.'

He laughed at this and focused on me with his fevered eyes.

'Not Jack Waits then.'

'No.'

'Friend of Glen Dobie,' he said.

'That's right.' There seemed little use for caution now, with Glendon gone, and Siringo in this condition.

He struggled to get a line on me and I moved round to the foot of the bed where he could look me straight on.

'Did you shoot me, lad?'

'No.'

'You were with him, with Dobie.'

'I didn't shoot you.'

He rolled half over with an agonized shout – it made me jump, but he calmed and lay still.

The doctor said, 'You were shot, Mr. Siringo, by a gunman who is still at large and whose identity no one knows for certain.'

This was a mild equivocation, since everyone at the ranch knew there was only one person who could've made the shot.

'And who are you?' he asked the doctor.

'James Clary.'

'You going to open me up?'

'If your fever goes down. If you live long enough.'

Siringo had a week's beard. A century's lines. He said, 'Well, you be careful in there.'

'I will,' said Clary.

'You keep your eyes open.' Siringo started to laugh – he

seemed onto a vein of comedy. 'Don't take out nothing I need, amigo.'

'You rest now, Mr. Siringo.'

Siringo nodded. His breathing guttered like flame. He seemed near lapsing into either sleep or madness, but he managed another quiet laugh saying, 'I got a burly old heart – you remember not to nick it, understand?' Then a pain got him and he swore at it, shouting in a blistered voice. Clary shook a bottle onto a cloth and I turned my face away while the room grew quiet.

'How well do you know him?' Clary asked.

'Not well at all.'

'Who is Glen Dobie?'

'The man he was pursuing when he was shot.'

Clary chuckled at my caution. 'That much I see – I mean, who is Glen Dobie that this old boy is so hard after him?'

'They have a grudge,' I replied.

Clary put a hand on the plaster wall – I think he would've tipped over otherwise. 'I must have some rest,' he said.

'I'll sit here with him awhile.'

'Would you do that? Since you know him?'

I nodded.

'I had a young man and two nurses. They went out on the wagons.'

'It's all right.'

Clary bent down and looked closely at Siringo's eyes and listened to his breathing. 'If he wakes in a frenzy, come get me. Don't try and dose him yourself.'

'I wouldn't do that.'

'I guess you wouldn't.' Clary lifted a muslin curtain and

went into the adjoining room. I heard a reserved sigh and the clink of a decanter. It seemed only moments later he was snoring. His snores were low and delicate – he was a particular man, even sleeping.

14

That is how I came to be Siringo's keeper – I would say his nurse, only I served him little except as company. I suppose I felt partially responsible for his condition, though his pursuit of Glendon was his own choice. For two full days he was on precarious ground – he would wake and carry on, lucid a small percentage of the time. When he roared his gibberish the boardinghouse residents cowered in the hallways, but then for minutes together he might speak with urgent exactitude as though narrating a preposterous memoir. He revealed many pieces of his life, including an account of his first meeting with Darlys DeFoe that made me blush to the eyeballs. He told how he left off cowboying when the profession of detective was chosen for him at a public demonstration of phrenology. The phrenologist's fingers strolled over his scalp like ten stubby prophets and he uttered the word 'detective' in a divine whisper, after which Siringo considered no other course. He talked about being dynamited out of his Chicago house by anarchists, landing literally in the street while pine shards and hot plumbing rained around him.

His sentiments for the most part were vengeful and emerged from experiences so long at a simmer that he spoke in what amounted to strong verse about those who had wronged him. I was surprised to learn he had been fired by the Pinkerton Agency years before; he gave an eloquent screed on the decayed character of Allan Pinkerton, whose 'spine went missing at birth.' To a cowardly pard who had fled gunfire he gave a scorching epitaph. Strangely his softest words were for certain of the outlaws he had hunted: Butch Cassidy, whom he never saw in the flesh through four years of pursuit; the surgeon and gentleman gunsmith Howard Cawley, whose talent for baking cinnamon rolls made him welcome at Hole in the Wall; and Glendon, whom Siringo referred to as 'that gentle bastard.'

Eventually James Clary taught me to douse a cloth with ether and lay it firmly over Siringo's mouth – it was the only way he would fully rest, but I never liked to do it and as in so many things my hesitancy proved expensive. Once as I hovered over him Siringo glimpsed the descending hanky and lunged up, getting my hand in his teeth. He got to the bone before the ether took him, so that meant a little more work for poor Clary, plus my hand looked like a hairless creature killed on the road.

On the third day Clary dosed Siringo heavily and went in after the bullet. He located it between the rib it had smashed and the lung it would've pierced otherwise. Waking afterward Siringo told the doctor he had strolled through a deepening valley at the bottom of which he'd glimpsed the gates of Hell – black as you'd expect with the usual smoke rising in the background. His voice amused, Siringo described an emissary who had come out from the gates dressed in shiny skin like an eel's. The emissary told Siringo they had a room reserved under his name but he wasn't coming in just yet.

Clary said, 'I know a preacher in Ponca City. I'll send for him if you like.'

'To what point and purpose?' said Charles Siringo.

'Well, in case you wish to make a reservation elsewhere.'

'Be an adult, Mr. Clary. It happened in my mind. My own good brain carved out that valley and built those gates; that eel-skin fellow was my own conjuring.'

Clary regarded him placidly. 'Most men would prefer not to take the chance.'

I will say for Siringo that he held to his convictions. Weak from days of fever and pain, he still found the strength to say, 'I can't believe I let an idiot probe my guts with a knife.'

'As you wish,' said Clary.

15

The earth slowly surfaced. Though I chafed to leave, five more days passed before the fusty waters withdrew enough to allow it. Even then the roads dried last, since they had no drainage. Mr. Bodes took the Packard apart, greasing it piece by cagey piece, and I packed my few clothes and watched from the window as mudcrackle peeled off the world. Redstart had often wondered aloud what we might find if a certain river or lake dried up – he imagined fishing tackle and anchors and human skulls and of course glittering doubloons. Well, I found no treasure as the Salt Fork retreated, but I did come across a decent wood frigate with a muslin sail set afloat by some youngster; also a drifting ox bladder inflated and tied with a knot attached to a note with the childish inscription, *Help help, we are dying of hunger on the See of Sinbad.* The note put me so much in mind of my own boy that I laughed aloud en route to a state of weepy fatigue.

The day came when Siringo crawled off the rank mattress and into a suit of clothes. He'd whipped the fever but I recall him trembling in the lobby after a wall-hugging journey down the stairs. How different he was; the suit was the same he had arrived in, a mossy wool, yet it now seemed his inheritance from a colossal ancestor. His beard had grown in almost pure white except for a streak of intractable red on his chin. For nearness to the next world he looked like one of your querulous great-greats with his damp eyes and his nodding jaw offset like a camel's.

He said, 'I'm afraid my driving days are over.'

'Not at all, you'll mend quickly now,' I said. It didn't hurt to be polite – he looked so frail, his clothes falling in over his bones, but then I said, 'You'll be back betraying old friends in a trice, I am sure.'

He seemed to enjoy that, wheezing like a gunnysack. He said, 'Clary has arranged to sell my automobile,' and even his voice was attenuated and of shadowy timbre.

I inquired whether he intended to take the train home.

'Yes. Thank you, Becket, by the way,' he added humbly.

I regarded him with surprise.

'For sitting beside me,' he said, nodding as though it embarrassed him. 'For bearing with me through the dark valley. It couldn't have been pleasant for you,' he said.

'It's all right.'

'Why did you do it?'

I hadn't an answer. I thought of Glendon saying, *Why don't matter.* I replied, 'You'd have done the same for me.'

'You're smarter than that,' he said, with a bit of his old pepper.

'I guess I am.'

'Now you'll be going home. Home to Minne-sota,' he intoned, lightly mimicking the grim Norwegians who had taken root on those northern plains. Noting my hand still bound up in cotton he added in a low voice, 'I understand that is my doing.'

'It's healing.'

'I am ashamed of that, Becket,' he said. 'I make no apologies for what I am, but that shames me.'

'You weren't yourself.'

'Is that a fact? Who would you say I was, then?'

There was a silence during which Siringo seemed to attempt by his will to stop the tremors in his fingers. 'And Glen Dobie, where did he get to?'

'Away from you, it appears,' I couldn't resist telling him.

He chuckled. 'It's true, I'm a reduced specimen now. Oh, I may hold off the grave awhile yet, but look how small I've become. How brittle.' His tone was of incredulity; I suppose small and brittle were conditions he had never imagined for himself.

'Is there anything I can do for you?'

'Do for me – when do you leave, Becket?'

'In the morning.'

'Well, then, I'll trouble you to take me to the train station.'

'Really? Are you strong enough to travel?'

He held my gaze a moment before answering, 'I'm strong enough.'

And did I see something in his eyes? Did I see a dark personage crouching, back in the shadows of his brain? No. If I am honest with you, I didn't see a thing.

16

The morning we left the Hundred and One I received a telegram from Susannah. The timing was dreamlike as Siringo and I stood on the boardwalk amid luggage while Mr. Bodes growled up in the swabbed Packard. The sun went sizzling up the bleached Oklahoma sky, which atoned for the fungoid exhale of the drying ranch. James Clary had stepped out to say goodbye, though he didn't offer to shake hands because his were covered with violet antiseptic. I didn't even notice the Western Union boy until he asked my name. Of course I fumbled and scrabbled at the envelope – I had been gone from home for twenty-six days, but they felt like years upon my shoulders.

The telegram said I MISS YOUR FACE, COME HOME.

I don't remember laughing aloud, though Siringo told me later that I did – it would become my greatest merit as far as Siringo was concerned, that a woman cared for me – I laughed, it seems, then flush with new generosity I picked up Siringo's two leather suitcases which he called his rhino grips and set them in the back of the Packard. When Bodes opened the passenger door Siringo fell into the seat. *Poor doddering oldster* was my thought, for he worked his mouth and finally produced the words 'Goodbye, Clary,' for the doctor was nodding to us in his delicate way.

'Stay away from the black doors,' Clary whispered to Siringo, leaning forward.

'You'll go through them before I do,' replied Siringo.

'I'll not go through them at all,' said the doctor.

'Got religion did you?'

'You are the completest argument for it I have ever met,' said Clary, at which Siringo with surprising vitality leaned out and grasped the doctor's violet hand, and so impulsive and free of calculation did this appear that I could only conclude the old monster was capable of gratitude after all, even toward the simpleton who had saved his life.

THE FIERY SIRINGO

Speeding north from the ranch, Charles Siringo grew light-hearted. He hummed and chortled; we tore along the peeling mudplains and the dust we raised got into our teeth and tasted of swamp. My final glimpse of the Hundred and One was, like my first, of an elephant. No doubt the same elephant. It was at some distance, seemingly confused, charging and tilting and changing its mind. I suppose it still woke each morning expecting an African sunrise.

After some miles we came to an intersection. East would take us to Ponca City and the train station; west – well, I didn't know where west would take us. In truth I wasn't thinking about west. I was thinking about Susannah in her orange skirt.

'West, Becket,' Siringo said.

'Ponca City is east,' I replied, pulling to a stop.

'East is not our direction.'

You may guess I felt a touch of frost in the old spinal column, though I still hoped we had merely misunderstood one another.

'You asked for a ride to the depot. That's where we're headed.'

'The depot was never my intent.'

'No? What was your intent?'

He didn't reply. Often, I would find, he didn't reply, and

these were usually times when I already knew the answer to the question I had asked.

I made to put the car in gear. In a tone of confidential humor he said, 'If you turn east, Becket, you will never get to Ponca City.'

Now you are thinking, Just a blasted second here – he was enfeebled! He fell into the car! But I am telling you that now I did glimpse the dark creature squatting behind the flatness of his eyes.

'I know what you want,' I told him.

'Why, I want you and me to travel west in company. That's fairly clear, I hope.'

'I don't know where Glendon is. I can't be your guide.'

'Then go as my companion. I need a driver. We'll have a pleasant time.'

'I'm going home, Mr. Siringo.'

Siringo said merrily, 'You are fibbing to yourself, Becket. You tell yourself I am infirm, but you don't believe it.'

'I believe my two eyes.'

He held out his right hand. 'Would you test my grip then?'

I looked at his hand. It quivered, which gave me confidence. I said, 'Don't humiliate yourself, you've had a hard time. You need to go home and continue your convalescence.' But I remembered Glendon saying *Keep out of his grasp*, so my hand stayed on the wheel.

'You daren't shake my hand?'

Feeling every ounce a coward I said, 'I do not trust you.'

'Very well.' And turning away he opened the door and got out of the car and hobbled over to the side of the road. He sat down in the dead ryegrass, bending in what I remember as an inadequate breeze against the heat. 'I'll wait here. Someone will be headed west, eventually.'

'Don't be absurd. It's going to be warm today. It's warm already.'

'I've been warm before. Get on your way.'

In fact I wanted to get on my way but dreaded my swarming conscience down the road. Siringo had nearly died from that bullet wound; we were miles from town and had yet to see another auto on the road. If he didn't get a ride, he would soon tip over and dry out. His mouth would draw open and he would become a leathery ribcage on that arid plain.

I said, 'I'd rather not leave you here.'

'West,' he said, as though at play.

'Oh, come on. Come on now,' and getting out of the car I stepped up to Siringo with the universal signal of entreaty.

I held out my hand.

He nodded and reached for it. Next moment came a pop and blast of creamy white! No doubt my eyes whirled back and caught a glimpse of my skull. I jerked my hand to my stomach and bent over it with a cry.

'Why, what's happened to you?' asked Siringo, getting awkwardly to his feet like any innocuous grandpa.

I couldn't answer. For that matter I couldn't breathe. I sat down in the rye where he had been and rocked and made a few high noises.

Stooping in he remarked, 'Well, that looks just terrible.' What looked terrible was the ring finger of my right hand. He'd given it a tug and a sidewise twist so it sat unhinged above its socket.

'Tell you what,' said Siringo, now taking my elbow and with disquieting strength lifting me to my feet, 'let's drive west.'

I stumbled along in his grip and he opened the driver's door of the Packard and settled me quite gently behind the wheel.

'How am I to drive,' I said, for though my breath was returned my vision still spun with pain and I sweated like the opium enthusiasts Redstart had described to me from Conan Doyle.

'It will do you good. It's soothing to drive, that is common knowledge.'

I had no words. I whacked the steering wheel with my left hand but of course that was the hand Siringo had bitten in his ravings. My wrath had nowhere to go. I started to pull at the agonized finger but felt the cool ghost of a looming faint. The finger was getting big and I couldn't put it straight.

'You'll feel better once we start moving,' he said.

So I steadied my breath and palmed the shifter and let out the clutch as if balancing tippy drinks and turned the Packard away from the sun. At the same time I began instinctively to bargain. 'I'll tell you where he is,' I said, as we began to climb off the caked floodplain into regions of spongy grass and cowland.

'You don't know where he is,' Siringo replied.

'I know where he's going. Approximately. I don't have a street number or anything, but I know roughly.'

'I'm glad to hear it. Roughly will be useful. I prefer specific, of course – but roughly will do.'

I opened my mouth to say, He'll be at a fruit orchard

in the Rienda Valley. You see how quickly I'd have betrayed my friend? But Siringo stopped me.

'Oh, I know it's California for Glen — Mexican Joe gave me that much! You clutch onto your details for the present, I don't need them yet.'

'But I can tell you now! Then you can go on, unencumbered by me, and I can go home.'

'Unencumbered, hey.' Siringo took enormous wheezy pleasure from the word. His laughs soon deteriorated into furious coughing, which tired him out but didn't ruin his cheerful mood. He said, 'Becket, I know you long for home. I expect you've a doting wife. A flock of tender kidlets! But I need to make sure of your candor.'

'I'll be honest.'

'You'll be honest if you come with me, because the consequences of dishonesty will be obvious to you.'

'But I'll tell the truth!' I'm sorry to say I nearly screamed the words.

'Why? I wouldn't, in your place,' he said. 'Also, Becket, I want your company. It comes to light we are both of us writers. Two authors traveling together — the discussions we'll have! Here, what do you think of this proposition? Men are built of words. Wouldn't you say that's true?' At this he leaned forward and slapped my knee heartily, as if we were a pair of thrown-togethers at the beginning of a long train ride, discovering our common love of bookish pursuit. 'Men are defined by the words they use, and I have always said so!'

During this conversation I had continued to perspire until my face and hands and even the steering wheel were rimed with salt and dirt; my dislodged finger was a proud little melon. Bitterly I said, 'Men are defined by their actions, Mr. Siringo. Yours define a bully and liar. I'll have no more discussions with you than I would with any thug you care to name.'

It was a righteous short sermon, delivered, I still say, in as tidy a style as a man with one hand broken and the other bitten is likely to possess; yet envision my surprise when Siringo blinked and drew back from me, as though I'd gone out of my way to injure his feelings.

'Why, there ain't any demand for talk of that sort,' he said, his voice turning back toward frailty and confusion. 'No demand at all. A little thoughtful discourse is all I had in mind.'

And the strange thing, as I watched his face struggle with my little flash of resentment, was that I was sorry I'd said it. All he had to do was turn from me to watch the passing ranch land, show me the back of his crabbed webby neck shrinking farther into that huge collar. For several long moments I truly believed I'd been too hard on the old vulture. Why deny him his thoughtful discourse just because my finger ached? I came that close to making a sort of apology. Go ahead and laugh. A time was coming when I would relate all this to Glendon Hale, confessing my weak-mindedness; but Glendon only nodded and said Charlie had more traps than anybody, so many in fact that Charlie himself didn't know them all; but his finest snare lay in believing every word that he said, until you believed them too and stepped readily into his palm.

2

We spent the night round a popping fire, having made some seventy miles. In that part of Oklahoma few trees grew bigger than cornstalks so we camped in the lee of a roof-less farmhouse from which I pried enough planks to keep a flame. Watching me scrounge boards sore-handed appeared to help Siringo rebound from my earlier terse remarks and he was in tall spirits again, pointing out telling features of the old farmstead; the skeletal mill tower riven by light-ning, a wide propitious chimney now rubbled, the lich-ened tilting posts of a vanished corral.

'It was a big corral once,' he said, as dusk faded. 'These folks must've thought they'd made it.'

'I guess they did make it, for a while,' I replied.

'Nope, that's vanity,' Siringo said. 'It came to nothing, you will notice. Grasping after wind,' he added happily. He had a way of pronouncing doom in buoyant tones as if reading aloud from the comics. It made me feel bitter toward him – and toward myself, for lacking the wit to have simply driven away that morning while he sulked in the weeds. It was worse than annoying to realize he'd guessed right about me – that I would not leave him there in the sun to bake.

My hand, by the way, was improved. After perhaps ten

minutes of knifing distress Siringo had abruptly reached over, taken my hand in his own and reset the finger while I yelped and jerked the Packard to and fro. One swift pull was all it amounted to – it shames me to tell you how strong were my feelings of gratitude. I am weak about pain. Immediately my outlook improved and the old strap seemed pleased with my advancing manners. When I thanked him he only cackled lightly, then tucked into a corner of the seat and fell asleep with apparent confidence that I would try nothing untoward. Sure enough I didn't. Pulling rotten planks off the farmhouse and stacking them by the fire, I was bitter about that too.

'Say – look what I got here,' Siringo said, as if remembering a treat held in reserve for this very hour.

Easing down on a precarious kitchen chair scavenged from the house he waved a copy of *Martin Bligh*. He said, 'Hey hey,' as if I ought to be tickled, but the last thing you want is for a fellow like Charles Siringo to know you any better.

'Guess where I obtained this,' he said, his cheeks burnished with firelight.

'I don't know.'

He propped an eyebrow and opened the book and angled it to better read the title page.

To my good friend Emma Davies, remember always the books that were your first loves –

'Stop!' I cried. It was unseemly that he should read my heart-felt inscription so breezily. 'You stole it from that girl!'

'No, sir. She gave it to me,' he replied.

'I don't believe it.'

That sat Siringo up a little straighter, across the fire. He regarded me, his mouth open in apprehension.

'I see. Yes, I do. You were a favorite of hers, weren't you?'

'Not that I know of,' I said, shutting my eyes.

'No, no – I see how it was. You like the notion that she kept your book on her little shelf of beloveds. That she read your words by golden lantern light. It makes a very pretty picture. It's nice to be admired by someone like that, yes?'

He had me nailed, of course. To this day I remember Emma, her eyes regular moons while I read to her Martin's close shave with the Apaches. Back to mind zipped her naïve compliment, that I was after Alcott but ahead of Frank Spearman.

Siringo said, 'Anyway, little Emma must've turned a corner after you left. Disappointment in your practical ethics, I would imagine. She more or less flung this book at me. Why would she have done such a thing?'

Well, that was simple enough. I'd stepped away from what might've become friendship with her grandfather, the dutiful Royal, and also away from law and innocence.

'I read it,' Siringo stated.

It took me a moment to realize he meant the book.

He said, 'It was real good for what it was. I enjoyed that Martin fellow.'

A great weariness pulled at me. I stacked a few more planks on the fire and lay down on my blanket. It was only a cotton blanket and no pillow. I could feel all my neck bones. It occurred to me, not for the first time, that I had perhaps glamorized Martin's blissfulness at sleeping on the open prairie.

Siringo said, 'A man of action, Bligh. Once he made up his mind, he wasn't much available to persuasion.'

I hoped to go to sleep on that affirming note, but Siringo wasn't finished.

'Man of that sort wouldn't be much use in this world, but I liked him all the same.'

The ground was full of hard knots. I sat up. 'Not much use, you say.'

'Well, no. Not much. He was honorable, as you mention forty or fifty times, but when a man has a chance to walk away from torture and doesn't, the word you're looking for is stupid.'

'We will disagree on this subject.'

'Nonsense,' said Siringo. He was deeply amused and not at all sleepy – I resented him for getting a long nap that afternoon while I drove the automobile through seventy miles of dust in the opposite direction from home. Now my eyes were all sandy and sore, while his were fresh and full of sashay. He said, 'For the sake of argument, let's postulate that you are my captive. If I abuse you from time to time on this our sojourn to the west, how long will it be before you bolt?'

'Bolt?'

'Try to bolt,' he amended.

'There wouldn't be the least dishonor in my taking leave of you – you aren't even a Pinkerton anymore, but only pretending. Your authority is counterfeit,' I told him.

If I hoped that would sting, I was disappointed.

'You are right about the Pinkertons but wrong about authority, as evidenced by our relative positions. We must raise the stakes. Suppose that by staying with me, you could convince me your position is the right one – that honor is worth whatever it might cost. Remember though that I am a rogue of brutish habits with a room saved for me in Hell. What would you suffer to make your argument?'

'I'd rather not answer.'

'Don't fret, we are only talking.'

'I refuse to answer. This is an ambush.'

He gave a thick chuckle. 'You have nine more fingers, Becket.'

I said, 'I would stay until my fear won out, and then I'd run away.'

Siringo reached for one of the boards I had stripped from the house. He poked the coals, then dropped the board amid them to smolder and pop. He said, 'Are you admitting to cowardice?'

'Yes.'

'Don't look so sad. The same end overtakes coward and champion. How about this proposition? Honor is vanity.'

'That's contemptible.'

He shrugged. 'As you will. Did you read my book?'

'No.'

'How come?'

I didn't answer. My eyes were still open and I could see sleep moving toward me like rain across the prairie.

'How come, hey?'

Honestly, I hadn't looked at his book because I hadn't the heart. It discouraged me to think of this reckless Siringo sitting down and dashing off his hundreds of pages while also being a cowboy detective and productive bounty hunter and living legend, while I might struggle a week to put down six sentences that mattered. I hadn't read his book because I was afraid it would be good.

'You got it with you?' Siringo demanded.

'No.' Though I did – it was still in my pack.

'That's all right. Here, I'll tell you a bit,' and he proceeded to narrate for me the first chapter of his memoir, wherein he leaves home as a stripling to get work driving horses. It was a swift involving tale, packed with ruffians and violent broncs and sweet-faced girls from the opening gun, and Siringo had it word for word and pause for pause like a man of the theater, even though he had written it all down some twenty years ago.

'Why, that's exceptional narrative,' I admitted, when he'd finished.

'Well, it's what happened, more or less. It's what should've happened, anyway. That's all I do, just lay down events without floral arrangement.' He leaned back, pleased with his recital. 'What about you, Becket? How do you work your stories?'

'I'm not writing anymore,' I said.

'What's that mean? Is your eyesight failing?'

'It means I can't do it anymore.'

'Can't do it?'

'I'm no good anymore – that's all. It's not the end of anything except one short career. Now I am tired. Good night, Siringo.'

He said, 'How can you be good once, and then not?' He seemed more awake than ever and also sincere in his puzzlement. Glancing at him, I saw a man watching me with something resembling concern. No onlooker would have guessed he had kidnapped me and put me in torment through much of the day. I shut my eyes and tried to drift. Siringo was stirring the coals. Abruptly he said, 'Say, Becket – is your mind all right?'

'It's fine.'

'Do you know your alphabet?'

'Yes, I know the alphabet.'

'Sing it for me.'

'Sing it?'

'You know: A, B, C, D—'

'I know it.'

Siringo threw something, a small rock, and hit me on the chest. I sang the little tune.

'Well, you got the letters.' He narrowed his eyes. 'You own a dictionary?'

'Both Oxford's and Webster's.'

'You got every tool in the box, and you still can't make a story.'

'Not a good one, it seems.'

Blessed silence while he thought this through; then he chirruped hoarsely and issued a diagnosis.

'Why, poor Becket – you got no medicine, that's what it is. You used it all up in only the one book. You got no medicine left at all!'

It put him in such a good mood that he let me go to sleep at last – down I went like a spoiled prince, hard earth and neck bones and all. Whether Siringo slept I don't know. When I awoke he was crouched over the fire. It was just dawn and his face was pale as smoke. It gave me hope; clearly he was weak. In those cold first moments the thought even came to me that Siringo was dying, that this would be his last day. It was followed however by the much worse thought that he had died already, during the night, and was up anyway, making coffee in the normal fashion, and that I would be compelled for some time to be the companion of a dead fellow who refused to acknowledge his condition.

3

We got bread and jam in a town called Ingersoll, plus cream and a pint of raspberries from a boy at roadside whose father had promised to take him to the Pacific Ocean if he sold every berry in their sizable patch by August. That's what the boy said. To this Siringo remarked that the Pacific Ocean was a long ways off.

'He's gonna get a boat and we'll fish for the big silver ones that live down deep,' the boy said.

'You'll never see the ocean in your life,' Siringo replied roughly. 'Drive, Becket.'

'We will!' the boy insisted – he was still insisting as we pulled away.

'That was unkind of you,' I said. 'You showed no grace to that youngster.'

He said, 'If I had the energy I would follow him home and show no grace to that papa of his. The ocean!'

'You don't know his papa won't take him.'

'Did you notice the state of his short pants?'

'No.'

'How about the dirt on his neck – did you see that?'

I confessed I had not.

Siringo looked at me in disbelief. 'Well, heavens, Becket! No wonder your medicine's dried up.' In disgust he settled back and shut his eyes. 'Wake me at the next town, we need fuel.'

The next town turned out to be Alva, which I remember by its colors – beds of petunias and black-eyed Susans and variegated daisies fluttered streetside, many homes wore new paint, the whole place seemed picked up. Horses and wagons and autos stood in a park beside a river which turned out to be the same old Salt Fork; an outdoor market had been set up with people selling pies and cakes and garden truck. Families spread blankets on the lawn and picnicked in the shade of cottonwoods; some boys had made a heavy kite out of butcher paper and the ever-present westerly had it humming over the lawn. All of it taken together seemed like a sign to action, and I began to look about and wonder what chance might show itself. A fuel station lay off the road near the park. I looked over at Siringo, who was waking up on his own.

'Where are we?'

'Alva.'

Maybe my voice betrayed too much interest.

'Charming town,' said he.

'Indeed.'

'First we'll get something to eat. Then gasoline and water. Don't you give in to temptation now,' he said. 'You've got no friends in Alva.'

I nodded, but felt lifted by the sight of people enjoying themselves. How could Siringo know who my friends were?

We pulled into a dirt lot where a team of Percherons stood in harness before a wagon bright with melons and cabbage and heads of broccoli. Stepping out of the Packard

Siringo leaned back in for a small canvas bag. He licked his forefinger and swabbed up a mixture of salt and baking soda with which to clean his teeth. This he did at leisure, scrubbing his gums while inspecting the forbearing Percherons; then it was back to his grip where he located a mottled tin badge and pinned it to his vest. 'Pinkerton issue,' he said, with what seemed an alloy of respect and irony. At last he pulled from his bag a clanking set of manacles and asked me without apology to hold out my hands.

'Are these really necessary?' I asked.

'I doubt it,' he said, with clear disappointment.

We ate chili in a café where my hopes of escape receded. The place was nearly full and we took a table in the center where Siringo made much of removing the cuff from my left wrist and clipping it with a brisk snap to the leg of the chair. Fixed thus I couldn't sit upright but had to eat slumped, like a chimp recaptured after brief liberty. The patrons peered at me over their newspapers while Siringo nodded smiling to all. He looked absolutely the sharp old lawman in charge of his situation. Craning round I caught the pitiless eyes of harried cooks so no doubt my felonies and punishment were being thrashed out fully in that kitchen. The chili was strong as poison and the reddest stuff in my experience; Siringo ate like a scavenging bird, in big swallows without evident pleasure. Afterward he called a waitress who brought out two wedges of coconut cream pie. I will say that even in my chimp slouch this pie seemed the work of angels.

'You pay, Becket,' he told me at the counter. 'Someone at the Hundred and One went and lightened my pocket while I lay sleeping.' I know he intended to humiliate me

– manacled I couldn't reach my wallet and had to have him get it for me, and ruffle through it, and pay for our lunch – nevertheless I had to smile, and nearly to laugh. For I remembered asking Glendon what I might do for Darlys DeFoe, as he was leaving, and Glendon replying he'd done it already.

I hoped Siringo had arrived at the ranch with a fat roll.

Heading back to the auto, he stopped and bent slightly at the waist. He was perspiring.

'Are you all right?'

He gave a nod.

'Is it your wound?'

'No.' His stomach made an agonized liquid sound. He said, 'Don't bother to live as long as me, Becket, it is only occasionally worth it.' Back he went to the café at a stiff trot after dispensing stern instructions to wait for him in the Packard.

The moment he disappeared I stepped round the corner in my manacles and through the first doorway I saw, a dim newspaper office with a counter and register and a man in repose behind a desk.

I said, 'Sir, if you please, I need assistance. My name is Monte Becket. Is there a police officer in town?'

'Yes, there is. Are you in trouble, Mr. Becket?'

Though I was in full view I don't think this fellow ever saw the cuffs.

'I've been kidnapped,' I told this journalist.

He said nothing.

'Abducted. Snatched,' I clarified.

He looked me up and down as though he had seen crackpots before. 'If that is true, why are you standing right here in front of me?'

Think of the thousand things I could've said that might've burst his cobwebs: *I've escaped! My assailant is upon us! Take me to the police!* But frustration muted me, and when I found words at last they were doubtless the most futile in our wide language.

'I'm a writer from Minnesota!' I cried.

At this the door opened and a woman came in – young and yellow-haired, lacy sleeves and large eyes.

'Wilfred,' she sang out.

'Hello, Trudy. Meet Mr. Becket, down from Minnesota.'

Trudy said, 'Hello, I need to place an advertisement.'

While Wilfred hunted a pencil to scratch down her twenty words, I noticed a copy of the local newspaper lying on the counter.

Slap on Page One was Hood Roberts, in deepening trouble.

He had come into Alva the previous week, stolen a nearly new Locomobile belonging to a well driller, and fled with a single passenger, a Mexican girl.

Of course neither Hood nor Alazon was named in the hasty article, but Hood's face had been ably reproduced by a local sketch artist. That artist was clever – he even caught some of Hood's natural shine, the faintly impudent eyebrow, the flair of the young immortal.

I said, 'Could either of you direct me to the telegraph office?'

'Bank building, down the street,' Wilfred said, and I stepped out the door.

4

It was a natty little bank with pressed tin on the walls and ceiling and proud black marble at the tellers' counter. I approached an oak desk in the corner where a man in baggy charcoal was writing with a fountain pen. There was a chair in front of the desk and I sat with as little clanking as possible.

'I'd like to send a telegram.'

He didn't look up but said, 'I'm not the operator,' while continuing to write.

'Where is the operator? Will he return soon?'

'Mr. Terrell is his name. Mr. Terrell is over at the café.' The pen scratched away. This fellow made beautiful script.

'Do you know when he'll return?'

At my insistent presence the man exhaled wearily and stood from the desk. He saw the manacles and said, 'What are those?'

'I have been abducted.'

He replied, 'Then you won't mind going to the police about it.'

It was tiresome, but I suppose I wouldn't be any different – you see a man cuffed, unaccompanied, a wary look on his face; the word *police* must feel like checkmate.

'I'd like that above all else,' I declared.

My eagerness to meet with law officers gave my tale of

kidnap a measure of credibility and the penman decided to take charge of me himself; out we went, him with lifted chin and me rattling beside him. He assured me Alva employed three municipal officers and that the sheriff and several deputies would also be available if help were needed tracking down my kidnappers.

'There is only one kidnapper, and he's right here in town. We had just come from the café when I slipped away from him,' I said, allocating myself a little unearned credit. We were going through town at a fast walk and he had hold of my elbow in a proprietary manner. To encourage a more companionable mood I said, 'Thank you for this. I tell you it's been a harrowing time.'

And he did believe me, I would swear it, for he lessened his stride and asked a question or two about my captivity and treatment and my place of origin. He seemed a very decent fellow after all; I would say we reached the police station on nearly equitable grounds. But my new standing was temporary, for when the door swung open there sat Charles Siringo, tilting back in a Windsor chair. He was holding a sheath knife by the tip, preparing to throw it at a pine plank tilted against the wall. The target was a jack of hearts and the riveted audience of six were all police or deputized citizens. Siringo's arm whipped forward and his knife struck the jack straight on the ear. What whistles! What fraternal hoo-hah! I stood helpless while my new friend the penman reached for the sleeve of the police chief, whose name I remember was Dick Speed.

'Dick, this fellow just came into the bank. Says he was abducted but has got away.'

Only now did Siringo look up. He registered no surprise

but smiled gently as though to welcome back my prodigal self. He didn't rise from his chair or act like any kind of authority, but turned expectantly to Mr. Speed.

'Well, Charlie,' said this Speed, 'you called it. Here is your specimen safe and sound.'

'Hello, yes, that's him,' Siringo replied. 'I'll admit I was skeptical, but you've proven your point; a confidence artist doesn't get far here in Alva.' Standing he shook the hand of the surprised penman. 'Sir, you'll be recognized for this. A public decoration at the very least. I cannot promise remuneration, though I see what you're thinking – the money ain't the point. Are you a deputy here as well?'

'No – no, I just work at the bank—' and though I willed the penman to look my way, he was in fact already useless to me.

'An ordinary citizen!' Siringo brimmed with admiration. 'It's what I tell the schoolchildren when performing lyceum shows: The path of duty is the way to glory. Old man Tennyson.'

'I thank you, sir – thank you,' said the penman, handing me over like a leashed mutt. More hoo-hah! A banner day for law enforcement in Oklahoma! I had time for one candid appeal and Dick Speed was my man.

'Would you hear my story before giving me wholesale into this man's custody?'

Speed met my eyes. I sensed a chance. 'Go on,' said he.

'I am Monte Becket. My home is in Minnesota, where many people will vouch for me if you take the trouble to send one telegram. Send another, and you will learn that the famous Mr. Siringo is a lone operative supported by no authority but his own. I am being held unlawfully by a bold fraud. That is as plain as I can say it. I petition your conscience.'

During this speech Siringo watched me with an expression of gravity from below his hooded lids. Somewhat belately I noticed that Speed was holding a copy of Siringo's Pinkerton memoir. So were several of the others. No doubt these precious articles were personally inscribed.

Then Dick Speed said, 'What is your profession, Mr. Becket?'

'Why, I'm an author,' I replied, blinking.

At this Siringo looked down with an expression of modesty, and Dick Speed turned to him saying, 'You fellows best be on your way,' as though my answer had instantly negated my solemn plea.

'No,' said Siringo. 'No, indeed. Dick, if you have one doubt in this matter you must follow it up. Here,' he added, 'is the telephone number of the Pinkerton office in Denver. I will wait while you place the call.'

But Dick Speed only shook Siringo's hand saying, 'I wouldn't detain you a moment longer – no doubt Monte here's got a book to write! No doubt he's got a deadline!' which put everybody in slick spirits.

My confusion at this response was only dispelled once we were on the road, where Siringo revealed his stratagem: he had described me as an oily academic confidence man who arranged to write old folks' biographies for an up-front fee, then fled with the money.

'Author,' Speed said again, as we left the police station. 'You be careful with him, Charlie, he's a greasy one.'

'Oh, I've had worse company,' said Charles Siringo. 'All the same, it's a good thing you boys got tougher minds than widows and shut-ins.' He shook his head. 'They used to give me more interesting jacks than this to chase. Read that book of mine, you'll see.'

5

'Tell me about the boy,' said Siringo, as I knew he would.

'What boy?'

'Hood Roberts, your recent companion who stole that couple's automobile. It's all those Alva rubes could talk about.'

We were well out of that handsome town, and Siringo had not made one peep of remonstration with me for trying to slip away – he was probably gratified to see I retained a small reservoir of unruliness, even if I had no 'medicine.'

I said, 'I don't know much about him. Just a kid anxious to be away from home.'

Siringo rolled his eyes joyfully. 'You're feeble, Becket! I know you picked him up in Kansas. I met his old boss Lewis. I know all that. I know he took up with that señorita at the Hundred and One, and I know what else he did there. What I don't know is whether he's worth my time. Worth deviating from the prime objective.'

'He's just a boy.'

'Billy McCarty was a boy. Tom Pickett was a boy. Cross the wide sea and Ned Kelly was a boy. Goodness, Becket, boys are trouble everywhere.'

'I thought it was Glendon we were after.'

'Hood Roberts is not his real name, did you know that?'

'He's a romantic.'

'That may be. I only want to know whether he is serious or playing at this.'

It was a fair question. Once I'd have said earnestly that Hood was playing. Now I didn't know. 'He's no outlaw, Mr. Siringo. He's just good on a horse.'

'Good on a horse ain't all it used to be, but it's still handy,' he mused. 'Of course he's got other talents. He broke that actor's neck: Swilling. You ask the girls in that boarding-house they'll tell you it was a serious thing.'

'Accidental. I saw it happen.'

'You go to the Swilling home next Christmas Eve, they might feel it was a serious matter.'

I said, 'You're giving the directions. I'll drive wherever you say, Mr. Siringo.'

He turned stiffly in his seat. His soreness had him for the moment and his breathing was shallow. He said, 'I'm going to sleep awhile. Can I trust you?'

I didn't reply. That he could trust me was my own disgrace. I didn't need to say it.

6

In this way I drove, and Siringo slept, through nearly a week of infinite days; of course he'd been shot and was recovering, but he was also an older man with a sluggish rebound, a fact that seemed strange – he was so competent, so concise. Yet old he was, and it showed in ways I began to see as we traveled toward California. His large joints hurt him, his knees and shoulders. He began to make certain his Colt's was near his hand at all times, and to go off suddenly into alarming coughing spells; they might last only a minute but sometimes refused to let off for a quarter hour or more. Sometimes jellied blood came up. These vile frogs he would spit with rage into the ditch, after which he would be in stormy humor, swearing or saying nothing or digging in his grip for the whiskey he never otherwise touched. I saw – and he saw – that his coughing represented a door to me. There were times it immobilized him so strictly he seemed near his final rigors. With right timing I might simply walk away or strand him beside the road.

In the meantime I tried to remain pleasant company. He loved talking about books, especially his own, and his other favorite, Ecclesiastes. That treatise with its severe rhetoric – 'all is meaningless' – he had by heart, often enlisting its author, Solomon, in his arguments against bothersome ideas like altruism and honor and clemency.

'That's the failure of most people,' he declared. 'They don't want the bad news. Everything's got to be good news! So they'll subscribe to the Proverbs, which feel nice and hopeful, and ignore Ecclesiastes, where old Sol is wiser than ever and has finally figured out what all those instructions of his are actually worth. They couldn't save him, could they? They were no comfort to him in his final years! He wrote those Sunday school lessons but perished anyhow and went to dust.' Nothing disgusted Siringo more than the necessity of perishing and going to dust. He was completely nonplussed at mortality, despite having had sixty-odd years to get used to it.

'All the same,' I ventured, 'since we haven't a choice but can only make the best of things as given, I would rather live among people who try to uphold the Proverbs.'

'And why is that,' he inquired, 'unless you believe in a hereafter?'

Having no wish to launch Siringo on the topic of the hereafter, I suggested that regardless of eternity the Proverbs seemed a reasonable-enough recipe for a pleasant life in this world.

'Well, then, bully for you,' he said. 'Yours is the prevailing notion of a weak and feminized generation. Let us see how it holds up.'

You may notice how many of Siringo's pronouncements have the ring of the last word. That is because they usually were. He felt entitled to the last word and would have it at all costs.

'Listen, Siringo,' I sputtered, but he stood suddenly and looked at the westward sky. It was a starless and moonless night, quiet except for our modest campfire – but now from afar rose the faintest orange on the clouds. There was a distant percussion or series of percussions, and I thought too that I heard something like a cry or wail, though my mind may have added that particular. Certainly the pale orange made for an eerie sky – a wail or two would've seemed at home.

Siringo walked a short distance from the glare of our little blaze and stood looking up and out. When I joined him he said, 'Something large is on fire.'

'How far away?' I asked.

'Fifteen miles, seventeen.'

'Is it the prairie?' I had heard about prairie fires – how they got to their feet and raced along under wind of their own making, easily catching your lathered horse as you galloped toward the river and safety.

But Siringo, gauging the pale cloud, said, 'No. No, that ain't grass, Becket. That's a town burning.'

7

Like old Israel we rose in the morning to follow a pillar of smoke. I didn't want to head for that oily ghost, but we did — it was due west of us and seemed to twist off the vanishing point of our narrow road. As for the road it never veered left or right. Mile by mile the ghost grew and warped, the sun leaned hard on our heads, my hands got slicker on the wheel; meantime Charles Siringo tipped forward in his seat and peered around, glittering. No nap this day for Charlie! Instead he talked, talked as though his mind were rekindled, making observations on the sere landscape and the brown spines of cacti and the sorry graze and cattle we passed, so thin their eyes jutted like blisters. He talked of crossing the Mojave on a mule in 1880 pursuing Billy the Kid, who as it turned out was in his final months of life. Siringo was still excited by those ancient events. His sentences grew short and hooked. It galled him that the Kid, whom he called Billy McCarty, had eluded him. It stung that the youngster had been a favorite of certain spicy girls whose attributes Siringo minutely recalled, and he summoned down eloquent blights on young Billy and also on Patrick Garrett, the sheriff who had stepped armed into a darkened hut and ended the chase forever. This stream of talk discouraged me. The smoke stood up over us with a hundred smells in its clinging scrim. A pit opened inside my ribs. The nearer we came to the burnt place, the heartier Siringo appeared.

The pile of cinders we eventually reached was called Spigot – Spigot, Texas, subsequently absent from maps. Never a large town, Spigot until last night had hosted several bustling concerns including a general store, a livery, a tele-graph office and a petroleum garage. Now it was black rubble emitting vines of grease smoke amid which people stooped picking items out of the char. One building only had escaped the fire so we parked near it, a brick foursquare bordered by a sodden moat of ankle-deep mire. The letters I.O.O.F. were mortared into its pediment. Three men in brass buttons sat on a bench in its shade. Charles Siringo stepped out of the Packard like a general, wiping his hands together – even among strangers he assumed authority – and said, simply, 'Well?'

'Well, what,' replied the shortest man on the bench. He had a sullen aspect but let us allow him his exhaustion. He matched the others in his burgundy coat and white sash. One wore a plumed bicorne hat like Napoleon's; the other two had similar hats but had removed them in the heat and placed them on their knees.

'Quite a little barbecue,' said Charles Siringo.

The fellow wearing the hat stood wearily and said, 'Your levity is misplaced, my friend, there is death here today.'

'I guess you've got no monopoly on that,' Siringo remarked. 'Who's died?'

'Who is asking?' the short man demanded.

'Charles Siringo of the Pinkertons,' was the ready reply, which carried, as I'd learned, far more weight than it should've. 'Tell me who's died.'

'Felix Fly or Langston Cree.'

'You don't know which?'

'We ain't sure. Janssen here found a hand,' said weary Napoleon.

'It's Felix Fly's hand, his left hand; I told you that,' said the sullen one, Janssen. 'I done played baseball with Felix Fly. He had a fastball to drop a sow. I know that hand.'

'General store sells black powder in the ten-pound kegs,' Napoleon explained. 'Felix and Langston lived above the store. Janssen, tell where you found the hand.'

'A good ways out on the prairie,' said Janssen. 'Sitting upright. Like it climbed out a badger hole to have a look around. There's nothing where the store was but a dent in the ground. My nephew got gashed by a falling teakettle. Every window in Spigot went bust.'

Siringo looked up. 'These windows look fine.'

'But this is the Odd Fellows Hall,' Napoleon said. 'These windows are stout.'

'Odd Fellows build things beefy,' added the bald lieutenant.

'Spigot was founded by an Odd Fellow,' Napoleon informed us. 'He dug the well himself, hauled the bricks from Galveston. Look,' he added, nodding at a stocky little well house attached to the building. A dripping iron pipe poked from it at knee height. 'Yonder's the town namesake – best water in a hundred miles.'

'Any other dead?' Siringo asked.

'Not as we know about. It started at the telegraph office. We were in session here at the hall when the cry went up. A boy ran in yelling. We fought it at the livery, fought it at the houses, but after the store blew we had to see to our families.'

'Where are they, the women and youngsters?' Siringo inquired. In fact, no women or youngsters were in sight – only a few stunned men standing in their trousers, murmuring through the ashes.

'We put 'em on wagons and hauled 'em to Gruver,' Napoleon reported.

'Who was the boy?' Siringo asked.

'What boy?'

'The one who rousted you out of the hall.'

'I don't know. I'd sold him some gasoline, earlier,' said the bald Odd Fellow. 'That was my petroleum station yonder. You would think the pump would explode, but it only had a flame on top like a candle. That boy had a pretty car – a pretty girl too.'

'Curly-headed youngster?' Siringo asked.

'Yes, sir. Curly and pale. Went and got sick on himself, the poor whelp, the fire scared him so.'

'And the girl was Mexican,' said Siringo.

'That's right.'

I kept an eye on the old vulture now, for he stooped and swayed in deliberation.

Napoleon mused, 'He wasn't a Spigot boy, but a good lad. He gave us the warning, though it didn't help much. He carried buckets. We owe that young man something.'

At this Charles Siringo straightened and pronounced, 'You do indeed. You owe him one swift trial and ten feet of rope, for he set the fire that killed your Felix Fly.'

Well, that enlivened the Odd Fellows! Nothing lights up a party like a surprise accusation of murder – not that it surprised me, for I'd observed Siringo long enough to know he trusted his hunches, and to trust some of them myself.

But I doubt it had occurred to these men that the Great Spigot Fire might've been caused by anything more malicious than a tipped candle, a wayward cigar.

'The little shyster!' cried Janssen.

'However,' Siringo said, 'I am already traveling in straight-line pursuit of a desperate fugitive. Your greenhorn arsonist is not my charge.'

'But if he killed Felix—'

Siringo said, 'It is worse than you know, for he is on the run after murdering a famous actor of the screen at the Hundred and One Ranch.'

'Why, then, you've got to help us. He can't be far away!'

'Contact the Texas Rangers. People here put stock in them,' Siringo replied, with polite disdain.

'By the time a Ranger shows up, this ruthless boy will be dancing in Mexico,' complained Napoleon.

But Siringo held his ground. 'It is not a job I can take on frivolously.' Plainly, he wanted to be clamored for. Moreover, he had accurately recognized in these Odd Fellows his very favorite audience: men with a pure faith in officers of the law, in sheriffs, in Texas Rangers, in Pinkertons. Here followed several minutes of the most abject supplications which I have wiped purposefully from my memory. I can tell you that during this simpering display the Odd Fellows seemed to shrink in height by several inches while Charles Siringo rose and shone and regained a significant measure of what must've been a notable prime.

'Well, he did burn a whole town,' he reflected at last, catching my eye. 'These days it usually takes a marching army to make that much fire, though the Comanches used to do it without much exertion.'

'Felix Fly is dead,' said the bald lieutenant, hopefully, 'and probably Langston Cree too.'

'Two dead and a burnt town, on top of that killed performer back in Oklahoma,' said Charles Siringo. Oh, his cup was overflowing! He heaved a deliberate sigh and concluded, 'It ain't convenient, but he seems a serious lad after all. I'm a servant of the law, gentlemen. Which way did you say that he went?'

8

Spigot is now an open field with a road through it, though I am told the well is still there if you know where to look, and that the water in it is still cold and of high quality. In compilations of Texas history you mainly find mentions of Spigot in connection with its ruin by fire – the Roberts Fire, it is sometimes called, for Siringo's intuition turned out correct.

Hood's intentions in Spigot seem to have been innocent. Presumably he wanted to send a telegram, though to whom we were never to learn because the operator recognized him from a description wired from Alva. The operator, James Pell, did not look refined but had great curiosity and discernment. Charlie Siringo disliked Pell instantly for what he later called 'the man's warped gaze,' though I suspect it was actually Pell's straightforward speech that rankled.

'You're singular old, for a Pinkerton,' Pell said.

That set Siringo on his heels. He had set up shop in the Odd Fellows hall and was conducting interviews of anyone still lurking around Spigot; most of them were tired as ghosts, but here came Pell rolling in like a sailor, sneering round the stem of a lit pipe, a red bandanna tight to his scalp.

'Old or not, you still have to answer my questions,' said Siringo, who nevertheless seemed reduced by Pell's discourtesy. 'I'll trouble you to start with the first appearance of the boy, Hood Roberts.'

As Pell told it, he had endured a long day at the telegraph box. He was bored and had gout in his feet, which is why he walked like a sailor. He knew that a white boy and a Mexican girl had stolen a car and some money up in Alva; when Hood Roberts entered his telegraph office, James Pell nodded to him and looked out his window. Sure enough, a beauteous Mexican girl sat craning round in an almost-new Locomobile. Hood tapped on the counter and said he wanted to send a wire.

Pell nodded. After obliging the young outlaw, he thought he might send a wire himself, to the Texas Rangers. Spigot had no law officers of its own, and it rarely had trouble, either; Pell had sent telegrams out of Spigot for more than twenty years, but he had only once before sent one to the Rangers. It had given him a small thrill at the time. Pell said, 'Where and to whom, son?'

Hood was silent a moment. 'You know me, don't you?'

Pell didn't answer right away. For one thing, he wasn't at all intimidated by this curly cherub.

'That's why you looked out your window,' Hood said.

Pell replied, 'You are the young man who stole the automobile in Alva.'

At this Hood leaned over the counter, picked up the telegraph bug, and threw it hard to the floor.

This offended James Pell, who said, 'You little milk toast, that's hardly broken – that won't buy you ten minutes.'

Hood looked at Pell in disbelief, then kicked the bug across the floor, where it smacked a wall and came into pieces.

'How about that?' Hood asked. 'Can you fix that?'

'You want to wager on it?' said the furious Pell.

Hood then walked over and jumped on the telegraph bug with both feet until it was like a puddle. He said, 'What about now?'

And Pell replied, 'The thing is, Milk Toast, I am reasonably handy.'

Then Hood said some bad words, and tore a lantern off the wall and waved it about; next thing we hear there is a fire in the telegraph office, a dry structure built in the very shadow of the livery, with its straw bedding and thirsty shingles.

As I think about it, it was probably the James Pell interview that prompted Siringo to go after Hood Roberts full steam. James Pell was unconvinced by Charles Siringo. He did not fall at his feet as the Odd Fellows had done. James Pell in fact was not an Odd Fellow but a cranky Texan from San Antonio. Probably he longed for the old Republic. At any rate he wanted the Texas Rangers to catch Hood; he was unimpressed by Pinkertons. They hadn't caught Butch Cassidy, had they?

'Butch is dead,' growled Siringo.

'Really? Has somebody got him then?'

'Butch died in a storm of gunfire in Bolivia seven years ago.'

'Begging your pardon, Butch came through Spigot December last. He had an automobile with a canvas tent folded up in back. He had a limp you could hang your hat on. He stood at my window and sent a telegram to his baby sister up in Wyoming.'

Siringo was not a stammering man, but this seemed to

cost him his footing. He said, 'If he was here, why didn't your darling Rangers catch him?'

'I don't know about that. I am only saying he was here.'

'I am not going to debate Butch Cassidy with you. I am tired of Butch Cassidy. This Roberts boy has killed three men. Tell me anything else he said.'

After Pell, nothing else remarkable came to light. Siringo talked with another half-dozen char-stained men while I looked out the second-story windows of the Odd Fellows lodge. I saw where the telegraph office had stood, and the livery, and a dark little crater where the general store had been. It was a dent in the earth, like Janssen had said. I got out my pencil and paper and wrote, *Dear Susannah, there is nothing I miss so much as you.*

9

In Siringo's mind, he never left off the pursuit of Glen
Dobie. Though we changed course after the Spigot fire,
following Hood and Alazon toward Mexico, Siringo still
spoke of Glendon as his primary quarry and even as his
rival. I asked him once what attraction Glendon held, to
be worth hounding still.

'It ain't attraction, it's attrition,' was his gruff reply. 'He's
among the last from those rough days. We're all that's left,
you see.'

'Then why go after Hood?' I asked.

'For the bounty,' Siringo said. He meant the reward, but
also the gain in eminence. The death of Ern Swilling and
the burning of Spigot had put Hood in the newspapers. A
new memoir was in the making. To that end we bounced
along in the ailing Packard through village after village
toward the Rio Grande.

I will credit Hood Roberts with some of Glendon's
outlaw talents. He could, for example, seem to vanish. On
that dusty journey we crossed the lovebirds' trail half a
dozen times – they'd stolen rice from a grocer, blankets
and a plump ham from a farmstead, grease and gasoline in
Doyletown. Never did we see the vaunted Texas Rangers
or encounter any sign of their pursuit. 'Supposed to be such
bloodhounds,' jeered Siringo, who viewed the Rangers as

though they had jilted him in his youth. At any rate we were on Hood's very heels while the adored Rangers were nowhere in sight. Twice Siringo thought we had the boy pinned down: once at a smithy where Hood had an axle hammered straight, again in a rooming house outside which we sighted the stolen Locomobile. A day and a half we waited for Hood to come out of that bleak-windowed place, but he never did; Siringo finally realized Hood had given up the car and proceeded by other means. Hours later we learned of a rancher named Pompey who had a horse and mule stolen the previous night, along with riding tack for each. People in town spoke wearily of this fitful Pompey – thirty years old and still roaring to get his way. He had hired a local man of skillful reputation to track and retrieve the animals. It measures Siringo's grit and the warp of his ambition that we sought out this disagreeable rancher and rented two horses ourselves. Pompey was suspicious of the arrangement even when Siringo said we would leave the Packard with him as collateral.

'What corrupt security is this?' cried Pompey. It's true the car smoked a lot as we stood beside it on the brown grass.

'I see that you don't know how to drive,' said Siringo. His voice was cracked and quiet and lent him something fearsome.

'I drive,' said Pompey uncertainly.

'Then you will recognize this Packard as a foremost machine,' Siringo replied.

'It's a shipwreck,' said the rancher, but conviction had deserted him. In the end Pompey supplied us with two decent nags, also saddles and tack and canteens and enough of his wife's bricklike bread to see us through a thin week. These horses were small and knobby with the flat eyes and cloaked aptitude of Indian ponies. I was startled at their paltry appearance, but Siringo went to the one that had caught his fancy and waved his hat in friendly style at the side of its face. The beast didn't shy but took the hat from his hand, lipped it a moment, and dropped it to the ground.

'All right then,' Siringo said.

This was just north of the town of Columbus, New Mexico. I won't forget my dread in scrambling onto that ribby paint, for I was never a good rider. Nor will I forget the crooked way Siringo sat his dun gelding. He was tipping always one direction or another and resembled an effigy or rigored cadaver strapped to a horse by pranksters. His every moment aloft seemed a lucky coincidence, but he never fell and in fact commented several times on the comportment and soft gait of the brute he rode.

In this teetering manner we followed the tracker up into the hills. Pompey had told us the man's name, Ericsson, and his specialty, which was not chasing dangerous fugitives but recovering animals lost during storms or stampedes. It seems Ericsson was well liked: a quiet single fellow nearing fifty who maintained a fastidious home in the hope he would one day attract a comely wife or even a plain wife. He sewed leather hats and sheepskin gloves, which provided his living but took a toll on his eyesight and spine. Saturday nights he crouched over a Ward's crystal radio, and he had a cool cellar in which he maintained a cache of orange soda.

We dry-camped in a rocky wash. The moon had set early and Siringo could not make out the trail by stars alone.

Under his guidance I hobbled the horses with lengths of hemp. The horses didn't seem tired and whickered to each other for company. We'd traveled at such a deliberate speed on those rented animals I couldn't imagine we were catching anyone.

'Tracking's always slow,' said Siringo. 'You're generally moving more slowly than the person you're after. However that person stops now and then, while you keep moving as long as it's light, sometimes longer.'

'We aren't moving now.'

'Are you griping about that?'

'No.'

'You think I'm tough, and I am. But I'm old too. Moreover, here is this bullet hole – it's still making me a little sick,' Siringo replied. 'The moon will be up two hours before the sun. When it rises we'll start again.'

Under that weary prospect I got out some of Mrs. Pompey's bread for a cold supper – it was unleavened and hard as a salt lick. Siringo gnawed the piece I handed him but soon gave up and surrendered the damp remainder to his horse, who bit it and dropped it and walked away but kept returning until it was gone. Siringo lay down in his blanket, twisting about as though the rigid earth surprised him; I could hear him breathing with his porous lungs. Clearly, a punishing day for the old sinner. Embarrassed by his suffering he said, 'When you're eleven you don't ever think it'll change.'

That's when he'd gone off cowboying, of course – I recalled his recitation from the opening chapter of his memoir.

'You must've been homesick, though,' I said.

'I scarce remember.'

'You remember.'

He made a noise in his throat. 'I suppose I was home-sick. Gladys helped me out of it.'

'Gladys who?'

'A girl, Becket. What did you think?'

'Eleven is young to have a girlfriend.'

'She wasn't a girl as you'd think of. A paid companion is what she was. She told me that straight out but I didn't know what it meant. She was a girl to me.'

Siringo left it there and I listened to his settling lungs and tried to fall asleep. But instead of sleeping I imagined him eleven, with curiosity and expectation written in his round face, along with neglect and ignorance. He suddenly continued. 'I suppose I was in love with her, young as I was. She had blonde hair. She'd hold my hand while we walked. We used to walk beside the train tracks outside Bay City and she'd tease me about hanging around with a paid companion.'

His speech tonight was different. This was no poised recitation. 'We liked to play cards. Five-card and monte and gin. Men's games. She had a pretty cockleshell necklace and unstrung it and we used the cockles for money. She was not a good player.'

'Why, you remember her well.'

'It wouldn't have mattered what she asked me. My answer would've been yes.'

'That's a dangerous position.'

'I was a boy. She didn't ask much.'

'Tell me about your wife,' I said.

'I don't scarcely remember.'

'You said she couldn't see you,' I reminded him.

'At first she saw me fine. It was only later.'

'What happened?'

He said, 'That's the mystery, ain't it, Becket.' A snort. 'She was incompatible with my profession.'

'You were gone too much,' I said.

'It was more than gone. Lot of men are gone and their wives happy enough. It was what I did gone. As I've said my talent lies in pursuit. Therefore it fell to me to befriend the worst of us. Robbers, anarchists. Stranglers. Wouldn't you know it I got along with them well. I have drunk the most putrescent rotgut with companions fresh from the bombed-out homes of policemen. I have raised toasts in their honor and more or less meant it, but it was always work to me and when the time came to call them down I never slacked or stayed my hand. I was a good detective.'

I said, 'Most men never have the chance to be both things at once, the hero and the devil.'

'That is ignorant. Most men are hero and devil. All men. That is what ruins it with wives.'

'She wanted just the hero?'

'Bad man or good she would've had me either way. She couldn't endure both, however. She said to pick one and to be that thing only so that she might trust me until the day of Jesus. It disturbed her that I could work up a friendship to a man, eat at his table, pattacake with his babies, bury myself under the surface of his life for six months or a year and then call him to account. She feared its effect.'

I said, 'It sounds like costly work.'

'All work is costly. I quit a few times and came home and lived like she wanted. We bred horses and some redbone

239

hounds I couldn't sell on account I was well-spoken and had all my teeth. We speculated here and there on riverfront and ranch land. Miserable work. There's your costly job! I wrote some newspaper editorials that paid by the word, and I did enjoy that. Opinions come easily to me. And yet I had this history, Becket. I am not a regular man. What is history if you don't own to it? She knew this at the altar. There was not a doubt in her mind she was marrying a man whose name would carry beyond his own time.'

'Do you still believe that?' I inquired.

Siringo didn't reply. He rolled onto his back; he breathed noisily; maybe he examined the heavens. If you are tempted to interpret his silence as self-doubt, I say don't do it! Charles Siringo had no doubts of his own; for the sakes of Glendon and Hood Roberts, don't lend him the benefit of yours.

10

I woke before Siringo to a moon just up and nearly full. There he lay like bones in blankets and beyond him the hobbled horses asleep on their sprung hips. I'd have slept longer but was stiff from cold and hoisted up with a groan. At this Siringo woke coughing, coughed himself to an elbow and spat the wicked day to life.

The tracker Ericsson had himself left a comprehensible track. By sunup even I had begun to discern where his horse had trotted, where it walked, and where his small dog transited the horse's path – staying behind always, like the well-behaved animal it proved to be. Time to time Ericsson dismounted to stoop back and forth and crouch on his toes, reading faint prints upon the dust. At first I could see very little sign except in my imagination but mile by mile it became more distinct until I found myself able to pick it out on the earth and animate it in my mind. As the day warmed, we warmed to the man we followed. 'See how he tends his dog,' Siringo remarked, as we wound through a patch of spiny low cacti.

'How do you mean? I don't see the dog's prints at all here.'

'Right, he's carrying the little chap,' Siringo said.

'How far ahead?'

Siringo didn't answer but less than an hour he reined up in a place where the earth sank and softened and blue-green moss appeared on the stones.

'Do you smell that?' he said.

'No.'

We moved ahead at a quicker pace. The smell he had mentioned came to me first as a mere sense of reassurance. Only eventually did I recognize it as pipe tobacco. Name a more heartening aroma! Thus Ericsson became in my mind a painstaking man who smoked a pipe, as Glendon did, and was generous to his animals. I felt somehow as though we were in Ericsson's steady hands and so am all the sorrier to report that upon crossing the little stream known as the Antelope we emerged onto a rocky shelf to discover Ericsson lying tipped over beside his embers and his apprehensive spaniel pacing to and fro before him.

Siringo eased down off his horse and said a few words to the spaniel. The tracker lay on his side with his legs tucked up as if sleeping cold. He had not thrashed about. There was an oval cavity like a winey thumbprint next to his left eye. Ericsson had set about breakfast with a tidy camp table, which was a flat board fastened to an iron pike stuck in the earth – a clever arrangement with biscuits still on the table and a little jam pot and a white stoneware cup of pekoe tea.

'Well, now he's serious,' said Charles Siringo. 'Yes, he is.' With that he pulled the clasp knife from his pocket and stooped about the campsite poking it here and there, muttering 'Now he means it,' poking the blade in the cold ashes and through a sheaf of booklets and papers I had not previously noticed lying on the ground. Among them was a small bound atlas and Siringo turned a few of its pages with the knife.

You would think I'd remember this more clearly. Ericsson's face, for example, or the look of his hands – you come on a man shot dead at his breakfast and oughtn't the scene write in blood ink on your memory? Yet what I chiefly recall are how my belt-buckle chafed when I slid off the horse, or how the spaniel wouldn't come to my hand until I offered him a biscuit from Ericsson's table. The biscuit crumbled in my fingers so I fed it to the dog piece by piece after which he went and lay down putting his chin in the crook of Ericsson's dead old arm.

'His horse has departed in the company of two other animals,' Siringo said. He stood at some distance, reading the ground. 'Two horses. Or a horse and a mule.'

I said, 'I need to go home,' a useless statement to which Siringo didn't rise. 'I'm going home, Siringo. This is enough.'

'Poor Becket. Is this business troubling to you?'

'It would be troubling to anyone with a shred of soul left.'

Siringo took his time walking back. Looking in my face he said, 'We knew little of Ericsson besides that he was a decent man. That is his tragedy. If he had been more careful we might be having coffee with him now. I am not hypocrite enough to pretend his death matters to me. On the other hand, it does add some dash to your Hood Roberts. It gives him more value. You understand that.'

I said, 'You don't know Hood Roberts. You are only adding him to your tale of yourself.'

This piqued Siringo. 'So you know the reckless boy, and

243

his work here bothers you. What do you imagine you know of him?' He reached for the reins of his gelding.

'What are you doing? Shouldn't we bury this man?' But Siringo was already aboard, setting forth after the fugitives. I followed suit and whistled for the dog. When he refused to come I climbed back down and retrieved the little fellow and set him in my coat where he propped himself as if from long practice. That spaniel was a patient rider and didn't whine for the next several hours as we followed the track in its southerly course. Now with three horses, or two and a mule, the trail was easy to follow, and I came up and rode next to Charles Siringo and asked where he guessed they would be.

'In some tilty farmhouse, I suppose,' he mused. 'Do you know, they always find some idiot farmhouse to hole up in.'

'Hole up? But aren't we close to Mexico?'

'Mexico. Oh – you mean if he gets across that border, he has gotten away.'

'Away from you, anyway.'

He regarded me with amusement for some moments. 'Becket, do you actually know anything at all?'

I believe it was an honest question.

He said, 'Do you know even one thing that is true?'

11

The trail led more or less straight to Columbus, which we entered at the supper hour. It did not look like the doomed village it was. We smelled meat and squash and, unmistakably, corn on the cob and saw the lively fires of the U.S. Army camp to the west. A light breeze was turning the town's considerable number of windmills, and we met a creaking wagonload of boys returning from a foray down to the Rio Casas across the Mexican line. The boys wore the weary glee of successful disobedience and were laughing at everything they saw. My memory of Columbus is, of all things, musical – through its screen doors I heard no fewer than three pianos being played with varying degrees of success. Also one woman sat on a porch moving her hands across a harp taller than herself, the first harp I ever saw.

The grocery was closed but Siringo took out his revolver and beat the door with such resolve that the grocer himself, plump and compliant, looked out the window above the store and came down to sell us whatever it would take. While he tallied up our bread and bacon and coffee, Siringo asked whether a young white boy had come through with a Mexican girl.

'Are you the boy's granddad?'

'I am no such thing. What did they buy from you?'

'Six fresh eggs and two slices of nice pink ham.'

'The boy loves breakfast,' Siringo noted to me.

'A good-looking lad, I thought so at the time,' said the grocer. 'Would you like some of the ham? I have a little left.'

'No. Did the boy talk to you?'

'What kind of talk?'

'Any kind.'

'Not as I recall. Maybe you gentlemen would care for a tin of peaches; these are refreshing after a taxing day.'

Siringo said, 'You seem not to grasp what's transpiring here. I am in pursuit of a bona fide desperado whose trail is gory despite his cupid appearance. If the boy said a word to you beyond yessir, then out with it; otherwise shut up and let a man work.'

The grocer was taken aback. I felt bad for him – he'd only spoken in that yielding way lonely people do, and here was this tall raw-hide standing over him and brooking no twaddle. Frowning at Siringo, he said, 'There's a place on a little tannin creek just to the south, belongs to Michael Raban who fought for Stonewall Jackson. Mike ain't around much, but he leaves the place open. Travelers come through they often stay there.'

'We'll take a look,' said Siringo.

12

And so it came down to a farmhouse. As it so often does! Remember Dan Champion, valiant of the Johnson County War, who crouched in that hovel until they lit it on fire then shot him forty times when he ran out? We rode down the dirt trail toward Mexico and sure enough came to a grove of trees in which we saw the shine of a tin roof and heard the creek rattling. It looked deserted from a distance and we doubted whether this was the Raban property; then we heard the strange bray of a mule and 'Hold up,' said Siringo.

We got off our mounts and tied them in the brush and Siringo got out his annoying manacles and stuck them on my wrists. I judge he was gone half an hour before he returned, up on his toes for quiet and a little out of breath.

'Well, we found them,' he said. 'The animals are in a lean-to by the creek. There's a well on the other side with an elevated tank. Look, there is the windmill.'

'What'll we do?'

'We could wait them out, or we could go down there and walk right in.' Siringo smiled. 'They got music playing.'

'Music?'

'A cylinder recording of some kind. It's pretty music. Could be they're dancing in there. You suppose they're dancing, Becket?'

He let me out of the cuffs and leaving the horses tethered we moved up through willows to a shallow rise. Peeking over the top I was surprised how near the cabin was. And how civilized, with its trimmed square corners and its door painted blue. Sure enough we could hear a faint symphonic orchestra. We could smell ham frying. Ericsson's dog pranced a bit because of the ham until Siringo took a length of cord and tied him to a willow trunk.

'Hood's stubborn, you know,' said I.

He reflected on this. 'I expect he is.'

'What if he fights?'

'What if he does?'

'What about Alazon?'

He said, 'I won't shoot a girl, unless it seems to me that I have to.'

'How long will we wait?'

'It doesn't matter.'

'Suppose you fall asleep,' I said, recalling how he'd slept all day long sometimes when we were driving.

'I can sleep or I can not sleep.' He seemed to shift a gear and said, 'Becket, what do you think that I am?'

I shook my head but he persisted.

'The question is not rhetorical. What do you say that I am?'

'Well, you are liable to sleep like anyone else after a long day. That is no particular weakness. I would say that you are human like everyone else.'

Siringo replied, 'I was human, but now I think I am changing.' He made this dread and puzzling statement with an air of hushed merriment. 'I have been noticing it for days. Perhaps I am only part human now.'

Noting what I suppose was my hesitant expression he

248

added, 'It's a change for the better. I can sleep or not as I will. I feel no anger. I am not thirsty. Hot and cold have no purchase on me.'

I replied, 'You are describing death.'

He frowned. 'I should have known you would think something morbid. Well, get comfortable, Becket.'

So I settled in. Plainly Siringo meant to wait the sun down, sleep a little – or not, as he willed – probably taking Hood in the morning when he came out the door. I had no plan to thwart him, no scheme at all.

We hear much about moments of decision, but often you don't know they have happened until later and there you stand in your cooling skin.

Siringo coughed, trying to keep it quiet lest Hood be alerted; he smothered the cough in his arm. He didn't notice when I took his old Colt's from its holster. He didn't notice until his coughing fit had passed. When he saw me holding the revolver something warmed in his eyes, and 'Becket,' said he, 'I thank you for holding that for me; I'll take it back now.'

'No, sir.'

'Come on. Ante up. Do you think it's my only gun?' he asked, when I still refused.

I didn't want to shoot Siringo. Now that the old Colt's was in my fist, it didn't seem possible to me. Even a pretend willingness to shoot him seemed out of my grasp; therefore I pointed the revolver straight up and fired in order to warn Hood. It was my first firing of a true Western *pistola* and its kick was not as troublesome as expected. I fired the revolver until it clicked empty, Siringo watching me balefully as though I were dead already.

First, all song and dance ceased from the cabin.

Second, Siringo with an expression of extreme aggravation rose over me and got hold of the gun and swung the barrel down hard on my collarbone. I went down writhing, while we heard frantic scrapes in the cabin that turned out to be window shutters sliding into place.

'Now, look, he aims to wait us out,' complained Siringo. 'Now it's a blasted all-night event. Moreover, someone else is likely to arrive.' No doubt he anticipated the despised Rangers. Hood Roberts had become a prize, after all.

'You broke my shoulder,' I gasped, for it seemed I could feel the astonished collarbone rubbing against itself.

'Well, there ain't nothing for it,' he said. 'We had a chance to take them in flagrante. You spoiled the surprise, and now you have to wait hurt.'

The good part is I didn't faint. Soon I remembered how to breathe, how to bear resentment.

'I thought you felt no anger,' I told Siringo, which made him laugh so hard he leaned forward and gave my poor shoulder a comradely slap – I must've gone pale, for he gave me still another slap, laughing all the harder.

13

From our slight hill in the cover of willows we had a good view of the cabin. If Hood came out the front he was finished; out the side window lay fifty yards of open ground to cross; if he tried to escape from the rear we would see him before he reached the creek. Swelling large with confidence Siringo called out, 'Hood Roberts!'

'Yes, sir, who is asking?' came Hood's voice.

'Charles Siringo of the Pinkerton Agency.'

'Hello, Mr. Siringo.'

Despite all that had happened, he only sounded like himself. Like a boy speaking respectfully to his elders.

Siringo said, 'Hood, things do not look good for you. I am offering you safe passage, followed by fair trial in the murders of the tracker Ericsson, the actor Ern Swilling, and Mr. Felix Fly.'

There was a pause before Hood called, 'Who's Felix Fly?'

'The brave fellow who perished in the fire you set back in Spigot.'

Again Hood said nothing for a while, then: 'It got away from me, Mr. Siringo. I didn't mean for it to burn so.'

'You're calling it an accident?'

'Yes, sir.'

'I am comfortable with that. You are free to make your

case at trial. If you will come out now, you'll not be harmed.'

'I'd rather not, Mr. Siringo. If you don't mind,' he added.

'Is the girl in there with you, Hood?'

'Yes, sir.'

'You think highly of her, correct?'

Again a silence. I can guess why – it's because Alazon was right there. That's the way Hood was; he might wax like smitten Shakespeare to me or Glendon, but he was far too shy to say such things in front of the girl herself.

Siringo called out sternly, 'Do you care for her!'

'Well – sure I do.'

'In that case you should send her out at least, son. You see it's shortly going to rain down six kinds of Hell on that little love nest. She ain't culpable for your crimes.'

There was a scuffling from the cabin and Hood called, 'Can we have a little time to talk about this?'

'Go ahead,' said Siringo.

We had now a rest of perhaps a quarter of an hour. We heard nothing from the cabin; short of breath, I tried to ease my shoulder by lying flat on my back; Siringo took a deck of cards from his pocket and played a hand of solitaire.

'Mr. Siringo?' Hood called at last.

'Yes.'

'She won't come out. I ast her and she won't leave.'

Siringo sighed. He called, 'Hood, if that girl's really in there have her sing out. I got to know whether she's truly inside with you.'

He reasoned of course that Hood might well be alone in there and would believe himself safer if we thought the

252

girl with him. Almost immediately, however, the door opened and Alazon stepped out of the cabin. Insolent as a raven! A whirl of her dress and she vanished back inside.

It put Siringo in a temper. It jarred him that a pretty young girl thought so highly of this accidental outlaw as to stay with him in such hopeless circumstances.

We waited a long while. Siringo said, 'Becket, we can't wait for dark. They'll slip off if we do.'

This fretting was so unlike his usual sangfroid that I allowed myself the pleasure of a snide remark. 'You seem out of sorts for a man with six kinds of Hell at his beck and call.'

He replied, 'I am thinking, that's all. The thing would be to burn them out, but I guess you're unwilling to help.' Nonetheless he stooped away through the willows to return minutes later with an oilcloth packet from his saddlebags. Gauging our daylight he unstrung the loaf-size parcel and began a brisk inspection of its contents, chiefly waxed tubes of gunpowder but also bundled heavy matches and stiff gray strings of various lengths which could only be fuses. He fiddled and made small gratified noises: plainly, the stuff made him happy.

I said, 'You have carried these things all this way?'

'I learned a few tactics from those anarchist boys in Haymarket. Never snub an education, Becket.' He uncapped a paperboard tube, sniffed it, rolled a pinch in his fingers. 'I was concerned about the integrity of the powder after that wet business at the Hundred and One, but nope – it seems to be fine.'

I said, 'Let me go down and talk to them. I know Hood. I can bring him to reason.'

'Reason? More likely they'll take you hostage. I'll pass on that particular bag of snakes.'

He had laid out half a dozen small tubes of powder and now took from the packet a length of iron plumbing threaded and capped on one end. The cap had a small hole and a groove across its center. He took his clasp knife and set its spine in the groove and twisted counterclockwise until the cap loosened. Squinting against dust, he blew into the pipe to clean it.

'Hood trusts me,' I said. 'He knows I want the best for him. Let me go down to the cabin.' Even now, you see, I had hope for Hood Roberts. His killing of poor Ern was an accident. The fire in Spigot had outrun his modest design for it. Another accident! I remembered what the Odd Fellows had said, how Hood ran to and fro with buckets of water, fighting the flames alongside them – a mitigating factor, certainly.

You see how quickly I forgot about the poor tracker Ericsson, killed that very morning at his jam and pekoe – I forgot him just like that, though his bereft spaniel even now sat sighing beside us in the willows.

'Suppose you do go down,' Siringo said. 'What do you know about the principles of negotiation?'

As he seemed quite serious I replied, 'That I need to offer them something real. That I cannot betray them.'

'That would be a noble start if you were meeting union thugs on strike terms, but it's poor fare here.' With that Siringo bent down and gently heaved me up. It brought a sweat to my brow, yet he brushed the grass and twigs from my shirt and straightened my shirt collar, taking special care about the collarbone he'd ruined. Like a sage old papa he spoke kindly to me; like windy Polonius he instructed me. As he talked he cut the tops off waxen cylinders of gunpowder and sampled each with a fingertip to test for aridity.

'Remember first that he is not a boy. He has killed three men we know of so his standing there has changed. When you walk down to the shack, watch your bearing. You carry what he most wants, another day of life. Therefore walk like a man with the goods. Know your own mind and what you can truly offer. Safe conduct to Columbus, New Mexico aboard a horse of my choosing. Trial by a jury of his legally chosen peers. Nothing more nothing less. It's a charitable proposal.'

'It's only proper,' I said.

'No, it is generous. Think and you will see I am right. It is his noteworthy good luck to be offered anything at all.'

He had emptied a number of the cylinders into the iron plumbing and was tamping a fuse into the powder with his bent thumb. It occurs to me now that Siringo was fully enjoying the story he was part of. He lifted the cap toward the failing sun and squinted into it – a drop of light came through the tiny hole and made a bright mark on his cheekbone. He fished the fuse up through the hole and threaded the cap tight. He said, 'Also, you must admit no argument. There is no time today for nuance. In truth there is no negotiation to be made. Look at the sun, Becket. There's only the offer and its acceptance or rejection.'

'If it is that simple, call out the offer yourself and spare me the walk.'

'No, amigo, you requested this opportunity. Besides, I

agree the terms might be more appealing from your mouth than mine.'

'Suppose he tries to redraw the terms?'

His plumbing job finished, Siringo laid it aside saying, 'What is this to you? Would you call it a mission of mercy?'

'I suppose so.'

'Mercy is a detour. Your mission down there is to get what I want, which is Hood Roberts. Alive is better but dead will do.'

I said, 'The sun is setting. Give me your word.'

'My word?'

'That you won't harm them, either one. Hood gets his trial and no abuse from you.'

'What do you think I am?' he asked again.

'I think you lie if lying suits you.'

'Let us say you are correct. It suits me now to tell the truth. Get the boy out and no harm will come to him.'

And so I called out, 'Hood. It's Monte Becket. I'm coming down,' and not waiting for a yes or no I stepped from the willows and crossed the clearing. The windmill screeled away in the orange breeze, cicadas droned, the dying heat came up off the brown grass.

At the entrance I called hello again and pounded on the door. It drifted open under my hand. The cabin was a single room and it was empty. My instinct was to cry out *they're gone* but I checked myself. I went in closing the door and walked through to the back and unbolted a shutter. There were the four rusty cross-wired legs of the mill tower, the heat-struck prairie grass greening where the creek jolted through. There was no root cellar, no adjoining outbuildings. It was a marvel, a clean disappearance under scrutiny. I looked around the cabin at the sturdy trestle table in the middle of the room, the Edison machine with its wax tube in the middle of the table, the four Windsor chairs of excellent build finished in dark oil. A deck of cards lay on the table and I sat down and dealt myself a hand.

'Becket,' called Siringo. 'Are you coming out?'

'We are in negotiations,' I replied, which struck me so funny I nearly wrecked it laughing. I looked at my cards and quietly reshuffled them and dealt another try.

'Becket!'

'Be patient,' I shouted, but Siringo couldn't be patient. Maybe he heard strangeness in my voice, or maybe he just had the celebrated intuition of the ancient plainsman. Next thing I heard him coming like a rock rolling downhill. The door flew open and in he came with his hitching step to rifle-butt my stomach. I crumpled inward with my collarbone rubbing against itself and even when breath returned it came with difficulty since his boot was on my throat.

So complete was his rage that it made him mute and he might have simply choked me, but a noise distracted him and he moved to the door. The noise was the earth ringing as several horses pounded away. Siringo leaned against the doorframe in the day's last sunlight. Our horses were gone; even I knew it. We would find the other horses gone too, their tracks confused; the animal identified as Ericsson's horse would appear the next day on the outskirts of Columbus, a milk-can lid tied behind to keep him running.

Siringo came back in – I hardened my stomach muscles, just in case, but his energy was spent. Down he sat in a

Windsor chair. He looked exactly like a man who should say, I'm too old for this.

But I could never predict Siringo. What he actually said was, 'Get up, Becket. We're walking back to town.'

14

Gimping through Columbus I sighted a moonlit clock in a bank window – it was 4:30 A.M. Ericsson's poor spaniel was still with us, though from time to time he looked back whimpering. Who knew how many miles we'd covered but my feet were burgeoned lumps and my gait irregular; collarbone and left shoulder had calcified so my shadow sloped apelike up the road. The El Paso & Southern was arriving, dark except for the lamplit engine and caboose and one coach window, where a frosty gentleman toiled at papers by a kerosene flame. When the train sighed to rest a knot of soldiers tumbled down and away toward Camp Furlong on the skirts of town. Siringo, sagging also, prodded me before him up the street – past the post office and adjacent newspaper facade, past the Hoover Hotel and the lonely grocer's, and also past Ravel Brothers, dealers in arms and ammunition. Lastly we stood at the window of a lit bakery; it was still closed, but seeing us standing at her glass the proprietor, a big agile blue-eyed Norsewoman, opened the door and in we went. The dog too – he padded wearily away to the kitchen and that was the last we saw of him.

Siringo crumpled at the table. I'd have dozed if I could, but the collarbone prevented it, and after a while I purchased from the woman a half sheet of yellow paper and got a lead stub from my pocket and wrote *Dear Susannah* at the top. That's as far as I got just then. Siringo woke murmuring, I sat becalmed. Presently the woman carried out a tray of buxom doughnuts; the door slapped and a butcher came in, betrayed by his unseemly apron. With him was a slow-moving fellow in a cleric's collar and behind them several officers from the army camp to whom Siringo complained disjointedly about being robbed of his horses. The officers paid him little heed but cast glances at each other as though he were simple. We paid for the doughnuts and went out into the dusty sunrise and back up the street.

Just as we passed Ravel Brothers, Hood Roberts came strolling out.

He recognized me and smiled widely, only to recognize Siringo a moment later.

'You are no more,' said Siringo, dropping his bags.

Hood shook his head and reached with clear reluctance for his revolver. He'd begun to wear it down low on his right leg – I suppose someone had told him all declared bandits wore their guns in this manner.

'Don't do that, Mr. Siringo,' Hood said, as the old man unslung his rifle.

But do you think Charlie listened?

In the time it took Siringo to lever up a cartridge Hood drew his revolver and shot four times. Four shots! At a distance of no more than ten feet!

It sounds foolish, but all I could do was throw my hands over my ears like a boy frightened by firecrackers.

Siringo meantime paid no attention to the shots but shouldered the rifle and thumbed back the hammer and fired. The bullet struck slightly left of the sternum; Hood half spun and fell on his left side. I couldn't hear anything but a teapot whistle, so shocked were my ears by these concussions; I couldn't even hear Hood's revolver fall to the dirt, though I watched it topple and bounce. The air nipped with powder and Siringo's jacket and shirtfront were aflame in places – it was an odd sight, him patting out the flames with his hand. Stepping forth he picked up Hood's pistol and looked at it curiously; he opened the cylinder and emptied the unused cartridges into his palm and put them in his pocket. He brushed at his jacket and the smoke lifting off it. The shop door opened – a sallow man came out, knelt at Hood's side a moment and retreated whence he'd come. Siringo found me and grasped my ailing shoulder bones like a surgeon. 'Look at my face, Becket.' I think that's what he said. His cheeks were mapped with powder burns. I think he said, 'Is my face all right?'

I knelt at Hood's side. He was breathing. My ears rang like wire. Hood's eyes were open but I don't know what he saw. Me, fading? The next world? Whatever it was his tongue refused to report. He did not seem to struggle against death, nor did he appear surprised. Death arrived easy as the train; Hood just climbed aboard, like the capable traveler he was.

15

When the teakettle finally died away, I could hear the other men smacking flies and playing cards in the short row of cells down the hall. It didn't really bother me to be in jail – I was grateful, in fact, because a physician appeared and arranged a brace that put my collarbone at ease. Also the solitude was a respite. I had a cell to myself, with a narrow cot and tiny square window and a jailer who let me have paper and pencil.

For a long time I could do nothing but stand looking out at the dust pluming in that merciless sun, and mourn my young friend. It's said grief is more easily borne in company – well, I didn't want to bear it easily. I wanted to think of Hood laughing and meadowlark free; to recall how he tried to warn Glendon with an owl sound, or the way he drew near Alazon with the stolen teacup in his hands. Never mind his violent trail, his orphaned goodness, the gun on his leg, he was very like my own son in those startling moments.

When it became too much, I sat on the cot with the paper on my knees and wrote to Susannah. Bleak colors of sandstone and dust were all I had to offer her, but offer them I did, and it helped me to do so.

To back up: when the echoes settled, there stood Siringo

in front of a small but deeply impressed crowd. Twenty people are enough to make a legend, as I said before; here in front of their eyes a young desperado had shot four times into the body of an oldster at point-blank distance. They saw the barking *pistola*. They saw the flames catch in Siringo's clothing even as he levered a shell into the chamber of his rifle. What bravery! they thought, and they were right – I would never dream of disputing it. In days to come the people of Columbus attributed all sorts of outlandish powers to the old Pinkerton; they pronounced him a rough angel, a defender of innocence under the protection of God, or at least a possessor of the most bounteous luck.

Of course there was more to it than that, as you will see.

In the meantime, Siringo's courage was every credential a man could want. By the time he'd unloaded Hood's revolver and set it empty on the boardwalk, Hood's spirit was taking its first sip of eternity and people were beginning to press. Siringo gave them immediate answers. The boy was Hood Roberts, famed outlaw, murderer of the screen star Ern Swilling and the renowned police tracker Rupe Ericsson; perpetrator too of the conflagration that destroyed Spigot, Texas, and killed Felix Fly, a fine left-handed pitcher and dedicated Odd Fellows Lodge 225.

'I heard about that fire,' said a man pushing to the front of the gathering. 'I heard a youngster started it.'

'Yonder's your boy,' said Siringo.

'And who's this,' asked the man, indicating me, 'a deputy of yours?' As it turned out, this curious fellow was the night jailer in Columbus just coming off shift.

'No, sir, a charge of mine: a confidence man, Jack Waits by name, who I am delivering to justice.'

And that is how I ended up in the restful cell, on the same street as the unofficial coroner who arrived to take charge of Hood Roberts. I met him briefly when he came asking for my version. He too was puzzled at Hood's close-range ineptitude but informed me a sharp young army lieutenant was studying the scene. 'He was a police detective, before he joined up,' said the coroner. 'I saw him on the way over here – down on his hands and knees, right there on the street.'

In the meantime Siringo was a living hero, rising from the smoke like a leathery old god out of Homer. Two days I stayed in that jail while Siringo was feted and dined and photographed alongside Hood's propped and pallid corpse. I still have a copy of the newspaper article citing his heroics but can't bear to read it – my eyes are drawn to Hood, his face flat and foreshortened, his jacket pinned shut over the wound. I don't think they should use such pictures in newspapers, which youngsters might pull out and look at. It isn't good. To this day I cannot pick up a book and gaze at the poor posed dead of history.

While I sat in the jail and Siringo ate braised beef and onions at others' expense, someone went to the trouble of putting Hood on display in the window of the furniture store. I could see people gathering there from my cell. At first it was unclear what the commotion was, but when the crowd thinned there was Hood positioned in an armchair with his legs thrown forward on an ottoman and a pillow under his neck. Like a young man just come in from a long day. Just resting his eyes. Someone had placed a small blackboard on an easel beside him. There was printing on the blackboard but I couldn't read it from my window.

I spoke to no one else in that jail, except a man one cell over who'd fed his neighbor's dog a poisoned fish. He told me the fish was a fine channel cat he meant to smoke for himself, but then he thought of the dog. 'A demon, a barker at all hours,' he said. 'It had a shrill yip, but I oughtn't have done it.' He'd hated that dog for keeping him awake; now, having killed it, he was even more wakeful. Two nights I spent on that thin cot, and both nights noticed the poisoner moving to and fro behind his bars, whispering to himself or God.

I didn't sleep well either. The tugging question was this: Why was Hood in Columbus anyway? With a good horse under him and Mexico so close, why did he come back to this little town?

The answer, I was to learn, was for pastry. On their way south, he and Alazon had stopped at the bakery that had so generously opened early for Siringo and me. One of the pastries was a triangle-shaped bit of dough filled with such strong cinnamon you had to close your eyes when you ate it. This treat so captured Hood that he insisted they go back for more. Aswagger with triumph, having scattered the horses of his enemy, Hood had his mind set. Mexico was a large nation. You could spend years there and not find another cookie like that! And so they went back. No doubt they thought we'd be busy tracking our dispersed mounts – how could they know we would walk a dozen miles at night through snake country and find them still in town? It was Alazon who revealed these things – much later, after her capture. Convicted as an accessory, she was briefly imprisoned in a facility for women. I am told she kept her dignity there, which wouldn't surprise me.

Released finally into Siringo's custody, I walked past the furniture window. This was my last look at Hood Roberts. I wouldn't have known him. I can see why some people refuse to believe they are seeing the body of a loved one; there is an immediate wrongness, a sense that a switch has been performed. The printing on the blackboard said:

HOOD ROBERTS
NOTORIOUS BOY ASSASSIN
Killed Here by the Prominent Detective
CHAS. SIRINGO
of the Pinkerton Agency

Propped beside the blackboard was a framed photo of Siringo. His eyes were bright as Venus. That is how you want to be remembered, my friends. Take a picture in your moment of conquest, when your luck is high and bullets still bounce off. That will do for the ages.

16

The army lieutenant was straw-haired and burnt, with shy humor and curious eyes – you could see the farm boy he had been. He was waiting for us on the platform as Siringo and I prepared to board the train for California.

'Good day, Mr. Siringo, I've been needing to speak with you,' he said.

'At your service, Lieutenant.'

'Thank you.' The young man looked at me as though unwilling to divulge a confidence in my presence.

'What is it, then?' said Siringo. 'This train won't wait forever.'

'Of course. Do you have his cartridges, sir?' asked the lieutenant.

'Cartridges?'

'Yes, the boy's cartridges. The ones he fired at you.'

'No, I don't. Of course not.'

'You unloaded his weapon, as I recall.'

Siringo said, 'Yes, there were a number of people about. I thought it wise to unload, in case there were live rounds in the chamber.'

'But you didn't keep them?'

'I put them in my pocket. My clothes, however, were burnt with powder,' Siringo replied. 'Mr. Hansen downtown provided me with two new shirts, also these nice trousers. I threw the old ones away – the cartridges must've gone with them.'

The lieutenant said, 'Mr. Siringo, the Roberts boy fired four times. I looked everywhere for evidence of bullet strikes. A gouge in the street, chipped siding on nearby structures. I couldn't find a thing.'

'Tough to find bullet marks on a dirt road, sir.'

'There's only one sign he shot at all – the powder burns on your clothing. You would agree that suggests an accurate aim.'

A conductor stepped out on the platform and nodded to Siringo. The lieutenant said quietly, 'Mr. Siringo, I believe Roberts was firing blank loads.'

'Blanks!' I exclaimed.

'A charge of gunpowder but no projectile,' the lieutenant said, adding, 'Your bravery's remarkable by all accounts, but four shots at eight feet – I am trying to see how you lived.'

Siringo studied the young man. 'Perhaps I am immortal.'

'With respect, Mr. Siringo: no.'

'Did Roberts have any other bullets on his person?'

'One full box of forty-four-caliber rounds,' said the officer. 'He'd just bought them from Art Ravel, apparently.'

'And were they compromised?'

'No. Regular cartridges, nothing suspect.'

Siringo gazed almost fondly at the farm-boy lieutenant. 'So this blank-loads business is conjectural. It's imaginary.'

The young man didn't answer. The train chuffed inching forward; laughing now, Siringo pushed me aboard and climbed up after.

17

Whatever had struck him funny didn't last long – when we pulled out of Columbus, things were already going south for Charles Siringo. He'd acquired Hood but the price was high. I am no medical man but have wondered whether the nearness of those four gunshots set off some realignments in his body and brain. Is that possible? For the pigment on his hands and face began from that day to separate into brown and tan. He acquired the look of weakening preservation. His cough, already frightful, became worse; he might now spend thirty minutes hawking up a tadpole. Most unlike himself, he withdrew into silence. It was disturbing after so long in his voluble company. At first I mistook this for a mere meditative state of mind, even a sign of conscience. But when the conductor came through to collect our tickets Siringo looked at him in simian fashion, then went slowly through every pocket in his jacket and trousers before discovering the tickets in his right-hand pocket where he had placed them five minutes earlier. I found myself wondering whether the sheer proximity of that barrage – his *jacket* caught fire! – had begun to dismantle him somehow.

Or perhaps it was only that men must fall apart at last.

'You think I am depraved, but I'm not,' he said finally, over strong coffee in the dining car. 'Art Ravel is depraved.'

It took me a moment to see what he meant. 'The lieu-tenant is right, then. They were blank loads.'

'I was looking down the barrel. Anything but blanks and he'd have shot me through the eyeball.' Siringo pulled a spent cartridge from his pocket. 'Don't give me that accusing look. Observe this shell. Strange, isn't it? See the tip? It's crimped, not smooth.'

I looked it over. I wouldn't have known it from any other cartridge – a bullet was a bullet, I always supposed.

Siringo said, 'I had a drink with Art. We came to terms.'

'What terms?'

'Listen, Becket. He used to have a sideline selling blanks to film companies. You know how much shooting goes on in pictures. But business dropped off. There sat Art with a roomful of blanks.' Siringo leaned across the table. 'He's been selling them to the ignorant to make back his losses. Prospectors, amateur militias. Mexicans. He buried five thou-sand rounds in a shipment across the border.'

'But that's monstrous!'

'Most people have never seen a blank load. They're like you – they aren't conversant with ammo.'

I said, 'So Hood had no chance.'

'None.'

I was unable to speak for a minute. Finally I said, 'Did you know? Did you know somehow?'

'I suspected that would matter to you. No, I did not.'

'But the bullets in his sack,' I remembered. 'They were real bullets. The lieutenant examined them.'

'Of course they were real. Art was on hand, you'll recall, after the shooting,' Siringo replied. 'It's trouble for him if the blanks are discovered. He made a simple exchange.'

Looking wearily at me he added, 'Depraved, as I said. Though I'm grateful to him — if not for Mr. Ravel I guess you'd be annoying Hood Roberts right now, instead of me.'

'Why tell me this?'

'Because who would believe you?' He fell quiet again and turned away. 'And because you liked the boy.'

18

Sometime in the night the train slowed and jerked me forward; I woke with a flinch. Siringo, however, stayed sleeping even when the train lurched to a halt. People rose wondering from their seats, and still he did not wake. Finally a conductor did come through, swinging his lantern, to explain that the locomotive had stopped for reasons unknown and that two railroad mechanics were on the job at this moment. I looked down at Siringo, who slept on. He looked shrunken and his teeth gummy. I said, 'Charlie. Charlie,' and for long moments it seemed he might not wake. The conductor held his lantern close and said, 'What about your pard here? Is he all right?'

I didn't know. I put my ear to his mouth and couldn't hear him breathing. But when I pulled away his eyes were open and he said, 'Why are we stopped?'

'The engine broke.'

We waited. In half an hour a stalled train smells like cattle. People were up and restless, not angry but wishing for food or some way to pass the time. A boy went up and down the cars offering limes and other citrus. I remembered Glendon, who had done this as a boy. I said, 'Let's have a lime.'

Siringo nodded but didn't speak.

It was at this time I felt freedom coming toward me like clear weather.

I took the lime and cut it in two with a paring knife loaned me by the citrus boy and sucked at my half while Siringo turned his inside out and ripped the flesh with his teeth. He sucked it down thirstily then began to cough. He coughed a long while, occasionally spitting into the empty lime skin. Soon the conductor came round again, saying the engine could not be repaired that night. The town of Aztec was ten miles to the west along the tracks. Those willing to walk could be there in three hours. The rest of us must wait until another locomotive was sent to pull us in, which would be sometime the next day.

'Let's go,' said Siringo.

'You aren't ready for it.'

He stood there weaving.

'For goodness' sake, Siringo, my collarbone is broken.'

But he would have none of my refusal. Energized by crisis, he said, 'Get our bags.'

The night was cool and dewy. I placed my bag over my good shoulder, Siringo took a grip in each hand and we set off west along the tracks with perhaps sixty fellow travelers tripping and laughing and a few singing as we went. Once again Siringo surprised me with his strength – every time he seemed at the end of his vitality, some kernel of anger or inquiry took hold and brought him back.

'I don't know what happened to the girl,' he told me, as we walked.

'Alazon?'

It's true we hadn't seen her. She had not been in the arms shop with Hood. It nagged at Siringo that she was unaccounted for.

I said, 'I am sorry for Alazon. She was in love with him.'

'Manure,' he cheerfully replied. 'The older I get, the more I doubt that whole business is anything but manure.'

'She sacrificed everything to go with him. Her family. Her prospects – she had hopes of acting, you know. Wouldn't you call that love?'

'Nope. No, sir. I've known eight or ten girls in my life who'd of sacrificed their baby brothers to be with me, they were that devoted.' Siringo set his grips down and stretched his arms and lifted them again. 'Of course when it come down to it they wouldn't do what I said. They hadn't any obedience in them but wanted this or that according to their wills.'

'So love is defined by unquestioning obedience to you, no matter the circumstance.'

He thought about it. 'Yes, that states it nicely.'

'Your version of love is a rare strain.'

'Mock if you like, I had it once. My little Darlys loved me like that, before Glen Dobie sent her away.'

'Darlys DeFoe?'

We walked on for a minute. I know – the merciful thing would've been to let the conversation die, but you will understand I felt little mercy for Siringo just then.

I said, 'She is the person who shot you, you know.'

'No, sir.'

'Yes, it's a certainty. She tried to talk to you and you rebuffed her. I saw it.'

'I was shot down by the handsome boy outlaw Hood Roberts,' Siringo said, so whimsically I had a glimpse of him writing it this way in another memoir.

'You know the truth,' I said.

'Can you prove me wrong then?' In the chill starlight he turned his eyes to me; they looked near laughter.

I said, 'It doesn't matter what you say, you and I will always know.'

We hiked along the rails. Between Siringo's infirmity and my own, we were well to the rear of our fellow passengers. Someone in the forefront had begun leading rounds of choruses which kept breaking up in laughter, then beginning again.

He said, 'I will outlast you, Becket.'

19

We reached Aztec shortly after sunup. It was cool and blue as a morning painted on canvas, and though my shoulder and feet ached it was clear I felt better than Siringo did. He'd said nothing for the last hour but seemed to wither into himself until he roused somewhat as we walked into the village. Pointing at the mountains beyond he said, 'From that peak you would see Arizona.'

'Do you want breakfast?'

'I want a room. I want to close my eyes.'

The hotel was full of what the desk clerk called 'distressed travelers,' but we found rooms above a stark café. Straight to bed I went, drifting wretchedly through a long nap. Siringo was across the hall and his torrid coughing was present at the edges like a curtain blowing into my sleep. Sometime later I rose and went to his door.

'Charlie?'

Receiving no answer I went down to the café and ordered eggs and ham. It was the best meal I'd had since leaving the Hundred and One, yet Siringo and his bitter cough stayed on my mind. He still didn't answer after breakfast, so I went to the proprietor. When I suggested one of his boarders might be ill he looked at me as though I were bringing this news to spite him – sulkily he handed me a key.

Siringo was alive. He was propped in his bed at a perilous tilt. He said, as he had in Columbus, 'Is my face all right?'

'No, Charlie,' I replied, since it wasn't. The left half of his face was wayward or fallen. It had drifted out of communication. I want to say his left half had died. The eyelid had failed him and stuck midway. I remember the chalky glaze behind it.

He said, again, 'Is my fay zaw rye?'

Endings are rarely what we wish. Hood Roberts, for example: He hadn't any brave last words. I doubt he had time to think of any – if so, he was beyond using them by the time I knelt at his side. When writing of Hood to Susannah I had to stop from time to time and collect myself, for an old lyric kept returning to me – that verse about the young cowboy *wrapped in white linen and cold as the clay*. When Redstart was a certain age he would refuse to go to sleep until Susannah stood in his doorway and sang him that song.

> *Get six jolly cowboys to carry my coffin,*
> *Six pretty maidens to sing me a song;*
> *Put bunches of roses all over my coffin,*
> *Roses to deaden the sods as they fall.*

Say what you like about melodrama, it beats confusion. The truth is we ought to have a chance to say a little something when it's getting dark. We ought to have a closing scene.

Now I sat by Siringo watching his ending come into

his face. The resentful proprietor fetched a doctor, a bald big-headed Scot in his sixties, late of army service. Peering in Siringo's eyes he diagnosed a stroke of paralysis. Siringo's mind was in disarray and his body wouldn't listen to orders.

'What's to be done?' I asked, in the hall.

'Rest,' said the doctor.

'Here?'

'I would not move him now. Let this be his hospital.' The old Scot rubbed his large hands and said, 'He was famous once, that old rooster.'

'Yes, I know.'

'Charlie Siringo. I read one of his books on a train. Long ago, but I have a great memory!' The doctor had a generous smile. 'I think he told more lies than Jacob, son of Isaac. It was a good book though.'

The doctor stayed a long time, talkative and wholly unruffled by his patient's condition. He was newly retired. He'd been stationed at Camp Furlong and spoke of it wistfully – he still looked strong enough to whip any number of sergeants so I imagine he was happy, some months later, to be summoned back into service for what was termed a punitive expedition in Mexico.

'Well, this has been something,' he said finally, heaving lightly to his feet like a colt. 'Charlie Siringo! Man knows not his time.'

'When will you come back?'

The doctor allowed he had a granddaughter being christened and would be away several days. He watched my eyes and asked was anyone willing to stay and nurse the old man until his return, and I said I would.

'Are you his relative then?'

278

'No. I am his captive.'

The doctor smiled. He did not ask for clarification. He said, 'Well. Get ready to be set free.'

20

Siringo ate because he had to. I fed him tiny meals ground up with the head of a mallet: shredded beef, corn, black beans. He was determined to live despite his dead half, despite the slackness creeping across his face. He had lost the ability to pronounce words but would write legible notes, balancing his right hand on a tablet in his lap. There was a small steadfast Calcuttan man who came and took care of Siringo's private tasks and this Siringo would not mention. The notes were of necessity short which only magnified their snappish character.

Dr. is a blind — , he wrote. *More sauce on the meat*.

Meantime he thinned. If he had been a strap of leather before, he was now an attenuated membrane near ripping. Once I went in and his face was wet. I asked if he was frightened, at which rage entered his good right eye and he wrote on the tablet, *You weak — Becket*. I think he believed his anger would blockade death. Even so, he was like a boat that sinks at its mooring and all you can see is the mast.

When a week had passed and there was no change, only further thinning, I went to bed and had myself a dream. It was hard as life. I was on the bank beside moving water, and a woman rode along the opposite shore. Downstream she cantered, away from me, a scabbarded rifle across her back. She sat the horse impeccably and watching her I thought she might be Susannah until she cantered back upriver searching a place to ford. She was a fierce and beautiful Mexican woman. She never saw me. I woke feeling I had stumbled into another man's mind.

In the morning I spoke with the bald doctor, then went to see Siringo and give him his tepid breakfast.

'I am leaving today,' I told him, when he had managed a few bites.

He would not reply but put his right eye upon me. Certainly there was some pepper in there but he would not pick up the pencil and write.

'I am leaving you in the care of Dr. Slane,' I said.

His gaze slid off me toward the wall. For no good reason I felt like a betrayer but bucked up and said, 'I see you are worse this morning, I am sorry about that. I doubt we will see one another again. Goodbye.'

Only then did he lurch and get hold of the pencil. *I will outlast* is what he wrote.

I left him that way and picked up my bag and went down to the train station. The man behind the window said, 'Well?'

'Well what?'

'East or west?' said he.

THE RAROTONGANS

A group of young women was also heading for California. Zealous botanists, they left the train at every stop to hunt local wildflowers, which they suspended in bunches from the coach ceiling. The drying blossoms swayed overhead, purple asters, orange skyrockets, white blooms plain as your chin but with the stunning name of heliotropes; most dangled low enough so passengers had to dodge them to walk, but it was also true we had the best-smelling coach on the train and no one minded except a soft banker in a homburg who sneezed hard under the waving flora.

Straightaway I got out pen and blotter, meaning to write Susannah an explanation – to describe why I was continuing west, though I had already been away longer than my intended six weeks. Certainly my reasons were passable. They had to do with allegiance, with my implicit promise to Glendon to help him 'see this through.'

Indeed my travels – willing and forced – had already carried me too near completion to turn back now. Yet once again I found the letter quite impossible to write. As New Mexico rumbled past, then blanched Arizona, I searched through the cars until I found a conductor familiar with the Rienda Valley. He didn't know Blue or the name Soto but knew the river itself because he had fished it once for three weeks with his father and uncles.

'At first it comes down fast and steep and it's a long way between pools,' said this conductor. 'We thought we'd lost one of my uncles, Bret, in the rapids, but he was sitting underwater in one of the deep pools hanging onto a rock. Bret could hold his breath for two minutes – until we started to think, Where's Bret? Then he'd bust up out of the water right behind you, frighten you into old age.'

'Where do the orchards begin?'

'The gradient lessens, the river levels out. It slows, gets wide, the hills are broad and tillable. That's your citrus country. If this Soto is there, someone will know him.'

I thanked the conductor and returned to my seat. On the way I picked up a recent Los Angeles newspaper that had a front-page picture of a marching army. Skipping the weighty headlines I meandered to the book section. There was a new Zane Grey, but then there is always a new Zane Grey; also a novel called *Freckles* about a disadvantaged boy who lives in the woods and falls in love with an angel. In the gossip corner was mention of Boyd Singleton Ample, who'd recently passed through Los Angeles. Boyd let drop he was working on a book about five brothers who go adventuring to sea and are all killed in a freak storm that then whips ashore and kills their parents too, so that no one is left of the family except the grandma who goes on lighting candles for twenty more years. Shutting my eyes I imagined Boyd: a destined figure in the grasp of his story, perfect strong sentences pouring out of his pen. I fell asleep that way. When I woke in the dark I was smiling – it's a happy thing to brace for a visit from old friend Envy who then for some reason never shows up.

2

A boy in a Ford A gave me a ride far down the Rienda
Valley. I had made inquiries after disembarking and the
conductor was right: People knew Claudio Soto. As for the
valley, it looked distressed. The boy informed me there had
been frosts the previous two winters; many orchards had
been abandoned or fallen into the hands of bankers. This
youngster was roughly Hood Roberts's age, yet he faced
forward as Hood had never done, driving the Ford with
an eyebrow raised as though on the lookout for better
prospects. He expounded on the nature of citrus trees and
how they grew, how they responded to cold weather. Himself
the son of citrus growers, he couldn't wait to get away from
the business. He wanted to design buildings – he'd seen
architecture in San Francisco that made him short of breath.
It seemed to him a better life than orange trees could offer.

'I read where an ice age is coming,' the boy remarked.
'There is a glacier in Canada moving in our direction. It's
coming faster all the time! Dr. Horton of Los Angeles says
in fifty years we'll all be Eskimos. We'll eat seals and live
in buildings made out of ice.'

'Do you believe Dr. Horton?'

'I used to,' was his cheery reply.

We drove on. Beside the road appeared a long low wall
of native stone. The stones were placed without mortar and

some had fallen and the wall wound to and fro like a dog on a walk.

'We're close,' I said, but the boy was talking about his plans and didn't hear.

The orchard behind the wall looked starved and skeletal. I sighted an ox harnessed to a flatbed wagon. A man on a ladder was trimming a tree and tossing the branches on the wagon. His movements were fluid and careful, his hair white as cotton.

'Pull up,' I said.

He steered the A to the side of the road. 'See, I've got to make money for school. Otherwise it's back to the orchard for me. I'll end up like that hired hand there, on a ladder my whole life.'

I opened the door and stepped out and leaned back in for my bag.

'What – is this the place you're looking for?'

The ox regarded us and the man kept at his work. He worked easily, twisting carefully on his ladder. We could hear sharp cracks as the cut branches struck the flatbed. We were at a distance and I knew his eyes weren't the best.

I handed the boy some money.

He said, 'Hey, if that's your friend—'

'It's all right.'

He was a very decent youngster. I shook his hand and started to tell him good luck – my voice caught, though, so I just waved him down the road. Partly it was the boy and his easy talk and high hopes. Partly it was just that I hadn't been around a friend in so long, and now Glendon was climbing down from his ladder, looking quizzically in my direction with his bad old eyes. For the first time in weeks I felt that lights were on somewhere for me.

3

Until he was within fifty feet he couldn't tell it was me but angled up slowly as though I might be the tax man or maybe Siringo himself. When I said hello, his face changed to certainty and he dropped his pruning saw and charged, in his delight not even saying my name but laughing and getting me round the middle and lifting me straight off the earth, slight as he was. I laughed too — I couldn't help it. He lifted me a foot in the air, set me down, then lifted me again. Whoop! Something was new about Glendon; it took me a little time to discern it.

'Why ain't you home with Susannah?' he said, poking my chest.

'Where's this Blue of yours?' I replied.

'How'd you shake off old Siringo?'

'What did she say when you showed up?'

We tossed up questions like confetti, as long-parted friends do; but in fact we had not been parted long, it only seemed that way. Soon the weight of undelivered news bore in and I turned quiet. Glendon looked dismayed.

'What news of our friend Hood?' he asked, in a reluctant tone.

I looked at his eyes and he turned them from me.

'Hood is dead, Glendon. I'm sorry to say it.'

He nodded as though expecting these dread tidings. I

waited for him to speak but he couldn't and ran his rough fingers over his head.

'Do you want to hear about it?'

He nodded again. I kept it short but tried to give him some context with the Spigot fire and the empty farmhouse and the counterfeit bullets. Siringo's stint as the toast of Columbus I left out, as well as Hood on display in the store window with his feet up.

Glendon sat on the flatbed with his legs dangling. Though built small he'd always given an impression of nimble strength. Now he just looked small — meager, I want to say. He didn't look at me but at the ground or the gray webwork of trees. A locust buzzed close by and the compliant ox shifted his feet. Glendon made no reply to Hood's tragedy.

Finally he got up and clucked to the ox, who moved forward at a walk as though a switch had been thrown. I rode on the flatbed with a pile of loose dead limbs while Glendon walked at the ox's head. In a few minutes a pale pyramid rose out of the gloom and became a pile of branches. The ox stopped at its edge and Glendon and I unloaded the flatbed. The limbs were light but stiff and spiky — you didn't want to get one in the eye.

He said, 'How did Hood seem to you — before Siringo shot him, I mean.'

'We didn't really get to visit, Glendon.'

'But you saw him. You heard his voice.'

I thought it over. 'Well, he was courteous — he said *Mr. Siringo*. He sounded like Hood, you know.'

'Good, that's good. I'm glad to hear he was polite. That's our boy.' Without another word he walked away into the trees. I didn't follow him but stayed with the wagon. Night arrived and stars came out by their thousands every minute. After a little time I heard Glendon returning, walking slowly, picking his way. He put a hand on the ox and said, 'All right then, it's late in the day. Come on, Monte, you should meet Claudio.'

4

Glendon had reached the Rienda Valley two weeks earlier, riding a sand-colored cowhorse purchased from a shrewd Arizonan midget. He told me this while we moved through the orchard at the rate of a plodding ox. The midget was a hard negotiator with a voice like a kazoo but had the quality atypical in horse traders of stating a beast's flaws alongside its heroic attributes. He knew horses like no one Glendon had ever met, especially their legs, where so many animals are prone to catastrophe. The mare he sold Glendon was named Sparrow and carried him without complaint clear down the Gila River to Yuma, where he stood on a hill overlooking the adobe ramparts of the famous territorial prison. Glendon's voice hushed at the word *Yuma*, of whose ravages he had heard from experienced compadres: the sun beating through latticed ironwork, the brazed manacles set into the stone floor. Viewing the penitentiary from his far hilltop Glendon had no way of knowing it had been shut down years earlier and posed no threat. He crossed the Gila and a short while later the weedy Colorado before veering northwest toward a bank of dunes he knew from long ago. He was in familiar country and so was surprised when a lake appeared shining where there had been only dry and saline earth. The lake was too large to see across, too large to be misplaced. Riding Sparrow along the water's edge he wondered at his memory until an Indian woman emerging from a tilted house informed him the Colorado had breached its banks a decade before and created this new ocean. At its bottom lay the bones of a town named Salton. Glendon had stopped in Salton twenty years before and done a little business in the saloon – he told the woman so, but she wasn't interested. She hated the lake. Its water grew more bitter year by year. Glendon rode on.

While I was still in New Mexico, waiting for Charles Siringo to emerge from his ravings, Glendon trotted down out of the Vallecitos into a watershed of bubbling streams and species of flowered prairie grasses he had not seen in thirty years. At the bottom of this valley a slender river twisted through farms and small ranchos where the cowhorse Sparrow had to be dissuaded from testing herself on the feral longhorns lurking against the hillsides. The vaqueros Glendon encountered in this promising valley didn't look like the desperates with whom he had rustled thousands of cattle in his youth. They were clean and strong with straight lustrous teeth and direct eyes suggesting a hold on the future. Their horses were muscled and full-barreled, larger and prettier than Spanish ponies. These cowboys didn't mind a lone horseman traveling through and confirmed for Glendon that the river he followed was in fact the Rienda. Yes, it went all the way to the ocean. Yes, a region of citrus orchards awaited him downriver. No doubt the cowboys sensed in this veteran horseman a lush deposit of stories, for they asked him to stay for an evening of music and fiery drink, but Glendon said no, he was too near the end of his own tale now. He nudged Sparrow and they continued on, keeping the river on their left.

Days of asking brought him to a valley of crippled trees. Some had leaves in the lowermost branches but many were dead brittle. He rode Sparrow through this shinbone copse, hopeless all of it except for one small quarter of dwarfish citrus with branches underfed but at least green below the bark. Emerging from these Sparrow stepped into a broad grassy lane that led to a painted two-story wrapped in a porch. A man sat on the porch in a ladderback chair. He was sleeping but woke as Glendon rode up. An ash cane lay across his lap and he took it up and touched the floorboards with it.

'Are you Claudio Soto?' Glendon asked.

'Yes.'

'Did you marry Arāndano Ordonez?'

Claudio stood from his chair and held onto it for balance. He had long graying hair that thinned and reached his shoulders in coarse wisps.

'Is she at home now?'

'No. What is it you want?'

Glendon sat on his horse wondering what to say.

'You may come in if you like,' said Claudio.

'Maybe we could talk out here.'

The two men stood in the dusty yard, Claudio leaning on his cane. He bore Glendon no hint of a grudge. In fact he seemed pleased to meet at last the man he had long thought of as a fabled rogue – the winsome gringo who married the local girl only to vanish just ahead of horse soldiers sent by then-president Díaz. Claudio saw himself as the beneficiary of this desertion. He was a gentleman. In all his years with Arāndano, he had not asked her for the details of her first marriage.

'But you have had quite a life,' said Claudio, for word of Glendon's exploits and the company he kept had drifted back from time to time.

'No, I expect yours has been the life,' said Glendon. He then described how Blue had ridden into his mind, persisting there day and night, carrying her rifle. He described the dread and regret that came over him. 'Now I am getting old and wish to lay things down. I came to make apology.'

'Apology.'

'That's right.'

Claudio appeared to think about this for a while. He had gotten the habit of thinking a long time before he spoke. Sometimes he seemed almost to go to sleep.

'She will be home by dark,' he said. 'I will talk to her then. Don't come up to the house until I put a light on the porch.' He turned, then added, 'The bunkhouse is empty. Go clean up if you like. There is a well in the back.'

Glendon washed and put on a clean shirt he had carried all the way from Minnesota folded in tissue paper. He shaved the whiskers from his face and took the end of his whiskey and poured it on the ground outside the bunkhouse. He had nothing left to eat in his panniers, but after a while Claudio hobbled down with a covered plate. Glendon said it wasn't necessary but Claudio left the plate in his hands and went back to the house. Lifting the lid Glendon found cold chicken and green beans and two slices of Spanish bread flavored with anise seed. At this all his nervousness went away. He sat down saying over the food a blessing taught to him by Crealock the preacher, whom he suddenly missed. He took the plate to the back door of the bunkhouse and ate standing outside, looking up at the hills while the shadows lengthened. Afterward he returned to the well and pumped up some water and cleaned the plate and the knife and fork, then sat down to wait for nightfall.

'It's peculiar, to reach your destination,' he told me. 'You think you'll arrive and perform the thing you came for and depart in contentment. Instead you get there and find distance still to go.'

I nodded and he went on. Sitting in the darkening bunkhouse he could hear noises from the house – a gramophone, a pan being scraped. Then a horse entered the yard trotting. He knew it was Blue. He didn't go to the window but sat in the bunkhouse knowing she was there. He felt something he couldn't identify, as though he might be someone else entirely from the man he had become.

She left the horse tied in front of the house and went in. Forgetting his clean shirt Glendon walked out and patted the horse. He unslung its reins from the porch rail and led the animal to the barn. It was a compliant bay a full hand taller than his Sparrow, and it nudged him forward to a tie stall where he removed its saddle and lifted its feet one at a time. He spoke to the horse in congenial tones – there were oats in a canted bin and he measured some into a bucket and brushed the horse while it lipped the oats. When he got back to the bunkhouse his shirt was full of horsehair and he had no other to put on. He looked out the window and saw Claudio stepping out on the porch to hang a lantern on a nail. Glendon crossed the yard brushing off his shirt and saw Blue standing in the lit entryway behind her husband.

I said, 'Was she glad to see you?'

Glendon smiled. 'She didn't honestly say much to me,

Monte. No – up to now, Claudio has pretty much done the talking. He's a rare fellow. I hadn't reckoned on it.'

'And what have you been doing, these two weeks?'

He nodded round us at the lopped and suffering grove. 'Working. They employ this fellow Joaquin who shows me what to do. He's got one arm and talks Spanish twenty hours a day. I can't hardly keep up with him.'

'How long will you stay?'

'Until she lets me talk to her. Or until she tells me to go.' There was a cumbersome pause, then he said, 'What about you, Monte – how come you're here? Ain't you going home to Susannah?'

'Yes, pretty soon I think.'

He held my eye. 'Oh, now, Becket.'

I dropped my gaze.

He said, 'You know what I've discovered?'

I shook my head and he said, 'The world's unkind to fools.'

He seemed altered, as I said; taller, even. His motions more exact.

I said, 'Glendon. You are sober.'

'Yes, I gave it up.'

'Are you glad?'

'Sometimes.'

'I have heard it is a tough habit to leave behind.'

'Tougher to keep up,' he replied.

5

'Are you a bandit too?' said Claudio Soto.

I stood on the lamplit veranda shaking hands with our vivid and crumbling host. His hands were purple and his hair a white phantom. He wore the cavernous pants of declining men.

He said, 'This is your plan, Glendon? Fetch up all your *compañeros* and rob an old man of his orchard?'

I said, 'I'd be grateful for a place to stay a few days. I'll work with Glendon if I may sleep in your bunkhouse.'

'It's more and more interesting,' said Claudio. 'Who will walk in next?'

We followed this old ruin into his house. It was adobe and cool as a shovel of earth. When my eyes became accustomed I saw patterned rugs, furniture of massive build, on the west wall Christ crucified, and a low bookshelf on which half the volumes were dictionaries and reference works in diverse languages. Later I would discover biographies of poets and musicians, histories of conquest, theoretical investigations into alchemy and the physics of time and the character of God, but for now Claudio pitched away toward his kitchen and we followed out of fear he would crash to the floor.

'Sit and rest,' he said. He opened the icebox and got down on one knee and selected a clay pitcher of water and two ripened limes. Slowly and at some cost he stood and retrieved three crystal glasses from an open shelf; he wiped them with flour sacking, sliced the ends off the limes and with startling vigor in his purple hands squeezed the limes over the pitcher until their juice slid into the cold water. The clay sweated and ticked. Claudio wiped his hands on the sacking and filled the glasses and set them before us.

'How have you arrived here?' he inquired of me.

I never tasted better water. It made my words run together. 'Glendon's my neighbor up in Minnesota. He asked me to come along but we got separated. It's taken me some time to catch up.'

'You are not one of his friends from the earlier days?'

'No.'

'What do you know of those times?' Claudio seemed amused.

'That they are long over,' I replied.

'They have no bearing on your friendship, these bygone sins?'

I was quiet and looked at Glendon across the table. Clearly he had told this man something of me already, for Claudio said, as if to clarify, 'That your friend was something besides his appearance – this was not important to you?'

'It seemed important, once or twice.'

On the kitchen wall hung a painting in a gilt frame. It was large for kitchen decor and represented a melded geometry of parabolas and planes. Its colors were reds and browns and there was a gold hoop at the bottom like an eclipse. Watching my gaze Claudio said, 'My grandfather is responsible for that. Do you like it?'

It is better to say I aspired to like it. It was a peculiar painting – though it first seemed a portrait of confusion, it soon began to take the form of a landscape with trapez-oidal fields, wishbone rivers, and orchard trees standing straight out from the curve of the world. The gold hoop was not the sun but a solar reflection in a pond or ocean.

'Was he famous?' I asked, to gain time. For the old man's sake I wanted to like the painting, and felt it beginning to happen.

'Only a little, and too late to make him rich. Fame arrived when his worship Porfirio bought several of his works, but by then my grandfather was old, he was prac-tically Moses.'

Glendon said, 'Monte here, his wife is an artist too.'

Claudio nodded at the picture. 'What would she think of this, then?'

'She would enjoy it,' I said, with increasing certainty.

'He spoke with an angel once – my grandfather,' mused our host. 'The angel told him there were colors deep in the heavens that have no correlatives on earth.' He watched me with his merry weasel eyes. 'Your wife the artist, has she spoken to angels?'

'Not that I know of.'

'God Himself loves artists,' said Claudio, adding, with a wince, 'However, He is ambivalent about doctors.' He sighed and tottered with us back to the porch, where he lit two additional kerosene lanterns and lifted them onto ceiling hooks with his cane.

He was hoisting the second lamp when we heard the horse coming into the yard. Claudio was holding Glendon's arm for support. Glendon himself wore a paralytic expression, and I knew I was about to meet the woman for whom he had crossed a country to express regret.

She cantered into the light on a leggy bay mare.

She was in her late forties, a little slumped, her silvering hair roped up in a braid behind her brimmed hat.

'Hello, *carina*,' said Claudio.

'Who is the visitor?' she briskly replied, looking me over. I confess to being surprised by her plainness. In all Glendon's telling, Blue had appeared as a snap-eyed Guinevere, yet here was an ordinary round-shouldered woman with a lined and skeptical expression.

'This is my friend Monte Becket,' Glendon said. 'Monte, here's Blue.'

'Call me Arāndano,' she said.

'I'm glad to meet you.'

She smiled and swung down from the horse. She wasn't plain to Glendon, of course; she was the most gracious part of his long history and evidence of the life he might have lived.

She half-hitched the reins to the porch rail and climbed the steps to Claudio, where she took his arm in a way that made him appear the strong one. She stood at his side with her arm around his waist. I felt a mighty sadness for my friend.

Claudio said, 'Monte would like to stay with us a day or two.'

I said, 'If it's not convenient I'll be on my way.'

But her eyes softened toward me and she said, 'The writer of *Martin Bligh*.'

'Why, yes.' I was only startled for a moment – by Glendon's sidecast eyes I understood he had given over his copy.

'I read your book,' Arāndano said. 'You describe horses fairly well, Mr. Becket. Do you enjoy riding?'

'Honestly, no, ma'am. Horses don't think much of me, as it turns out.'

She said, 'Are you writing another story?'

'I'm afraid not, ma'am. That was the end of that.'

Nodding as though this were probably for the best, she shifted suddenly and said, 'You arrive at a busy moment. Tomorrow my tenacious Claudio must cook supper enough for twenty men working at Pond's. If you are rested, I will ask you to help.'

'Thank you, of course,' I said, and watched Arāndano grip her husband's arm as he moved back into the house. When the door shut I turned to see what Glendon made of this request, but he had disappeared.

6

Pond's was another frostbitten orchard a few miles up the Rienda. If anything it had suffered worse than the Sotos' because, according to Claudio, it was another hundred feet above sea level where winters were incrementally colder. The twenty men were neighors from other farms and fruit concerns who threw in together when need occasioned. Sometimes the needs were fortifying ones such as a heavy harvest, but not lately. As Claudio remarked, 'Turning a citrus grove into bonfires is depressing work all by yourself.'

Glendon was gone with the ox and flatbed before I woke. The world seemed old and in disrepair as I walked through heavy dew to the house, where Claudio had already set round loaves to rise under a floury cloth.

'Do you want breakfast?' he inquired, by way of greeting.

'I'll wait.'

'Good. There's an oven in the yard. Clean it out and make a hot fire. Wait – where are your shoes?' he demanded.

'They were wet.'

'Put on your shoes, then start the fire,' were his stern instructions.

The oven looked like a clay beehive or troll hut with its black chimney hole and scorched iron door. Ash ghosted out when I opened it; when I reached in with a shovel two pale scorpions slid into the sunshine. I felt a little sick

– I'd gotten all the way to California without seeing any scorpions; honestly, a Midwesterner isn't accustomed to scorpions. Peering into the oven I could see there was also a robust tribe of spiders in residence but hard luck for them.

I made the fire, watching where I knelt and where my hands went. Claudio had pointed out kindling and the woodshed, and I found an old bellows on the shed wall and wheezed at the flames until they drove me back. Leaving the iron door open an inch I returned to the house, where my host was stewing hens.

'Is it lit?'

'Yes.'

He nodded toward a counter. 'There is a knife. Quarter the peppers and leave the seeds in. I am cross this morning, thank you.'

The directions seemed urgent so I blistered along, chopping and quartering until we had a pot of gravy to water your eyes. I said, 'Did you always cook?'

'No. Arãndano used to cook; then she began taking in bookwork and left the kitchen to Joaquin. Now Joaquin works with the trees.'

'A big job, it appears.'

'Not as big as it used to be,' Claudio said. He touched a loaf under its sheet. 'Go check the fire.'

It had burned to mostly white ash which he had me shovel out. We then lifted the loaves one at a time into the oven with a long-handled implement like an oar. It worked reasonably well, though one of the loaves tipped off and deflated on the earthen floor.

Claudio said, 'Now the pies.'

Peach, blackberry, apple – he set me to peeling while he

cut lard into flour with a pair of knives held between his fingers. While we worked he explained his orchard. Seven years earlier, 'in fat times,' he'd read in a newspaper that a man near Sacramento had imported some dozens of young citrus from Tahiti. The trees were described as dwarfish with shiny leaves and knobby twigs; the oranges they bore had a greenish tinge but were dawn-sweet, with so much juice they burst when dropped. Claudio at that time was well-off enough to fund intuitions. He sought out the captain of a trade barkentine running salt pork and liquor to the Cook Islands, sandalwood and native exotica back. The trader agreed to deliver three hundred saplings in watered burlap but required a stiff deposit. Five months later the bark arrived from the island of Rarotonga. The trader refused to see Claudio but sent one of his crew to demand he pay in full before the trees were off-loaded to the dock.

'It felt like a robbery in progress – what would you have done?' he asked.

'I have no idea,' I admitted.

In the end he accepted a cargo of bare sticks bagged in salty loam. Seeing his aggravation, one of the crew confided that the trees had been healthy when the voyage began – the problem was fresh water. The bark's drinking reserves had been compromised by leaky barrels, and the sailors resented having to water young trees when they themselves were thirsty.

'Why didn't you just buy grafts?' I asked. 'They could've been kept damp with little trouble and perhaps brought home successfully.' I knew an apple grower in Minnesota, a proud amateur geneticist, who was forever sending away for new grafts – he loved to confound people by showing them three or four obviously different fruits all hanging on the same tree.

'It wasn't the bearing branches I wanted,' Claudio replied. 'It was the rootstock. That is what you rely on. The rootstock is where a tree survives.'

He'd set the famished sticks immediately in crates of fresh damp soil and rigged canvas over them to prevent scorching on the ride home. It was months before he knew which ones would live and which would die. In the end, nearly two hundred of them made it. Since then they had survived several hard freezes while trees around them perished – a lucky development, Claudio said, since you wouldn't expect hardiness from those tropic latitudes. Of course the Rarotongans hadn't borne a crop yet, either.

'The past two seasons, no harvest at all. We sold most of our land. Arāndano feeds us with her bookkeeping. If she were not solid with numbers we would be back in Oscuro, eating frijoles with her relatives. I like her relatives and frijoles but prefer to be here.'

'You're a fortunate man,' I said.

He placed a lump of dough on a smooth board and worked it flat with a rolling pin. 'When I was young and not as you see me now,' he said, 'I used to have a little influence. I was listened to in chambers. Once before a jury I argued the case of a neighbor accused of theft and won his acquittal, although I am not an attorney. Some people believed I should run for this or that office.'

'That's not hard to believe.'

He laid a sheet of dough into a pie pan and turned to the next lump. 'Now I am older, my clothes fit wrong. My work has gone out with the tide.'

'Tides turn. It won't freeze every year. There are the Rarotongans,' I pointed out.

'You are kind to say so. All the same I am decreasing. There is a hard growth in my guts the size of a pigeon. I am told it will kill me.'

To hear this news in such a guileless tone deprived me of words. I could only sit back and watch him.

He said, 'Fatigue is a rotten condition and entirely new to me. Energy was never my problem.'

'You've been to doctors, of course.'

'I felt something happening years ago, before the trees arrived – a pain like a faint taste in my center, a metallic taste. I thought it would disappear but instead it took hold. I picture it as a brave little colony. There is a craven doctor in Lury who diagnosed a frenzied imagination, as if I was too happy and must create myself an agony. In the meantime the colony prospered, it declared statehood. By the time the doctor could be convinced, it was too late for him to do much. He did recommend a priest, although I was friends with one already.'

'That's unforgivable,' I said.

'Nothing is unforgivable, although I admit I have yet to pardon this doctor. I will have to do so before the end lest the Almighty rethink my standing. There are certain unfairnesses I don't much like, but then it is His story to tell.' Suddenly Claudio looked up. 'Do you smell the bread? Don't let it burn!'

I went out on numb legs and indeed the loaves were brown as buckeyes. I removed them with the long paddle and wrapped them in sacking. When I returned with the steaming bundle Claudio was crimping the edges of fruit pies – dipping his hard fingertips in a cup of water, pinching the top and undercrusts together. He took a knife and slitted the crusts in a cordial geometry, dashed them with cane sugar, and stooped to examine the pies one by one as though vigilant for things to fix. I could imagine him arguing the accused neighbor's case – oh, yes. It was easy to see the defendant feeling at least reasonably confident with Claudio Soto walking to and fro before the jury. Aware of me watching he said, 'Don't feel bad for me, Monte. The smaller I get, the better I cook. If I am given another year I will shrink to the size of a large dog but my pies will be extremely famous. Here, help me put these in the oven.'

7

Arāndano returned with Joaquin in the late afternoon. They drove a tall unsteady truck with thin tires aslant on their axles. The truck was Pond's. Arāndano was tired and kept blinking her eyes to make them focus – she'd spent the day cutting a path through a two-year jungle of Pond bookwork.

'It's worse than he knows,' she told Claudio. 'He's a poor bookkeeper, the ledgers are frantic. He is at the end of his funds.'

Joaquin and I were packing pies and bread into blanketed fruit crates in the truck bed.

Claudio said, 'I'll go along. Pond should have his friends there,' but his voice was changed from earlier. I was jolted to see him suddenly withered; the day's baking had cost him his vigor and several inches of height.

'Joaquin will go to Pond's,' said Arāndano. 'You will go to bed.'

He didn't argue and in fact lowered himself onto the grass.

Arāndano said to me, 'Why don't you help my spent hero into the house?'

Claudio's eyes were closed. He said, 'Hero, yes. Baker intrepid. Captain Bread.'

I took his hands and lifted him to his feet. We got him

into the parlor where there was a bristly purple sofa full of pillows. These Claudio shoved onto the floor minutes before falling slack-jaw into a nap. His wife motioned me to sit in one of the armchairs nearby. I thought we would be quiet on account of Claudio but she spoke right up.

'He's your neighbor then – Glendon.'

'Neighbor and good friend.'

'Does Glendon have many friends there?'

'Not many.'

'He used to have friends,' she said. 'In Oscuro it seemed everyone was his friend. Tell me, what is it like where he lives?'

'He has a little place near our own on the Cannon River.'

'What kind of place – a farmstead? A shack?'

Encouraged that she wanted to envision Glendon's home, I provided a few scenic details – how the structure sat on a bend of the river and so had water on three sides, how it rose out of the fog if you arrived early in the day. I emphasized Glendon's orderly habits, his swept workshop, and omitted the fact that his house was a barn. 'He has a little garden of herbs,' I concluded, 'and always brings some fresh-cut when he comes for dinner.'

'So he didn't go to drink,' she said. 'I half expected he would go to drink.'

I made no answer and for a little while we sat listening to Claudio sleep. He breathed in through his nose and out through his mouth, his lips making faint pops on the exhale.

She said, 'What has Glendon said about me?'

Again I felt the need to choose well. 'He told me how you met, while he was repairing your great-uncle's boat.'

'He was a handsome boy,' she admitted. 'He made that job last a long time.'

'He said it took him three weeks just to make you laugh.'

She smiled. 'My uncle told me laughter encouraged young men. If I had laughed, he would've told my father about it. That would've been the end of things.'

'He told me about the casita where you lived.'

'It had a nice garden.'

I said, 'It tormented Glendon, that he never came back to you.'

'He left for himself. I doubt he would deny it. He stayed away for himself. Now he has returned for the same reason.'

'He came back out of repentance,' I replied. 'It would be generous of you to hear his apology.'

She turned to me with surprising tenderness. 'Do I look angry to you?'

'No.'

'I was for a time, but Claudio is a man who turns away anger. Eventually I lost the habit. However, I am not silly enough to believe I owe Glendon anything. If he wants absolution let him seek it from God.'

'Maybe he wants it from you as well.'

Her voice was kind but without concession. 'You're his friend, Monte, so listen. His conscience doesn't concern me. His apology does not benefit me. His work for us on the orchard is another matter — that's real enough and comes at a good time. That is why we allowed him to stay. There is no other reason.'

I nodded. Sometimes it seems every woman I meet is more than a match for me.

8

In the morning I borrowed Glendon's horse Sparrow and ventured down to Lury. Glendon had described the horse as temperate and amenable, but in fact he kept wanting to turn around and trot back to the orchard; I had to rein him up half a dozen times. On the other hand, he didn't flare when a red fox abruptly appeared smiling in the tall weeds beside the road. One moment there was the fox's grinning face, the next nothing but its white-tipped brush, and this horse kept its gait as if designed by the Swiss. I don't understand these animals. Down we went into that scraggy mission town and I located the telegraph office, a scantly built room with a lean-to where the agent had a hand pump and a copper sink.

'I need to send a wire,' I told the agent. He was probably my own age but looked older, so I imagined, in his brim and banded sleeves.

'Hold on,' he said, and found a pencil.

'Susannah Becket, Northfield, Minnesota.'

Even now I am not sure why I asked them to come west, why I didn't simply board a train for Minnesota. Maybe I wanted Susannah to prove her interest in me. Maybe I feared that old invisibility back home, or a return of the tepid fugue. What I'd have given for a dream or vision now, like Glendon had of Blue – in wavering times, a vision's what you want! Instead I confess to the most unrefined and selfish longings. I wanted to walk with Susannah and be solid and foremost in her eyes. I wanted Redstart to discover from its roots upward this place where I might be of use.

By noon I was back at the orchard helping Glendon and Joaquin — we had plenty of work before us, if not the wholesale clear-cut visited on Pond. My shoulder was still damaged so I drove the wagon while they cut lifeless trees and bucked them into pieces that Joaquin lobbed onto the flatbed. The stumps we pulled with the aid of the tolerant ox, King Richard, who leaned into the chains without grievance. Any trees with living green we climbed with ladders and relieved of dead limbs. We filled ourselves with sunlight and sawdust and the agreeable tumble of Spanish flowing always from Joaquin. He had a passable store of found English but rarely employed it. He sang in the mornings, narrated what seemed to be personal epics in the afternoon, and by evening was down to complaints and occasional confessions — Glendon got sick of Joaquin sometimes, but to me it was all just melody.

'He says he's getting baptized Sunday next,' Glendon remarked, as we fed a bonfire. 'He's having a picnic with some Protestants downriver, after which whoever wants can get dipped. Look at him — he's all keyed up about it.'

Joaquin looked over and said, for my benefit, 'Hooray.'

'Aren't you Catholic, Joaquin?' I asked.

He responded with a barrel of Spanish which Glendon did his best to reduce. He had been a Catholic but couldn't maintain it. At fifteen he quit confessing because he couldn't look at a pretty girl without wishing to kiss her. Also, he couldn't look at a man without coveting one of his arms. Both these desires were sins, yet Joaquin couldn't stop himself – the moment he exited the confessional, a pretty girl would stroll by, or a man with two arms.

'Now he's past the kissing part, or so he believes,' said Glendon. 'He's getting pain in the joints. He would prefer not to die wearing his sins.'

I looked at Joaquin, who was scratching his smooth innocent stub of an arm while maintaining a stream of syllables.

Glendon said, 'I am going also.'

'To get baptized?'

He nodded.

'I thought you were baptized already. By your friend Crealock, at Hole in the Wall.'

'Well, I was.'

'Isn't once supposed to do the trick?' I was teasing, but curious all the same.

'It is, yes.'

'And you're thinking it didn't take the first time?'

He answered, 'Crealock dipped me under the wrong name. I never was baptized under Hale.'

'If there's a God,' I said, 'don't you guess He knows your true name?'

And Glendon replied, 'If there's a God, then I better offer it up myself. Here, Becket, could you manage to talk and work at the same time, do you think?'

The telegram was waiting for me back at the house where Claudio had roped the Western Union boy into the kitchen for a game of cribbage and a pint of nectar. The boy was fourteen or so, tall and stooped, a red-haired gangle. His brimmed hat rested on the table with the yellow paper sticking out of the hatband.

'Here's your man,' Claudio told him.

'Mr. Becket,' the boy said, handing me the paper.

'Thank you.'

I opened the telegram while the boy made to leave.

'Sit back down, *nieto*,' said Claudio, and, to me, 'Well?'

'It's from my wife,' I said. 'I asked her to come and bring our son Redstart, and she has agreed to do so.'

At this Claudio became sunny and began to stand up – he changed his mind and sat again, but his face retained its light. Meantime I noticed minor electric tremors in my legs and lowered myself to a chair.

The boy said, 'I better go, Mr. Soto.'

Claudio turned to the boy. His tone was vibrantly instructive. 'That you have delivered good news does not release you from courtesy. I am a dying man. You may leave only when the game is over and you have finished your nectar, or else when it is clear that I am winning. Sit down.'

The boy sat. He looked uncertain and concave. No doubt he had had a long day.

9

When Arāndano heard the news she was slightly indignant at my proposal to stay with Susannah and Redstart at the lone hotel in Lury. A friend had stayed there once and suspected dicey margins.

'Your wife will be disappointed,' she said.

The alternative was to stay at the orchard. Besides the bunkhouse, already occupied, there was a disused sawmill built many decades earlier when the property was first cleared. I'd seen the structure at a distance through a reach of dead trees – a story of quarried limestone with a timbered loft.

'The wood part leans, and the rain blows through it,' said Claudio, but when Glendon and I rode out to examine it we found the tin roof sound. The stairs and beams were white oak and solid, though some of the floorboards had rotted and dropped. The river ran a few feet from the limestone and the loft faced what must've once been the handsomest part of the orchard, the very hillside where Glendon and Joaquin and I had done the bulk of our work. Also, you could just glimpse a corner of the remaining healthy grove, the Rarotongans filing round the edge of a rise, though with their pursed leaves and warped trunks they resembled no one's idea of deliverance.

The mill became my mornings. Poised on joists I tore

up what was rotten while Glendon drove the wagon to town for new. The bankrupt Pond gave us four sheets of virgin glass once meant for his own house and we spent a panicked few days fitting headers and sash. Arāndano even provided me with numerous pails of whitewash which I spread across the stickly walls, doing three or four coats in my anxiety.

'What's scratching at you, Becket?' Glendon finally asked. 'Your wife and boy are coming before long. This place is pretty and snug; there's the river just paces away. You ought to be merry, that's what I think.'

'I'm nervous about seeing Susannah,' I admitted.

'Now, what kind of sense does that make?' he inquired. I guess it made none to Glendon, who in the name of atonement had braved an absence of decades. Compared with that, what cause had I to worry?

And yet I did. Recently it often seemed as if Susannah were looking at the moon while I looked somewhere else – say, at a lake. If I saw the moon in the lake I believed we were looking in the same place, but let anything disturb the water and we were two people standing alone. We needed to look at something the same way, as we once had, or as it seemed to me we once had. I didn't know how to do it.

'You will know what to say when you see her,' Arāndano told me, while I fretted on their porch the next evening.

'No, that is not what will happen,' said her husband. 'No, Monte. You will be mute when you see her. Entirely lost for words! Speechless is what you'll be.'

'Contrary man,' said Arāndano.

'I am never contrary. No. Because this silence itself will speak to her on his behalf. Words pile up like a wall, but quiet will win back her heart for him – can you see it, Becket?'

He said this partly to tease his wife and partly because he really was a rhapsodist of the first order. He slapped his hands together. Good thing for him I'd come along, with my romantic burdens!

That was the first night I spent at the mill, on a cedar-framed mattress borne up from the house by King Richard. Despite the serene composition of waxing moon, the Rienda ambling past and leaf gossip on a subtle wind, no sleep arrived, so I rose and went down the cool stairs. The lime-stone breathed like castle walls. Emerging to moon and stars I stood by the river watching a large mink play among the rocks. Redstart had trapped a mink the previous summer, after it pried into our hutch and made an untidy meal of Redstart's docile rabbit – vengefully he laid traps for the predator who replied with glee, stealing bait nightly and defiling the traps, but Redstart polished up his wits and at last the mink misstepped. Redstart found it one morning afroth with pain. He had no choice but to kill it with a whip stick across the bridge of its nose. He cried into his sleeve most of that day, though later he skinned the mink and tanned the hide with gunpowder and salt and wore it like Davy Crockett.

Moving through the maimed grove I glimpsed a light and followed it. Night confounds your compass, or mine at least, so I was surprised to stroll out from the trees and find the light coming from the main house. From a second-floor window – the bedroom, I assumed.

A laugh of pleasure drifted down from the yellow square. Aware of my bad form I got a bit closer. Now came Claudio's voice, portentous and wry, and more of his wife's deep laughter. You never know what drama will spring from lit windows, but iambic pentameter was not what I expected. He was reading English poetry – farcical verses, it turned out, about a clever old manservant who ran the household while his lordship fled from aggressive women. It was funny, though maybe not quite as funny as Arāndano thought it was – I missed the ending, she was giggling so.

There was a pause, a flipping of pages; Claudio resumed reading but in a softer tone. This was neither farce nor English but Spanish and sinuous. It swirled and drove. Here was poetry of different intent. It made me wish I knew the language and also made me realize how humid the night had suddenly become. Warm and lonely I slipped away. When I told Susannah about it later she didn't reproach me for rubbernecking but only replied, 'Those people know how to live.'

10

While awaiting my family's arrival I worked with Glendon and Joaquin. Few trees remained, except those South Seas youngsters — for that matter, none could guess whether their robust health was owed to breeding or their fortunate placement in a fold or frost shadow in the hills. In any case they looked like the future if future there was. We examined their branches for blights and pawls; we pointed the crooked ones straight and tied them up with wrapped cotton. In the grip of these chores Glendon appeared to slide backward in time. His eyes seemed to regain some clarity, or perhaps he just learned his way around. His bucksaw procedure was efficient and tireless; when a bough gave way he stepped lightly aside and was busy on the next before it settled in the grass.

In the afternoons Arāndano slung cold canteens across her horse and rode out to see our progress. Then we'd release King Richard, who never roamed far, and Joaquin would unfold the thick saddle felt he always brought with him and disappear into a bottomless nap, and Arāndano would sit in the grass talking to Glendon and me about the Rarotongans. She was ardent about those trees, and why not? Three hard winters had threatened her assumption that the orchard would outlast her husband.

Several times I tried to leave the two of them alone, but

when I made to disappear Arāndano got up also and I understood that to leave her with Glendon imperiled her need for propriety. Therefore I stayed put and watched my friend grow more and more agitated. One day he could bear it no more and, twisting his hat, divested himself right out in the open.

'I'm sorry, Blue, I got no defense and ought not have left,' he said – with me reclining in the shade not ten feet away! He went on. 'My reasons were shabby, we both know it. You were the only right bearing my life ever had.'

Arāndano was abruptly on her feet. Much as I'd feared transparency I wanted some just then. 'Why have you come now?' she said, with a kind of fierce blush. 'Can I make you innocent again? How am I supposed to answer this?'

Mortified, Glendon replied, 'Why, I don't know – you were always the one who had the language, Blue.'

'You shouldn't call me that. I don't care to hear it,' she replied.

About this time I slipped toward King Richard, who was off some yards away enjoying a little grass. An ox enjoying a little grass is like a large chemist standing beside you grinding minerals with mortar and pestle – I didn't hear much, is what I'm saying. It would seem they talked guard-edly of their courtship and marriage; it is strange to hear the word 'devoted' spoken in bitterness. In a bizarre moment I saw Joaquin crawl out from his own shady siesta on two knees and a hand, fleeing his front-seat perspective.

'You could've come back later, to stay or take me with you. Why *didn't* you come back?' Arāndano said.

There was a long silence while King Richard consid-ered the anemic grass before him. When at last he dropped his head for a mouthful I dented his flank with a sharp stick.

Glendon replied, 'I was scared to death of prison, you see.'

She had no reply to that; his simple admission didn't gain him mercy but did reduce the temperature a little. Finally she said, 'Of course you were afraid,' her voice yielding a yard or two of the high ground.

'Claudio was better for you, anyway. Now you know that's true.'

'That is not in dispute. I am only trying to discover why you never returned.'

'Why, Blue – a bandit's of no value. I shot a fellow on a train. I couldn't come back – to you or to anybody I loved.'

Absorbed, I forgot about the ox. He picked up another mouthful and started again with the mortar and pestle. Of Arāndano's lengthy rejoinder I heard only the color, which was one of rebuff. Glendon said, 'I will be on my way tomorrow. I only came to apologize.'

'You've done so.'

'I thank you for hearing me out.'

She turned from him and found the empty canteens and looped them up on her saddle. As she mounted the horse Glendon walked over and untied its lead rope from a limb and coiled it and handed it up to her.

Grudgingly she said, 'You shouldn't go yet.'

'How come?'

'Because of Claudio. He isn't strong enough to do this work.' She shrugged. 'Besides, he enjoys your company.'

11

In fact, Arāndano's current and former husbands got along so easily I believe it was rough on Arāndano. Yet soon enough Glendon appeared to sense he was in the way. He and Claudio might laugh and revise their histories over cribbage if she were away in the evening, repairing the books of a builder or blacksmith; but once she rode in, Glendon would get up to check on the horses, to make sure a burn pile hadn't flared up, to work on this or that project. 'I got a little project,' he'd say, in believable fashion, and it turned out to be true.

Two nights before Susannah and Redstart were due, I entered the bunkhouse to find Glendon with a twig of charcoal, drafting up a boat on a sheet of newsprint.

'Hello, Monte, see what you think.' He'd found six or eight oil lamps and scoured their chimneys so the light was adequate. 'It's the first I ever drew. Do you like it?'

As a drawing it probably wasn't great, but as a foretaste of beauty it was at least persuasive. The boat was a stretched version of the Dobie Swift. He'd marked the length at twenty-two feet, the beam at seven. There was a short raked mast set well back with a gaffed mainsail and an unfussy jib, a low square coachroof, and round portholes with the word BRASS penciled below.

'See the tidy cabin? A fellow could just about live on it,'

he said. Nodding toward the window he said, 'Here's the best bit, Monte. That old tack shed's all but empty, except for a box of chisels and a block plane as thick as my elbow. And it ain't twenty yards from the water.'

'Have you talked with Claudio about this?'

'It was his idea. I been to the sawmill in Lury – the manager's an astute horseman, he'll take Sparrow in trade for plank oak and cedar. What do you think of this sheer-line?'

When I left the bunkhouse Claudio saw me and hailed me to the porch for a glass of cold water and lime. I'd barely sat down when his wife stepped out. She was in skirmish mode. 'You invited him to stay and build a boat? Why not a house? I hear he is going to the baptism Saturday, maybe he could stay and build a church!'

Claudio laughed. 'My dove, he has worked like a bond servant. You know it's true. To offer him no return is poor treatment.'

She answered this with a brisk good night and pushed into the house with such ferocity I remembered Glendon's vision of her armed and horseback. Her husband was unperturbed, however – he felt better that night, his stomach was sound, he'd enjoyed a beefsteak for supper. He invited me to a hand of gin rummy that he won in five turns, then another that he won in eleven. He told me he liked having more people on the orchard – he'd once planned to enlarge the house to include Arāndano's shrinking parents, but things turned a different way. His appetite vanished. His stomach retreated and reshaped itself as a knob of pain. His in-laws prayed for him diligently but moved in with Arāndano's sister.

Now Arāndano said, through an open window, 'How long does it take to make a boat? A long time, I remember. Monte, how long will it go on?'

It took me a moment to locate her, looking fretful and alone in the blowsy curtains of the window.

'Well, he's only got evenings,' I replied. 'I suppose it will take him two or three months.'

'Months!' cried Arāndano.

'To build a whole boat – that's not so bad,' said her husband.

12

We later learned the clergyman who'd planned to baptize converts was hosting a houseful of in-laws so contentious he received for his goodness a case of the hives, and that is why he didn't show up. For most people his absence was no heartache – it was a lovely morning on the Rienda. The place was near a ford where the water thinned and riffled and zippy little trout gathered in the pools. Some dozens of orchard people and ranchers were on hand, with a few autos and many picnic baskets containing marmalade and brown bread and the occasional well-found ham. Everyone was in a fine mood except for the few folks who had actually showed up to get baptized; these had come in broad-cloth trousers or other clothes designed to withstand a wetting and now felt disappointed and self-conscious.

Glendon for his part was as miffed as I ever saw him. Peevishness was a new slant on my friend – I wasn't sure what to make of it. He was as set on getting himself rebaptized as he'd been on finding Blue.

'Well, where do you suppose he went?' Glendon said. We too had brought along a picnic – some bread wrapped in cloth and a small bag of old oranges, bottles of ginger beer and a wedge of crumbly cheese.

'Look at Joaquin there,' he said, in a dark tone. Joaquin had ridden his squat gelding to the event, humming redemption songs; now he was across the clearing keeping company with a surprisingly appealing woman who thought everything he said was droll. 'Look at him laughing – he don't care if he gets baptized or not,' said Glendon.

'Maybe he's reconsidered the question of kissing,' I said. It didn't really land, but I thought it was funny.

'No doubt that preacher's on his way. He's late, is all.'

'That's probably it.'

'He's sent no word to tell us otherwise,' said Glendon.

'True enough.'

'We'll just wait awhile, then.'

So we waited. A little tribe of kids had driven a big pike up into the shallows. It was a striking fish with its leopard spots and thrashed menacingly in the gravel; once those kids glimpsed its sawtooth maw they backed away, and the pike finned off to the deeps without further discord. After a while Joaquin disappeared with his comely friend, and a boy spun a kite into a tree, and people devoured their picnics, though I did catch sight of one basket half sunk and tilting adrift down the river – you could see a heel of bread poking out. Eventually a genial man showed up begging to play his accordion. He was fresh from a few glasses of applejack but strapped the thing on with comprehensive decorum and performed with the pared dignity of a man who has lost everything else – which he had, for Glendon told me this was the bankrupt Mr. Pond. He played dance tunes and hymns until we all got sleepy, and soon people started filtering away.

'Hang that preacher!' said Glendon. I didn't understand his exasperation – his eyes were damp, even.

Finally, we were the only two people left on the riverbank. We'd spent the whole day there. The sun declined, the air cooled, and there was Glendon still in his dunking clothes.

'Well,' said I, getting up, at which he seized my wrist.

'You do it,' he said.

'Do what?' I inquired, though I knew very well – I knew before he even asked, as certainly as the boy knows he is about to be asked to answer the arithmetic that has always puzzled him.

'You baptize me,' he said.

'No. Don't ask it of me, Glendon.'

'I asked already. I'm asking again.' His eyes were alight. His fingers worked in edgy high spirits – he had looked exactly this way when talking of fast horses or the elephant at the Hundred and One.

'Please, no. The Almighty's a mystery to me. I daydream in church, when I even go. Doubt is my usual condition! I'm not qualified for this.'

'I guess you aren't, but do you see anyone else?'

He was resolute, not to say mulish. A new fear entered me. 'Glendon, what if it's wrong for me to do it? Suppose I imperil something?'

'Imperil what?'

I didn't want to say it but there he stood with perked ears.

'My immortal soul,' I rather hissed.

'Why, Becket,' he said, with a warm familiarity I found irksome.

'I'm serious. What if He's got a rule about this? What if He hates impostors?'

He looked bemused. 'If you're afraid, then I think you're no impostor.'

So rarely had I quarreled with Glendon that his ease in whipping me was a surprise. In any case, evening was upon us and it was getting cool. There seemed to be nothing for it.

I said, 'How did Crealock go about this?'

He didn't remember many details. There'd been no audience that day, either: Crealock wasted few words but recommended Glen Dobie to Glory in the name of the Father and the Son and the Holy Ghost.

I said, 'I still maintain it held the first time.'

'I didn't see it then. I got to give my right name.'

We waded out to the center of the Rienda. You wouldn't think the river would be so cold – southern California, for goodness' sake! There had been a hatch of large winged insects and the surface was beset with their drifting skins. Midstream I started to say something to Glendon about the cold or the hatch but he already had his eyes closed.

I said, 'Lord, excuse me, I am Monte Becket and here is Glendon Hale.' I don't remember what other words I used. They were not much to listen to I am sure. Glendon stood shut-eyed and now thought to remove his hat and hold it on his chest. The river ran around us. It was an absurd situation for an ambivalent fellow like myself – numb to the eyeballs, dispensing a grace I couldn't even describe. Then something moved in the water. Something large slid past my leg! Panicked to get out I said, 'Father, Son and Holy Ghost' and laid Glendon down in the river.

Coming up he blinked and swept his eyes clear. He nodded to me but was silent. The water moved past, the last sunlight showing its skin of dust and insects. It seemed a long wade back to shore with our slow footing, our arms lifting the wings of our drooping sleeves.

Then: 'Thank you, Becket,' he said.

When he offered nothing else I inquired, 'Well?'

'Well what?'

After all this I wanted an answer. 'Are you changed, from before?'

He smiled and for some reason I remembered him from that first morning when he came for breakfast. How he had charmed us all! 'Yes,' he replied, the agile old sprite. 'For one thing, I am quite a bit colder.'

And that was almost all I could get from him – a smile, a joke – though riding back to the orchard he kept a hand on the pommel of his saddle and seemed to ride like a younger man does, or an old man who remembers his youth.

13

The train was early, but I was earlier still.

Glendon came too and brought the wagon but refused to wait with me at the station, for which I was grateful. Instead he went to see about groceries and brandy for Claudio and copper rivets for himself. Letting me off at the depot he nodded at a distant jet of steam just climbing over treetops farther up the valley.

'Lucky man,' he said, and touched the horses, and moved away.

Redstart was first off the coach – moments after the screel and hiss, a door lurched and out he spilled as if he'd been leaning there for a hundred miles. The pug Bert was in his arms and the two of them fell down flailing on the platform. I ran up and collared Redstart to his feet and he was more of himself than ever, laughing and throwing punches at my hands. It takes time to settle a boy like that but time I did not have, for Susannah was being handed down by an appreciative old conductor.

'Thank you,' she told him, turning to me. She looked curious and tired and slightly undone. She had a shallow closed folio in one hand which I knew would contain paper and pencils and the drawings she had made on the trip.

As on the last time I saw her she was hatless – and as I reached for her she began to laugh.

'What is it?' I said, because she wasn't laughing from discomfort or the relief reunion can sometimes bring – these were surprised and spirited laughs. I said, 'Love, what is it?'

I tell you, she couldn't even answer. A porter appeared with her luggage and she sat down on a steamer chest and rocked. It was not what I'd hoped for. I'm not sure what I would've done had Redstart not cleared it up.

'It's your clothes, Papa,' he said.

Claudio, swept up, had offered me a well-kept suit from his own closet. It fit nicely with its cuffs and tails, so I suppose I looked the part of a California citrus baron circa 1880. Again I'd cast my lot with sentiment, and again I was its monkey. Then I forgot my chagrin, or most of it, for Susannah stood and kissed me and asked was everything all right.

I said, 'Besides the clothes, what do you see?'

'The man I have missed for a very long while,' she said, still smiling.

'I have not written anything except those few letters to you.'

'It doesn't matter. It doesn't.'

'That author business is all finished, you know. I am very much less than I once believed.'

She replied, 'Monte, what did you think I wanted?'

I still wasn't sure about that but said, 'I am no one's self-made man.'

'No,' she agreed, then her hands tightened on my arms and her eyes adjusted suddenly as though the light had changed. She said, 'Monte, what work have you been doing here?'

'Cutting trees and lighting fires. We are building a boat. I baptized Glendon in a river of water.'

She put a hand to her mouth. Her eyes were wide and bright.

'I'm glad you're here,' I said.

She nodded, touched her forehead to my shoulder. Put her hands against my chest.

That was what I hoped for.

14

It was dark when we reached the orchard, but the house was lit like a cake. Every window on the upper story showed lamplight – I thought Claudio in a fever of hospitality had planned some grandiose reception.

But things were not that way.

'Oh, now – that's the doctor's auto,' said Glendon, as the horses drifted up into the yard. He handed the reins to Redstart, who had ridden beside him, and went up the steps at a run.

It transpired we'd no sooner left for the train station than Claudio began to gasp and tremble. His stomach was climbing around inside him – that's what he told his wife, who fetched brandy and sent Joaquin racing up-valley for the doctor. His name was Fellows and he was the same doctor who had denied Claudio's earlier complaints. It would be pleasant to say this Fellows arrived with renewed humility but he was surly and pompous. Redstart later asked had I noticed the doctor's hands. Sure enough I had: weirdly small, soft, ductile hands with fingers tapering to witchy points. The only decency I saw in Fellows was his willingness to treat Claudio with morphine, which eased his twistings and set him breathing normally again.

When I accompanied the doctor to his car it was late, the wind bullying treetops, the moon at three-quarter. He looked about and touched my arm with those spooky fingers.

'A month at most,' he said.

It was only when Fellows had driven away that I noticed Redstart. He'd left his mother up at the house and had been standing close all along, in a clutch of black aspens. He came alongside now and walked with me. Against the cool moonlight his shadow was nearly as long as mine.

It was closer to two months – eight arduous weeks – yet at times Claudio's pain dwindled and he had access to his full mind and would talk about art or oranges or history or baseball with anyone available. His shortening span made him decisive. He decided instantly to love Susannah like a daughter and invited her to set up her easel in the parlor where he resided in his blankets. She sometimes painted whole evenings while Arándano read aloud. Of course there was no telling how long his intervals of sturdiness would last, but Arándano believed they stretched longest with Susannah humming and daubing at her canvas.

At first she made the paintings you would expect – the orchard at sunset, cattle in the distance, sometimes an invented sheep placed for effect where the sun could touch its glossy feet – but as weeks passed she began to paint other subjects, such as Claudio himself. She painted his face in variegated planes – in blues and shadowy grays, as of a man dying – but these somber tones were tempered by the lively reds and golds that described Claudio's essential jubilance as clearly as a poem. Though she had never painted portraits before, she embarked on them as though called. Her easel followed everywhere. She painted Joaquin who couldn't

335

rest long but would get up and march around then come back and sit with his good arm crossed over his chest; she painted Pond when he came with his accordion.

Redstart she couldn't paint in the usual manner but had to do so in quick dashes as he raced by. In less than two days he had found the burrow of a young raccoon and enticed the tricky beast into friendship with sugar lumps provided by Claudio. Boy and raccoon resided together in the peace enjoyed by creatures who recognize the same delights, in this case sweetmeats and an urge to move nocturnally over the countryside. For a short time there was little separation between Redstart and this small mammal, whom he named Lupin after the caped thief of French society; if Susannah were to paint the boy she must paint the raccoon also and thus discovered her skill with animals. She painted Glendon aboard one of Claudio's bright geldings, name of Wardlaw, who had the habit of curving his neck like a Roman horse and prancing sideways as if to make the person riding him look noble and skilled. He didn't seem like a gelding, Wardlaw, for he had an eye always on the mares – Claudio admitted he had lacked the heart to geld the youngster at the proper age and had let him turn five before letting one-armed Joaquin do the trick with his soft words and his clever knife. Thereafter Wardlaw was somewhat more ridable yet retained the arched neck and thought habits of stallions. He was a beautiful creature; Susannah even painted his portrait riderless in tones of burgundy and purple, which played up his undaunted character. Arāndano laughed, declaring the picture actually frightened her, but Claudio prized it so highly he asked Redstart to pound a nail and hang it on the wall of their bedroom.

One night when we were walking next to the river, a warm night, Redstart far downstream fishing or dam building, Susannah said, 'Do you think we ought to go back home?'

I was considering ways to evade her question when a lantern emerged from the house. Arāndano carried it. She walked steadily toward us over the dewy grass. When she neared, her eyes shone in the lantern light, her stricken eyes. She came and stood with us and put the lantern down in the grass and laid her head on Susannah's shoulder to weep. Looking at the house I saw Glendon come out and sit on the porch steps. His head was in his hands, and sometimes he looked about aimlessly, as though he were lost out on the prairie after a bad dream, or as though casting about for some work that he might do.

15

There was little ceremony at the funeral. Joaquin was upset about it, telling Glendon at length about the worthy funerals he'd attended in Guerrero, with solemn corteges and black ribbon and guitars played with such grief the fingers bled. It frustrated Joaquin that Claudio had forbade this business for himself. In fact, Claudio had promised to return as a shade and haunt Joaquin if he tried to organize any drama whatever.

'A shade?'

'He said he'd come back and wake Joaquin in the night,' Glendon explained. 'He said he'd wait for the darkest night, when Joaquin was already nervous, then drift up and breathe on his ears.'

So it was an unadorned service at the mission church in Lury. I suppose there were sixty people in that sanctuary of cool adobe and lit beeswax. By far, most were native Californians who knew Claudio as a citrus grower, but some of his relations had also arrived: a nephew and his wife from the horse country of Morelos, twin cousins famed once for their beauty and now for determined spinsterhood, a sister who kept to the side of the room in her black skirts and stood up the whole time, a hand on the wall.

Later the relatives gathered back at the orchard. Susannah

and I stayed out of the way. Someone brought bread and someone else chocolate, also a jar of viscous mescal Arāndano was unhappy to see. Pond showed up with his instrument and offered to play, but Joaquin put a finger on his chest and informed him music would displease Claudio's shade.

Drifting back to the mill house, Susannah said, 'Glendon's different now, isn't he.'

'He quit that whiskey,' I replied.

'Not just that. There's grace in him. He's reached some settlement.'

We didn't feel like going in. A westerly breeze had picked up and was laying a pink wash over the valley. It smelled like rain or the sea.

'You are also different,' she said.

I didn't try to explain that. You can't explain grace, anyway, especially when it arrives almost despite yourself. I didn't even ask for it, yet somehow it breached and began to work. I suppose grace was pouring over Glendon, who had sought it so hard, and some spilled down on me.

Susannah said, 'You seemed afraid before you left. Now you don't – that's what I think.'

Up in the yard we could hear Pond's accordion wheeze and blow – he had won out, it seemed. It sounded like a distant carnival. I said, 'Do you know who's going to be afraid tonight? Joaquin.'

This is what Arāndano wanted: to give the orchard one final opportunity to rebound from its hard winters. To see whether the young citrus trees that had voyaged so far would resist the cold and the blights and the various insects and bear a crop. Toward this end Glendon and Joaquin and I used up the end of summer, the smoky days and nights of cooling earth.

When it came time for school Redstart went each day to Lury while Susannah took work painting signs and I set about finishing the boat with Glendon. He had scratched out the envisioned keel and replaced it with leeboards, the better to navigate shallows. He had an idea it would be speedy under sail and pretty enough to build a business on. One night, thinking aloud, I said it could be prettier.

'Prettier, Becket? How?'

He'd developed a little pride about this new girl – he felt she would dance in any breeze at all.

I said, 'What if we built in a bowsprit and made room for an extra headsail?'

'A staysail and a jib,' he mused.

'One for beauty and one for speed. Let's make her a cutter.'

'A cutter,' he said. 'My goodness.' He stepped back and looked at the hull, at its lines and hefty scantlings. 'Yes, all right, Becket. A cutter it will be.' He grasped my hand and we grinned as partners do, but then a boat always takes longer than you think it will.

December arrived as a cloudy mist aspiring to rain – hardly difficult conditions for people accustomed to biting snows – yet the season brought down a hush that was not unwelcome. Evenings we lit a fire in the grate and read the tales of Chekhov and O. Henry and occasionally verse by Amado Nervo, which Arāndano would translate as she read. When these turned melancholy we put them away and looked at pictures in the stereopticon. Claudio had collected several hundred of these images, their edges so crisp they were nearly in motion – sinking battleships, the Great Pyramids, famous racehorses with their puny saddles on. We mulled over the photographs, and we grieved for Claudio. Christmas came, and for all our stuffing and fowl it was a beleaguered holiday. Late that afternoon we went walking round the orchard – it looked pockmarked and infertile and even the islanders seemed trancelike and forgetful in their little frost pocket.

Mostly what we did that winter was work on the boat. Among Glendon's board feet was a small cypress beam which we tapered into a sprit with a carved tip and iron bobstay. Claudio would have loved how that boat turned out; surely Arāndano loved it, for she ventured down evenings along with Susannah and ran her hands over its curved ribs. Sometimes she'd ask Glendon about joinery or design and he would answer her straightforwardly, in short complete sentences. Sometimes she smiled; if she did, Susannah and I might drift back to the mill house.

'She's being good to him,' I might say.

'What do you hope for?' she might reply.

'Well, I hope for his happiness. And hers.'

'Poltroon.' Susannah could not endure the safe answer.

'What do you hope then, if you're so brave?'

'All right: I hope she forgives him entirely, and mourns Claudio for as long as is right, and then I hope she falls for Glendon in a way that is just barely dignified and marries him, and that they live here on the orchard in perpetuity,' she might declare, and I would laugh, saying, 'Yes, that's it!'

So we indulged ourselves in romance; we wrote scenarios in which Glendon and Arāndano's eyes met, and she forgave him at last his flight from the *federales,* his nonreturn, his years of thievery and shift. It was much to forgive, but we talked ourselves into believing it would happen – indeed, into expecting it. Why shouldn't it happen? Weren't we living in a valley of orchards? In a house like a castle keep?

But Arāndano was not to be rushed. In fact, the two of them didn't talk much. Their conversations filtered down to formalized questions, to occasional citations of memories common to them both, or, more often, memories from their unconnected decades.

One night Glendon and I were at the nitpicky work of installing deckboards when he straightened and said, 'I don't know what else to do.'

'Do?'

'To make it up to Blue.'

I said, 'Haven't you done it already? You apologized. You worked here in the orchard as though it were your own. You stood by for Claudio while he was dying.'

'It ain't enough, Becket.'

'Maybe it just takes more time.'

He walked to the door of the shed and looked around and came back in. 'Monte, what is it you think I am trying for?'

The question made me nervous. I felt found out, I suppose.

'Go on,' he said.

'Why, I guess it's the thing you didn't dare hope for previously. The thing honor prevented while Claudio was alive.'

He smiled. 'You mean I should win Blue back again. No. That is the very thing I must *not* do.'

I had nothing to say.

'Do you think because Charles Siringo is dead or dying someplace, I am no longer a wanted property?'

'But no one else is looking for you.'

He smiled. 'Even if you're right, does it remove my debt?'

'But wait, Glendon – you love Blue,' I said. 'That is partial payment at least, I would think.'

'It's as you say. But if she loves me back, it deepens what I owe. There ain't no parity in that arrangement. That's what I did not see coming.'

I still didn't understand. He said, again, 'I don't know what to do next.'

So we worked on the deck of the boat, on its handsome coach-roof, but from then I understood that Arāndano's reticence was only partly her own. Partly it came from Glendon's refusal to allow her to come near.

17

Croplanders learn early to distrust good omens: A perfect planting invites epic drought; a burgeoning wheat field is a summons for hail. Arāndano had been examining the trees daily, awaiting nascent blossoms; when the first buds showed color in early January it put her in a precarious mood. A wet cloud descended and stayed most of a week and Arāndano became nearly hostile – mention the trees to her and she would look away, sometimes walk away while you spoke. When the cloud burned off we saw the buds emerging by such heavy thousands the limbs appeared to bend presciently. I wondered whether the brightening petals might actually drive Arāndano to violence, but instead she became precise and supervisory. Redstart and I set to cutting forked posts for later use supporting laden branches. Glendon and Joaquin took the wagon down-valley to rent honeybees and came back with a load of box hives, which they left covered until after dark and then stacked in the orchard. It was the bees that brought Arāndano around – you can't walk through a humming orchard with sun dripping off the glossy leaves and not admit that something fine might be about to happen.

It happened slowly, the fruits gaining until they lay clumped along the boughs like tiny limes. As we filled the days until harvest, I unrolled Glendon's boat sketches and made some adjustments that seemed appealing; Susannah completed her first California commission, of a priest's Great Dane that would obey at least twenty commands including *Sit still;* and Redstart got sent home from school when his own latest pet, a coyote, entered the building and bit an administrator through the meat of his hand.

Then in late spring a man drove up and didn't come to the door but walked out into the trees and began to grip the oranges. He put his nose to them and pressed with his plump fingers. He had a square-shouldered jacket on, a city hat, boots that looked much used and out of place with the rest of him. When Arāndano went out and confronted him he made a small accented bow, disarmed her fully, and asked after the character of the fruit. He was a wholesaler, not one she had met before. The oranges with their patina like verdigris beguiled him. 'They might be a risk. There are prettier citrus,' he said. 'They're sweet, though, am I correct? Island trees, I believe. They'll be sweet all right.'

Arāndano told him to come back in a few weeks and taste them himself. He wanted her to sign a contract but she said, 'No. Come back.' So he drove away, looking over his shoulder.

Later that day Susannah brought her easel outside. She meant to walk down and have a go at the oranges, but she was diverted. We had the boat finished right down to its paint: cream decks, blue topsides and the bowsprit aglitter with varnish. It sat on its launch boards one shove from freedom with the cold river running behind it. Also that day the gelding Wardlaw was tethered close by – he was a curious animal who liked the smell of wood shavings and oiled tools and would come snuffing right into the shop if we didn't prevent him.

Struck by something, Susannah set her easel down and laughed aloud. She prepared a vivid palette and began to paint a whimsical picture of our proud cutter. In the picture Arāndano is at the tiller wearing a green dress, and the speckled roan Wardlaw is on the boat too, his head peering out the companionway. Of course he would never have fit on the boat, but there was a curious appeal in the picture. It looked completely right and cheerful – Wardlaw's great Roman neck arching up from below, the cutter with exaggerated almost storybook sheerlines reaching along under full sail below a cerulean sky; and above, as in myth or song, a sun that was no ball of flame but a perfect round orange with a coppery skin. When Arāndano saw that picture she at once began to exclaim with pleasure and took Susannah to herself as though they were blood sisters; when Glendon saw it he could only laugh; but when Redstart saw it he said, 'That would be a good label for the new oranges.'

Susannah began at once to refine her painting, to produce in fact a number of versions from which Arāndano might pick the best for a lithographer's run. In this excitement and as the oranges swelled, we saw Arāndano continue to soften toward Glendon, so that it became common to see them talking in evident comfort. An observer stepping in without background might have said, Here are two handsome people entering a courtship. But that observer wouldn't have heard the sparring that went on, the tacit sparring of two people keeping themselves at a distance.

It seems to me now that if we did not witness the rebirth

of a union, a clasping of souls after thirty years' absence, we were at least privileged to behold a slow mutual rescue – slow in that Arāndano's forgiving of Glendon Hale took some months and might never have happened if Charles Siringo, ancient and infirm, had not come into our lives one final time.

18

On the day in question a Wells Fargo truck rolled up to the house and deposited a crate of prints from a lithographer in Los Angeles. They were reproductions of Susannah's painting of Arāndano at the helm of our delicate cutter, with Wardlaw's noble head looking out curiously from the companionway. We had awaited these prints like a boy waits for snow. The size of book jackets, they were orange, green, azure. They were labels for the new brand of oranges, which Arāndano had named Claudios. When she pried open the crate and cut the twine and lifted out the little bale we all whooped, and Redstart carried in ginger beer, and we sliced down some cheese and summer sausage and raised a toast to the tough little islanders, which at that moment were bearing a promising load of the oranges to be so labeled. It was a moment that had been unimaginable only months earlier, and it surprised us all; up to our chests in victory, I looked over at Susannah, whose face was rapt in lament. Arāndano clung to her, and Glendon clinked his ginger beer to Redstart's and said the name of the man we loved. So we ate and drank and mourned. I never enjoyed a party more, or so bitterly missed its absent host.

Then Redstart went to the window and announced that an old man was sitting in a car at the end of the yard.

When I looked at Glendon he was already looking at me.

'Let me talk to him,' I said.

I peered out the window. There sat Siringo behind the wheel of a black Chalmers automobile.

'I'll go out to him,' said Glendon.

'Who is he?' cried Susannah.

'Siringo,' Redstart replied, who had gleaned my adventure to the last bronze nail and now owned it as though he had been there himself.

'Don't, Glendon,' said Arāndano.

Recalling with what little ceremony the old Pinkerton had shot Hood Roberts I went out, not waiting for Glendon. As the door shut I heard Arāndano telling him to go out the back, to take the cutter.

The Rienda of course goes all the way to the ocean. I was thinking that myself, and of the boat, on which a man could neatly live.

Siringo saw me coming but didn't get out of the car. He was holding a long-barreled revolver. The barrel was resting on the car door.

'Hello, Siringo. I'm a little surprised to see you up and about.'

'Pursuit,' said he, by way of reply.

'Glendon isn't here.'

'Oh, he's here.'

'He *was* here.'

At this Charles Siringo looked mildly downhearted. How frail he was! His left eye was sleeping and his skin looked as if it might not bleed if pierced.

I began to think it was possible, then, that he was capable of giving up.

'How do you feel?' I couldn't not ask it, he looked so low. Under everything else, he was an old man.

'I've been better.'

Something kind, I am sure of it, dwelt behind his eyes. I'd have even tried his grasp now, if he had only put down the revolver and offered me his hand.

'Is that your woman?' said he, for Susannah had come out on the porch in her blue dress.

'Yes.'

'Lord Almighty,' said Siringo. 'Well, you don't deserve any such thing.'

He reached down, set the gun on the seat beside him. He was short of breath. He swung around and looked behind him and put his hand on the shifter.

At this point Glendon stepped out of the house. He had his hat on, a vest. He had a little duffel and came down off the porch in our direction.

Siringo picked up the revolver again. He looked at me with his old snap, admiring me, I think, for lying.

Glendon said, 'Charlie.'

'Glen Dobie,' said Siringo, and this is the oddest part of it: yes there was triumph in his face, yes the thrill of success at long last and all the rest of it. But there was also a longing there, as though he'd missed Glendon, as though he were meeting an old comrade – which, of course, he was.

Siringo said, 'It has taken me longer than usual.'

'But here I am,' replied my friend.

'Let's go, then,' said Siringo.

Glendon nodded. He shook my hand and tossed his duffel into the back of the car. He said, 'Goodbye, Monte.'

I had no hold on this. I looked round and saw the thin-shouldered form of Arāndano at the window, Susannah on the porch holding tight to Redstart.

'Goodbye,' I said.

He nodded again and in his open face and the grip of his hand, flexible and strong as my own, I saw again the remarkable difference in the two men – the one archaic and closing fast, the other seeming to get younger.

Glendon walked round to the passenger door while Siringo kept the revolver trained on him. The hammer was cocked. When Glendon opened the door Siringo actually dropped the gun. It landed on the floor of the automobile – somehow, it didn't go off. Siringo dug for it but he couldn't bend very well. A string of saliva came off his lip as he felt around for the gun.

Glendon got in the car, leaned down and retrieved the gun, uncocked it, and handed it back to Siringo.

Siringo said, 'You are not winning.'

'No. You win, Charlie.'

Siringo put the car in reverse. He said again, 'You are not winning.'

They drove out of the yard and up the road.

19

What am I to say here? I don't know that I ever saw a stranger event than Glendon's surrender to Charles Siringo, for at the same time that he lost everything — the very direction of his own steps — he won the thing he'd held so precious he wouldn't approach it in words.

He won Blue.

She didn't say so, even to Susannah; she gave no outward clue, except that she wrote to the Governor and to the California Board of Corrections; she packed up and spent time in Sacramento to lobby clemency for this man who had deserted her in order to go rob trains and shoot a politician in the face. It didn't make her popular, and if you read the newspapers of the day they are filled with the usual righteousness of the press: TREACHEROUS FELON CAUGHT AT LAST! As for Siringo, he was once again the man of the hour, though it's telling that in none of the articles does a current photograph appear. There is instead an old picture, the same one you may see today inside the covers of his books, a handsome devil with a mustache and in his eyes the ways of acquisition. JUSTICE TRIUMPHS, cried the newspapers, for there is no statute of limitations on murder, and murder is what Glendon confessed to; representing himself, he would plead nothing less than guilty and was handed eighteen years in the Los Angeles pentitentiary.

From time to time, he wrote us letters.

Here is part of one from that first year. I won't repro-
duce it all. I know the pains it took him.

Dear Blue & Monte & Susannah
Thank you for writing it is all fine here. They have
given me my 1st spectacles which are a true surprise,
also a fellow here provided me a book it is Don
Quixote should keep me busy til I get out. No
complaints. Hello Joaquin, how is that Maria? Red you
forgive that principle for it was his hand & not your
own.

I went back to Minnesota at last that spring and sold
the Cannon farmstead. The buyers showed up on a Saturday.
They were a young couple locally famed for having produced
triplets several years earlier – now those endearing babes
were inquisitive rascals bent on conquest, their parents
tattered refugees clawing at the door.

'Come in,' I said. The truth is I was glad to have so many
lives flood into that house at once, for I had spent two
whole days in rooms never meant for silence.

We didn't bicker but agreed almost at once on a price.
They were glad to get the furniture and especially glad to
have a barn – I think they envisioned the horde out there
at play, and a glimmer of privacy for themselves.

In one thing only were they disappointed. One of the
rascals came pounding up to where we stood, discussing
wells or windows. He was slick with snowmelt and mud
to his kneecaps. He poked my leg until I squatted down
and then said, "Ant the horse.'

'Sorry, amigo,' I had to say. 'Chief is going with me.'

It took me two weeks to finish it off – to sell what would sell, arrange train passage for Chief, and pack the rest. On the day I said goodbye to the lovely Cannon the weather was cold and the river ran below its sheath of ice, sometimes breaking through in patches to show its deep green self. I left the keys on the porch table, where I had made and abandoned so many words.

20

The trip back west was memorable for two reasons. First, I arranged to stop in Revival, hoping to find someone who could tell me more of Hood Roberts – who he was, where he came from. The car dealer, Lewis, had not heard of Hood's death and didn't seem overly affected by the news.

'Who killed the boy?' he asked.

The distant way he said *the boy* made me wonder whether Lewis even remembered Hood, or whether he was thinking of someone else.

'An old detective, Charles Siringo.'

Lewis hadn't heard of Siringo either. He seemed a little impatient with me for stopping. But then he must've remembered who Hood was, because all at once he remarked that he never knew Hood's family, that Hood just walked in off the plains one day with a grin on his mouth and a wrench in his hand. He asked Lewis for nothing except a job; he slept, Lewis said, in an empty cooper shack at the edge of town.

'Was Hood Roberts his real name?' I asked, for this had been picking at me. Lewis smiled at this strange question. 'His one and only, so far as I know.'

No one was living in the shack when I found it – there was nothing inside but a few corrupt hogsheads and dusty brown bottles and a dime novel entitled *Tom Knight and the Banditti of the Grasslands.* I picked it up. It contained the adventures of a rambling cowpoke who always got more than he had coming. I put it in my pocket, being careful, of course – those cheap little booklets seemed calculated to disintegrate.

The other prominent incident on that return journey was marked by a column of smoke, sighted as we rolled through New Mexico. People were exclaiming, crowding to the left side of the train. There was a lot of sweaty speculation about what was burning, though I had a queasy feeling about it. I'd seen such an oily cloud before. When we stopped at the station in Harkin, sure enough, word was Pancho Villa had swept across the border with an army of one thousand Mexicans and burnt half the town of Columbus to ashes. To this day there is speculation as to why he did it. It's hard to say. But if I were engaged in writing history, I would set aside for a day the darling motives of appetite and politics; I would search out and knock upon the front door of Art Ravel, erstwhile arms proprietor, who once shipped five thousand fraudulent bullets to General Pancho Villa. There might be no answer, for I've heard Art is shy about visitors, but it couldn't hurt to go knock.

I did build a second boat, you may wish to know, and a third, and several more after that. I'm glad to report people seem to enjoy these Dobie Swift Cutters, and I am usually behind in production. While dreading overconfidence I can say they are decently wrought craft, with solid joints and kindly motion, and I mean to go on making them; they seem quite alive to me, and if I can become a bit faster there might be a living in it. But there's this, too: After a while, a long while, without writing a word, why, a sentence arrived from nowhere. Not a great sentence – actually sort of a ragged one, in need of paring. I searched around for a pencil and wrote it down, a sentence about a white-haired man rowing upstream through the parting mists of the Cannon River.

'What are you writing?' asked Susannah. She was painting something, I couldn't see what.

'Just a sentence.'

She lifted her head, a daub of orange below her lip. 'Read it to me,' she said.

ACKNOWLEDGMENTS

I am surrounded by friends, kept safe by generous people. So it has been for as long as I can remember. Maybe being the youngest of four acclimated me early to a pattern of kindness: whatever the reasons, a surprising number of people have given me the benefit of the doubt.

Therefore let me thank Elisabeth Schmitz, who saw instantly to the soul of this story, and whose questions, confidence, and wit helped me do the same; and Morgan Entrekin, who welcomed an outlaw tale and saved a spot for me in the lineup. Thanks also to Paul Cirone and Molly Friedrich, whose counsel is reliably clear-eyed and practical.

Mom and Dad used to put me to bed accompanied by an album called *Songs of the West,* a loving thing to do. There is no sweeter sorrow than 'The Cowboy's Lament.' Moreover, Dad's friend Hood Roberts allowed me to borrow his name; I wish he was here to judge the result.

Ty and John spent hundreds hours in my writing loft, talking, listening, making me laugh – without their vigorous distraction, I might never have finished.

Finally, thanks to Robin, for hearing my pages with persistent grace. Sometimes heroism is nothing more than patience, curiosity, and a refusal to panic.

Community Learning & Libraries
Cymuned Ddysgu a Llyfrgelloedd

Newport
CITY COUNCIL
CYNGOR DINAS
Casnewydd

This item should be returned or renewed by the
last date stamped below.

To renew visit:

www.newport.gov.uk/libraries